TIGHTROPE

After entering a house where a commotion has been overheard, two community police officers make a horrific discovery. Detective Inspector Olivia Hardy and Detective Sergeant Lauren Groves are dispatched to investigate, triggering a major case that ends up with Hardy being usurped as the Senior Investigating Officer. It's yet another problem for Hardy, as she already suspects that husband Hal is having an affair. Meanwhile, as Groves descends into alcoholism after her husband's desertion, both officers' lives seem to be spiralling out of control. When a baby's body is found at the back of the police station, Hardy takes the unpleasant case, determined to succeed and show the world she's still capable— but things don't turn out exactly as planned . . .

TIGHTROPE

ANDREA FRAZER

LARGE PRINT

First published in Great Britain 2016
by
Accent Press

First Isis Edition
published 2018
by arrangement with
Accent Press

A catalogue record for this book is available
from the British Library.

ISBN 978–1–78541–592–0 (hb)
ISBN 978–1–78541–598–2 (pb)

Published by
F. A. Thorpe (Publishing)
Anstey, Leicestershire

Set by Words & Graphics Ltd.
Anstey, Leicestershire
Printed and bound in Great Britain by
T. J. International Ltd., Padstow, Cornwall

This book is printed on acid-free paper

Prologue

The door swung open at a touch, unlocked and unlatched, revealing a wide hallway. Dimly visible, the staircase rose from deeper in the house. There was a carpet, but its pattern was dirtied beyond recognition and the pile was matted and sticky. There was no central light fitting and the walls were scarred with pale patches where pictures had once hung, and the bloom of mildew. The whole scene was utterly bare and forlorn.

The one clump of real colour that caught the eye was a string of red, already turning brown, that ran like a thin river from just beyond the entrance to the house, through the house, disappearing into the gloominess of the interior. Silence hung in the air like a scream, and specks of dust swam through the sea of it, disturbed by the movement of the door.

A low moaning pierced the atmosphere; a spear of sound that was agonisingly loud in the dead house and drew the callers to the middle room on the right-hand side, from which protruded a lone foot, on the toe of which was a female shoe. A male counterpart was caught in a shaft of sunlight from a distant window in the depths of the large house, elevated on a step that indicated a slightly lower level in the ground floor.

Her jaw was broken, her teeth a bloody mass of stumps made jagged perhaps by the steel-capped toe of a boot, and the ends of her fingers twitched with a life of their own, but there was something wrong with her face which took a couple of seconds to comprehend. Her eyes were gone, the sockets bloodily empty.

And still her fingers twitched, and she moaned quietly, her limbs at unnatural angles.

The man's shoe came into contact with something gelatinous underfoot and he looked down. The woman looked from the face of the thing on the floor, then at the man's shoe, and vomited.

The man was in the kitchen, agonisingly close to the freedom of the rear door, sprawled in a pool of blood which surrounded the pile of his disembowelled insides, an expression of gut-wrenching agony and disbelief on his dead face.

The male caller half-dragged his companion into a room empty of everything except a worm-eaten wooden chair and settled her there, as a babble of voices intruded from the outside world and broke his mood of absolute horror. Putting a finger to his lips to keep her silent, although he didn't know why, he left her and crept through the rest of the rooms on the ground floor. Apart from the room where they had found that poor wretch of a woman, there was not another stick of furniture.

He made a quick call, *sotto voce*, and then crept up the stairs, wary of others present but hidden, his senses heightened for confrontation, his breathing shallow and careful.

The tracks in the dust of the first floor were numerous, and the inside walls were stacked to the ceilings in each room, but this was not the only unexpected aspect of the property. Looking up the next flight of very narrow and steep stairs to the attic quarters, he unclipped the torch from his belt, for he dare not flip on a light switch in case he disturbed somebody concealed up there. A creaking tread had his heart in his mouth but no shadowy figures appeared above him.

The second floor proved as devoid of people as the first, but he was unnerved by a bright light that shone at the bottom of the three doors at the top of the staircase. Should he risk going in, or should he collect his partner and just skip it? Taking his courage in both hands, he flung open a door as a pungent aroma assailed his nostrils, and the lit space, all knocked into one huge room, revealed a complex network of hydroponics and plants. An indoor forest of money lay before him: an expanse of evil triffids that could fill the mental health wards and fatten the coffers of whichever evil bastard had planted this "field of dreams".

He encountered no opposition and made no sudden movement, stunned into immobility, until the wailing scream of an ambulance siren cut through his thoughts with the precision of a lancet, and he flew down the stairs like a hunted animal.

CHAPTER
ONE

"And where exactly was this?"

DI Olivia Hardy, passing a fairly average day in the CID suite in the town's police station, held the handset away from her ear and stared at it as if it were a snake, her face livid as if what she was being told were an outrage. "And this was just down the road?" There were a few seconds of relative silence as she listened intently, and then said, with incredulity, "And the poor cow survived?"

DS Lauren Groves looked up at these words, scenting trouble. "Whassup?" she asked, still mentally embroiled in the paperwork she had been catching up with.

"Come on. We can walk. It's only in Gooding Avenue," was the terse reply. "It's a nice day: for us, anyway."

"What's happened?"

"You'll see. And right under our bloody noses. I don't believe it. The barefaced cheek of some criminals."

"What's going on?"

"It's quicker to look than to talk. Let's be off."

Nowhere in Littleton-on-Sea was far away from anything else, although this did not really include its new and rapidly burgeoning suburbs. The old town was small, and when Olivia had joined the police service, had little modern housing on its perimeter, with the exception of what had been, then, a brand new, sprawling council estate.

That had been in the days when the police station had been new as well, and the town was not a hotbed of crime. In the intervening years, however, it had spawned a huge ring of new and fairly cheap housing. The older buildings had continued to age and fall into disrepair and it was now like a pie, with a stale Georgian and Victorian filling and a hugely thick crust of rapidly ageing, jerry-built boxes.

The financial recessions of the last three decades had taken their toll on the economy of the town, as had cheap flights to Spain, and its mainstay — family holidays — had all but disappeared. There were precious few of the bucket-and-spade brigade left in England, most of them converted to kids' clubs and sangria.

The boarding houses and bed and breakfasts had slowly dwindled and died, along with the jobs that they provided, and the town was now a sink for petty criminals, illegal immigrants and the casual trafficking of drugs. Olivia had seen this transformation and often mourned the loss of the olden days which, with the benefit of hindsight, she now regarded as the *golden* days.

She was, after all, approaching the big five-o in the next couple of years, and she felt every day of her age some days. She was married, and suddenly, with the good weather, remembered fondly how the summer had been a string of treats for her and her two children. Her husband, a teacher, had a lot of free time in the month of August, and ice creams, paddling, sandcastles and candyfloss had filled a lot of days and produced suitably exhausted and happy children at the end of them. August had been a month of endless pleasure, negating the need to go away for a holiday.

Now the summer meant the endless problems of what students, released from the endless round of partying of which their term-time consisted, relocating their louche activities back onto home soil. There were precious few holiday jobs for them to come back to, and so her days were filled with incidents of shoplifting, petty theft, small-scale drug deals and weekend fights fuelled by alcohol, drugs and legal highs, the like of which didn't exist when she had been a rookie cop.

There had been no skunk then to suck kids into paranoia and schizophrenia, just good old hashish. There had been no alcopops to encourage kids to drink at a younger and younger age, and the concept of the legal high had not even been predicted. Life was so much harder for kids now. It wasn't just an unwanted pregnancy that had to be avoided; it was the other multifarious temptations that modern life threw at them and expected them to be able to cope with.

With the advent of all these temptations, Olivia's time in the service had had more and more to do with younger people getting involved in criminality, but a case that she and her fairly new partner, DS Lauren Groves, had dealt with late the previous year, and the personal problems that must have been forming for some time but which had eventually come to a head, had really piled on the pressure. Suddenly the presence in her life of her husband and children had been painfully highlighted, and she realised that she had not kept her eye on the family ball.

At least she still had Hal. Lauren had been deserted by her husband, Kenneth, who had run off with the family's nanny, and was now having to cope with life as a single parent. Olivia was keeping a firm eye on the three other members of her family, determined that her job should not distract her as devastatingly as it had done such a short time ago.

This was a lot of introspection in such a short walk, and in just a couple of minutes they had reached the perimeter wall of a large, three-storeyed Victorian villa, set four-square in its gardens. At the wall stood a whey-faced community police officer and her male partner, who leaned against its solidity trying to appear as if he faced such horrors every day. An ambulance was just leaving the kerbside, its lights and siren on, and a gaggle of neighbours clustered on the pavement, weaving the cloth of rumours and speculation in an excited undertone.

Shaking her head to clear her mind of everything except what she was about to discover, she said, "DI Hardy and DS Groves. You found this?"

"Yes, ma'am," replied the male officer. He was tall and broad with dark skin and reminded Olivia of her husband Hal when he was younger.

"You both look like you could do with a cup of something hot and sweet. Get yourselves back to the station and report to my office when we've finished here. I want a full verbal report and a written back-up. Don't miss out any detail, no matter how small."

The female officer looked after the disappearing ambulance and then whispered barely audibly, "Did they take the eyes? Please tell me they took the eyes."

As Groves looked nonplussed, Hardy, keeping her voice gentle, instructed them to give their names to her sergeant and she'd see them back at the station later. "What was she talking about?" asked Groves.

"I hope you haven't got a full stomach. Gird your loins. Let's walk this one through, and I'll get the station to contact the FME and a CSI team."

A couple of uniforms sauntered up to guard the exits but soon altered their relaxed body language when they caught the inspector's eye. The two detectives found the door on the latch, but not yet locked. Paper suits were donned in public view in the front garden, giving the goggling neighbours full value for money. This was the sort of thing that Hardy particularly disliked, being on the short and tubby side and managing to look scruffy even in her best clothes, whereas Lauren was tall and willowy and would have looked elegant in a bin liner.

Without a thought, the inspector yelled at them to disperse, as the pair stepped over the threshold into the drab void of the house. The flowers in the front garden, grown wild through lack of care, mingled their sweet perfumes, disturbed by the unaccustomed passage of visitors up and down the path, with that of the blood in the interior.

Within what seemed only seconds, they were joined by a white-suited horde, all eager to get involved in what promised to be a very unusual case. The position the woman had lain in was marked out, and numbered markers were placed where there was any sign of blood or other possible evidence. A photographer began to click away, occasionally pausing to take a sweep of video film on his small handheld camera.

Although the officers were fast, they were also thorough, and they soon moved ahead of the two previous arrivals on the crime scene. Hardy and Groves stepped slowly and carefully, observing each part of the house as they moved through it. The hall and ground floor rooms of the building gave the impression of a house, no longer a home, abandoned long ago.

The room, in the entrance of which the blinded woman had been found, was furnished only with two venerable but disintegrating sofas, each topped with a grubby sleeping bag and a filthy pillow. There was some detritus of everyday living, in the shape of a few empty beer cans, crushed and discarded, and a number of empty takeaway cartons, their contents long-consumed and casually discarded onto the already filthy carpet.

A room across the hall held only a solitary, rickety wooden chair — the one where PCSO Harris had bidden PCSO Strickland wait while he went through the rest of the house — and the remains of curtains, now in tatters, hung at the windows, doing their inadequate best to provide privacy for any inhabitants in the room.

The first foot or two of the kitchen looked like a tiny square of abattoir had been transferred there, so covered was it in blood, and numerous indications showed that there was a lot of evidence in this area. The victim here seemed to have been eviscerated and his face, even in death, showed his fear and incomprehension at the way events seemed to have overtaken him. Lauren had to look away from his eyes which appeared to be fixed in an expression of mute appeal for help that had never arrived. Without entering and contaminating the scene, the two women moved to the foot of the stairs where they waited whilst a couple of anonymous suited and masked officers scurried down. One murmured, "You'll be amazed at what you'll find up there," in her ear, scuttling off before she could identify his voice.

Before they could mount, however, a voice summoned Hardy to a cupboard underneath the wide staircase and showed her the electricity meter, which had been bypassed and was whirling away at great speed indicating a heavy usage of the utility. After a whistle of appreciation, they reached the first floor only to be overwhelmed by the amount of cigarette cartons, boxes of cigars and bottles of high-end malt whisky.

"Good God!" exclaimed Olivia. "Someone was planning a helluva party." The goods were stacked from floor to ceiling, with the exception of where there were windows, and several piles of exotic alcoholic ingredients were piled up in the middle of the floor. All the rooms proved to be similarly stuffed, but that did not explain the heavy use of electricity.

"Next floor," an anonymous voice advised them, and they headed towards a much narrower staircase, this one covered in worn linoleum rather than the threadbare carpet of their route to the first floor.

It was the smell of which they were aware first, harsh and pungent, making them catch their breath. "Has some idiot left that door open?" the same voice called out in disgust, and Hardy and Groves continued to mount the stairs, their hands over their mouths as they had not donned masks. "Get it shut!" Whoever was calling the shots was determined to contain the odour.

Stepping gingerly through the door and closing it behind them, the two women were dumbfounded to see a waving crop of marijuana plants. The temperature was high, as was necessary for them to thrive, the floor lined with thick plastic so that the sprinklers could do their work without leaving watery signs on the ceilings below. The lights of the heat lamps were blinding.

The rest of the vast space, for all the rooms had been knocked into one, had been thickly insulated and then covered in a sturdy silver foil to reflect heat back into the attic, including the skylights. There were also wide pipes snaking around the room, all disappearing into what was evidently a chimney breast, and there were large fans which directed much of the smell into these flexible pipes. No wonder so much power was being used and, thanks to the meter being illegally bypassed, free gratis.

"I've seen enough. I've got to get out of here. The smell's making me feel really sick and peculiar."

"That, Sergeant, is the smell of "skunk"; hybridised by an American chap who managed to increase the strength of the drug thirty-fold, but omitted to transfer an important chemical which makes the effects benign. It's from this evil combination of other strains that cannabis psychosis has emerged. Users become more and more paranoid and sometimes violent in the mistaken idea that they're protecting themselves.

"Skunk has virtually nothing in common with the hash the old hippies used to smoke and I strongly believe that instead of reclassifying it back up to Class B, it should have been separated out into its different strains and one made legal the way they've done in the Netherlands, the other stamped out with a viciousness that would leave its growers' heads spinning."

"I didn't realise you knew so much about it," coughed Groves, backing out of the doorway.

"I made a point of it when I had that trouble with Ben last year." The inspector and Hal, a steel drummer and retired teacher from Barbados, had two children, Hibbie and Ben, aged sixteen and eighteen respectively. Both had rather blotted their copybooks in the previous year, and Olivia was still smarting from the incidents that had so rocked her world.

Groves had understood how shaken her partner had felt, as she contemplated the end of her marriage at the end of the previous year, when she had caught her husband in bed with the au pair, and they had both fled back to the Middle East where he was working on contract. Her children, Sholto and Jade, were, however, far too young to be involved in drugs, but had also suffered from the wind of change that had dragged them from attendance at their prep schools and catapulted them into a faith school close enough to their home for them to attend every day instead of boarding.

With a similarly nauseated expression, Hardy followed her, bidding her to get a move on. "We've got two new officers starting today, now that Redwood's not coming back, and I want to be there when they arrive. We've also got a talk from someone from drugs and from traffic about some zero tolerance operation that's coming up. As if we didn't have enough to deal with here!"

Superintendent Devenish had decided that his force — strike that; his *service* — wasn't ethnically diverse enough, so two officers were being transferred, one from Brighton and one from Yorkshire. Both DCs, Ali Desai complemented Terry Friend from the uniformed branch in representation of the Asian community, and Lee Oh satisfied the Far Eastern sector. Winston Harris, the Police Community Support Officer, had been an earlier appointment when the idea had first crossed devilish Devenish's mind.

As the two women climbed the station stairs to the first floor CID office, the Super was on his way down from the second floor, his two new members of staff in tow. He seemed to have decided that he'd like to introduce them to the team himself. *Gosh, he must be feeling smug*, thought Olivia, as she tried not to stare at Devenish's intimidating features. These two new appointments, apart from being a necessary addition to the CID staff, were typical of him — to blow with the wind on current thinking, in the hope of extra brownie points from above.

"Come along, ladies. Where have you been?" he bellowed and then, without giving them a chance to answer, added, "Your place at the moment is with your team, settling in these two new officers." Both women clamped together their lips lest they should say something they might regret. Hardy was being particularly cautious as she had been under the senior officer's beady surveillance since they'd had a little professional difference of opinion at the end of last year, and she'd been trying to keep her nose clean ever since.

He entered the CID office with no clue to his imminent arrival therein, and discovered a cacophony that would've disgraced an unruly classroom. "Silence!" he bellowed, clapping his hands for extra volume and, as the noise tailed away, turned to DI Hardy and gave it as his opinion that she should teach her staff a little office decorum. "This is a place of work, not a playground — who threw that paper aeroplane?" he continued, raising his voice again.

An embarrassed silence greeted this question, and he resumed in a slightly quieter voice, "May I introduce you to your new colleagues, DC Oh and DC Desai."

He waved a magnanimous hand in the direction of the two embarrassed but smiling strangers. To this there was a smattering of applause and a couple of catcalls. "I want you to take them under your wing and assimilate them into your team as smoothly as possible, as there are important moves afoot."

"Do you mean the massacre in that drug den in Gooding Avenue?" called a voice from the rear of the office.

"What massacre? What drug den?" It would appear that the news of the community officers' find had not yet had climbed to the necessary height to make a superintendent aware of it.

"DS Groves will accompany you back up to your office and explain everything, while I get these new lads settled in, sir," Hardy cut across his spluttering, and pointed to two empty desks awaiting their occupants. "Sit yourselves down, lads. We've got an operation coming up at the weekend which I want you all to put your hearts and souls into, as well as your backs. We will be carrying out operation ZeeTee, which stands for Zero Tolerance, in regard to drink and drugs. It's a county-wide operation, with neighbouring services willing to cooperate if necessary."

"Why is it 'zee' and not just 'zed'?" asked the long-serving and long-suffering DC Lenny Franklin in a peeved voice. He hated anything that smacked of Americanism.

"Because it is. Now, pipe down and just listen. We have been issued with a number of the new drugalysers that can detect cannabis and cocaine in saliva. As you

12

will remember from a demonstration a few months ago, these are one-use saliva swabs so I don't want any of you messing about with them for a lark.

"For your information, a list of illegal drugs and their tolerance limits is posted in the medical room, along with a list of prescription drugs which are on the banned list whilst driving, and the limits under which these are tolerated. We don't mind people needing such treatment, but we will prosecute if these drugs are misused for other purposes. Feel free to check the list out in your own off-duty time.

"This is a full-on operation which will use every officer available, leaving only a skeleton staff. Traffic will be out with the ANPR cameras, and some officers not usually out in vehicles will be with them so that they can do single shifts. Anyone not involved in this will be out on the streets literally looking for trouble or following up leads.

"Uniformed officers will be picking up every drunk outside pubs and clubs, and we want to show this town a real crackdown. The colleges and universities have just finished their academic year, and students will be celebrating being home for the holidays. Remember that every available and vaguely suitable premises will be running English language courses for foreign students, and they need keeping an eye on too. No wonder they shoplift and pick pockets — considering what they're charged for the privilege of lacklustre teaching, I'm not really surprised."

This was a subject in which she was taking more interest this year, as her husband Hal had taken on a teaching post in one of these out-of-term-time language schools, some of which were pop-up. He had been retired for some little while now and had decided that he really ought to keep his hand in, and had also registered for some supply teaching as well, before the end of the school term.

Olivia and Hal had been married over twenty years and had been living in the same pretty cottage for most of that time, Hal's parents having retired early to their native island and leaving their home in two pairs of safe hands.

"Right, now about this incident that DS Groves and I have just attended: as you probably already know, the station grapevine being what it is, there's been a murder and an attempted murder in Gooding Avenue." None of the officers looked surprised at this. "It was originally called in by a member of the public reporting the sound of raised voices and screaming. What you may not have heard is that also uncovered has been a large stash of presumably smuggled booze and tobacco products on the first floor, and a cannabis farm on the second floor.

"It's been well-insulated, which is why we haven't had any reports, from the helicopter spotters, of the property giving off a large amount of heat. It's also been well ventilated, so we've had no reports from the neighbours about the smell — although I'm slightly surprised. It's our pungent old friend skunk.

"I want us to dive straight into this so, Desai, I want you to pick up our PC Shuttleworth — easily recognised as the only one of our uniformed branch who looks like he plays rugby for the county, which he does — and get yourselves over to the hospital. I want you to get fingerprints from both the dead man and the injured woman and run them through the Police National Computer, and see if that poor woman's conscious yet — he'll need to book out a Lantern machine.

"Tell Shuttleworth I want him to stay on duty by her side as she may still be in danger, and I'll arrange for him to be relieved at the end of his shift. To this end, please take separate cars. And make sure you bring back the fingerprint machine with you; don't let it stay at the hospital. And for God's sake, don't lose it or let it be stolen.

"Lenny," she called, fixing her most experienced officer with her beady eye, "I want you and Oh to do a house-to-house both up and down Gooding Avenue to see if anyone's heard or seen anything, no matter how small, either earlier today or in recent weeks. Plants that size don't grow overnight; they didn't sprout from magic beans.

"The ring road runs behind it, so ditto with any of the houses carrying on up this road that might have had a view of the rear of the properties. We don't know how whoever committed these atrocities got in or out. It is worth taking note of, however, that this all sprang from a call to the station about raised voices coming from that particular house, to the point that one set of neighbours thought it sounded like it needed checking out. Luckily for them, although not so for our victims, our community support officers, Strickland and Harris were nearby and immediately dispatched to check out the situation."

"So, what do I do?" asked DS Groves, who had re-entered the office halfway through the session.

"I want you to speak to Monty Fairbanks. He knows every face on this patch, and I need you to get a list of names to visit to see if we can uncover any rumours and gossip, and then collect PC Terry Friend and get visiting; it's safer in pairs."

"And what will you be doing?" asked Groves, sounding just a little bit peeved that, whatever it was, she wouldn't be doing it with her.

"Mind your manners, Sergeant. For your information, I shall be debriefing our two intrepid community officers, to discover whether they saw anything that they might have missed the importance of. I shall then be pushing for identification of our victims and the results of anything found by Forensics. Keep in mind that we'll be working in collaboration with the drugs squad and HMRC on this one. The only part of it that's ours is the violent side — as usual. And not a word about the cannabis farm or the contraband on your travels, or one of the other departments will have our guts for garters. Now, get yourselves out there and watch your backs; we've got someone very dangerous on the loose, and anything could happen."

They all left the office, Lenny Franklin at the back and dragging his heels. As he reached the door, he looked over his shoulder and said, pleadingly, "Guv?"

"I know it doesn't seem very exciting, but you need to be prepared for the unexpected. And, just think, in a couple of years, you'll be enjoying a well-earned retirement." Lenny's face creased up in a scowl, but he picked up his pace and caught up with DC Oh.

Looking out of the window of the now empty office, Olivia could see a van parked outside number three Gooding Avenue, and presumed that this was drugs officers taking a separate set of photographs and removing the highly commercial crop. She sincerely hoped that some low-life was watching so that he — or she — could put out the word that there were no pickings left. The last thing they needed was a spate of break-ins looking for crumbs from this table.

As she exited the office, she left a message on the whiteboard that any officers returning in her absence, for there had been a few, to get in touch with DS Groves to get a list of names to be checked out.

CHAPTER
TWO

Groves, being a diligent officer, decided to have a quick check of the drugs covered by new legislation while Monty Fairbanks was calling up names for her. To square her conscience for not doing this in her free time, she decided that she would work through her lunch break, and grab a sandwich to eat in the car.

Fairbanks' eyes had lit up at her request for names connected with drugs. "Do you want users or suspected dealers?" he had asked. If he had been a dog he would have been panting with anticipation.

"Both, if you can manage it," she'd replied without thinking.

"Suspected dealers, I can get a list together fairly quickly, but users, it'll take some time, there are so many."

"Just the dealers for now, then."

"I wouldn't go on your own, love. You don't want to go blundering in with faces like that. There'll be some pretty dodgy characters in there, and you'd probably have to have permission from the drugs squad."

"Firstly, I am not your 'love', and, secondly, I'll seek whatever permissions I need before I go. I do not intend to go 'blundering in', as you so delicately put it," she snapped, her face reddening, because that was exactly what she had intended to do.

That was why she'd settled for a list of persistent users and parked herself in front of the notice in the medical room perusing the list of drugs which had a limit on them for driving. She was familiar with the illegal ones, but her brain began to tie itself in knots with the legal ones, and she spoke them to herself under her breath.

"Morphine, methadone, diazepam, clonazepam, flunitrazepam, lorazepam, oxazepam, temazepam" — so that was anything that ended in -pam, but the legal limits were so diverse. A thousand micrograms per litre were legal for temazepam, but only fifty for clonazepam. At that moment, she considered herself lucky not to be a doctor, but was bounced out of her reverie by a resounding slap on the rump and the voice of DC Daz Westbrook wishing her good day, followed by the lazy voice of DC Teddy O'Brien stating that he wouldn't have done that because it could be considered assault on a police officer. Lauren blushed, but said nothing, her old-fashioned soul actually taking it as a compliment that Westbrook had been moved so to act.

Westbrook had been a replacement for former DC Colin Redwood, who had been dismissed from the service after leaking confidential information to the press. He had turned out to be not so much an improvement, as more of the same, in that he was young, mouthy and impertinent. Teddy O'Brien was in his mid-thirties and had retained his Irish lilt even though he had lived in England since the age of ten.

"We phoned Lenny and he said you'd be down with Monty, and he pointed us in this direction. What have you said to upset him? He seemed to be in a right old mood."

"None of your bloody business, Constable." Suddenly, so was she. "And if you lay a finger on me again I shall have you up on a disciplinary." Why had she suddenly become so defensive?

"Ooh. Aren't we in a mood? Time of the month, Sergeant?"

"How do you fancy joining the ranks of the unemployed, Westbrook? I shall speak to the inspector later about your disrespectful and sexist behaviour and, no doubt, she'll have a few quiet words with you — one of which I rather hope is "off".

"No need to be mardy, Sarge." Westbrook really was pushing his luck.

"No need to be bloody rude either," she snapped back at him. This young man had really got under her skin without her being aware of it. O'Brien, very wisely, kept his lip zipped.

"Are you aware of what was discovered in Gooding Avenue this morning? Allow me to enlighten you," she suggested, as they shook their heads in blessed silence. She was more unsettled than she had realised by what had come to light that morning; and practically on the station's doorstep, too. But how on earth could she do as she had been bidden without mentioning the drugs? She would have to get hold of a name from the drugs squad with whom she could liaise, before setting off on a wild-goose chase. What was Olivia thinking, giving her a task she couldn't carry out?

As she scuttled off to get a name and contact number, the two male detectives headed back to the office.

"Come on, Paddy, let's get out of here. She can find us when she's ready."

"My name's not Paddy."

"OK, Mick."

"You cheeky little bastard. Call me Teddy or I'll start calling you Ariel, and that's the name of a fairy as well as a washing powder, *Daz*."

"Fair dos — Teddy."

Liam Shuttleworth proved easy to identify for Ali Desai. Apart from being in uniform, he was easily the largest officer in the station. After introducing himself, he explained what Hardy wanted them to do, and that she wanted Shuttleworth to stay on in the hospital after they had taken fingerprints and seen whether the woman was able to speak to them, to keep a watch on her.

"If someone injured her as badly as the inspector told us, they might have left her for dead. If word gets out that she survived, they might have another go at her," he explained. "For that reason, she wants us to take separate cars."

"I'll just grab my newspaper," replied the uniformed constable, picking up his copy of the *Daily Express*.

At the hospital, they were shown to a single room in the ICU where the body of a woman lay in the bed, her face heavily bandaged with large pads covering her eye sockets. One of her legs was in a splint, as was one of her arms. She was hooked up to a number of monitors and had two drip bags slowly dispensing their contents into a cannula in the back of her right hand, the other being in a splint, the fingers separately bandaged. Her mouth was slightly open when she breathed, showing the place where teeth had been that morning when she woke up, and her nose was askew where it had also taken a heavy knock.

The nurse who had led them to the room commented. "She's had a good going over. We've got her sedated, and she's been for X-rays and a scan. Now we're just waiting for a theatre to be readied so that we can set her broken bones, but she'll possibly need her spleen removed. And then there's her eyes, or rather, lack of them. How she'll cope with living like that I've no idea. I don't think I could do it."

"What about her eyes?" asked Shuttleworth, Desai not having gone into specific injuries but who, nevertheless, was looking slightly nauseous.

"She doesn't have any any more," said the nurse, curtly.

"*What?*" Shuttleworth looked appalled. Desai kept schtum.

"Did nobody tell you?" asked the nurse with compassion in his voice. "Whoever did this to her gouged them out of their sockets — not even leaving them hanging, but actually ripped them out of her head — and the ambulance crew didn't manage to recover them. One of them they couldn't find, the other seemed to have been squashed — trodden on, I presume, when she was picked up by the paramedics."

Shuttleworth was speechless with shock and felt a chill run through his body. Whoever had done this to the poor woman was pure evil.

"Could you give us any idea of when we might be able to speak to her?" asked the DC.

"Certainly not before she's been to theatre, and probably not for some time after that. We'll have to keep her sedated while her body tries to recover from the shock of what has happened to her, not to mention the shock of surgery. She'll definitely need some metal plates inserted to hold her bones together. They've been quite badly broken. Given the bruising, I should think it was a baseball bat or something that was used on her, but that's not really for me to say."

The idea certainly raised some terrible pictures in the policemen's minds. "So, she's not likely to come round?" Desai wanted a definite "no".

"Absolutely not," replied the nurse, rubbing the beginnings of stubble on his chin with the palm of one hand. "She's sedated at the moment and, as I've already told you, that's a state she's liable to remain in for some time. We can let you know if there's any change."

"That's all right, I'm staying on. We don't know yet if she's safe, not even here, and I've been given the job of keeping an eye on her."

"She'll be off to theatre pretty soon."

"I'll just kick my heels while she's being operated on; maybe get something to eat. It's just about time for my trough."

"And a frame like yours must take some stoking," said the nurse, batting his eyelashes at the scandalised constable, who gave a sharp intake of breath and looked anywhere but at the member of staff.

"I'm afraid we're going to have to take her fingerprints," said Desai, hoping that this would not be vetoed.

"Do you have to?"

"We need to try to identify her. Nobody seems to know her."

"If you must; but be gentle."

"We will be. Shuttleworth, have you got that Lantern device? It's a mobile fingerprint machine," he explained, "so we'll only be needing the index finger of her right hand. And after that, do you think you could give us directions to the mortuary?"

He mumbled some instructions on the quickest route as Shuttleworth gently pressed the woman's finger on to the screen of the device, the nurse's eyes still on the constable's broad back. He then left them to go about his business, and Desai said, much to the uniformed officer's discomfort, "I think you've pulled, Shuttleworth," in an attempt to lighten the atmosphere.

"Over my dead body," the young man replied with an expression of distaste on his face.

"I'm sure he wouldn't mind too much." The DC sensed that he shouldn't push things any further and let it drop. "I'll get back to the station, after we've taken a quick trip to the morgue."

Maybe the instructions were a little awry, or maybe they'd been misremembered, but it seemed to take

24

them rather a lot of footslogging before they finally arrived at the mortuary.

One of the mortuary assistants led them to a sliding metal drawer in a wall of similar openings, and slid out a body shrouded in a white sheet, stained with blood about the middle. "We need the right-hand index finger," said Desai, and Shuttleworth once again brandished the device in front of him like a weapon.

Wishing them the best of luck, the assistant withdrew the sheet and waited for one of them to comment. The right index finger was missing its top two joints.

"What do we do now?" asked Shuttleworth, rearing back as if he'd been bitten.

"Take the middle finger, then do the left index finger just to be sure," advised Desai, improvising like hell.

"Do you think we should ring in just to check?"

"We can always come back. It's not as if he's going anywhere, is it?" Desai was nothing if not pragmatic. "Then give me the thing. I promised I'd bring it back with me in case it gets half-inched hanging around here. And you, don't forget to let us know if there are any developments — like a further attempt on the woman's life, any suspicious visitors or maybe her regaining consciousness. I'll arrange for you to be relieved of duty at the end of your shift. Now, you get back to that room and stand guard."

Lenny Franklin and Lee Oh, already dubbed "Leo" by the team, left the confines of the station on foot, as Gooding Avenue was so close. When it had been built, it had been an avenue of prosperous villas, but now most of them were split up, into what estate agents optimistically referred to as "apartments". Oh, they were flats all right, but when you were trying to sell something as expensive as a home, you had to advertise optimistically.

"So, what brought you down here?" asked Franklin, who had not worked with someone with Far Eastern origins before and was a nosy old sod.

"My parents," the other man replied with a rare economy of words.

"They Chinese?"

"Korean."

"They retired?" Lenny wasn't giving up that easily.

"No," came Leo's retort, and then he gave his colleague a break. "They've got three restaurants in Yorkshire, but decided they'd like a rather upmarket one down south. The weather is rumoured to be warmer."

"Don't you believe it, buddy."

"They want to do outside catering too."

"Like takeaways?"

"No, like weddings and functions."

"Well, bloody good luck to them. Are they far away?"

"About ten miles east. The next big town along the coast."

By now their leisurely progress had led them to their first destination; number one, Gooding Avenue. To the side of the door there were six doorbells, some with names, some with their little slots empty of any information. "I should start with the ground floor, then we're at least in the building," advised Lenny with a knowledge born of long experience.

"Just what I were about to do," added Leo, in his rich Yorkshire tones.

As they waited for an answer to their summons, Lenny asked. "So, whereabouts were you born, Leo?"

"Yorkshire. Can't you hear it in my voice?"

At that moment, their ring was answered by a grey-haired old woman wearing a baggy cotton sundress and a pair of thick-lensed glasses. "Who are you?" she demanded in terse tones, looking them up and down. "If you're them Jehovah's Witnesses, I'm not interested," and she made to close the door.

"Police," stated Lenny firmly, whipping out his warrant card and holding it up towards her. Relenting a little, she snaked out a hand and snatched it from him before he could restrain her, then closed the door sufficiently to put on the security chain. "There's been enough bother round here this morning, what with all that to-do next door," she declared. "None of us are safe in our beds any more. Is he from the local takeaway?"

Leo also produced his warrant card and held it out towards the slit, wondering how many times this was going to happen. Arthritic fingers whipped it out of his grasp, and there was a bit of quiet mumbling from the other side of the door, as the old biddy made up her mind whether to admit them or not.

"I'm going to call the station and just check that these aren't forgeries," she called, and shut the door again, leaving them to wait on the doorstep. She was

27

gone three or four minutes, and they spent that time looking around the front garden, which seemed to be well kept.

When she returned, she bade them enter in a haughty manner, as if she were deferring an honour on them letting them in at all. "It was me that phoned the police this morning," she informed them, as she led them into a sitting room which smelled of both dust and damp, and was as airless as a tomb. "Can't stand flies," she suddenly exclaimed, as if this explained everything. "Filthy little disease-carriers."

"Can you tell us why you called the police out this morning, Mrs Lucas?" asked Lenny, who had made a mental note of the name next to the first flat and had observed, however briefly, the presence of a ring on the third finger of her left hand.

"What happened in there?" She was dying to sticky-beak.

"What was it that alarmed you enough to call for police assistance?" Lenny wasn't falling for that one, and Leo was playing the foreigner card and taking notes or, at least, pretending to. "What did you hear or see that prompted you to do that?"

She took the bait. "There was all this shouting — which happens frequently enough, I can tell you — but then I heard someone screaming as well."

"And where did you hear this from, Mrs Lucas. These properties are detached and I wouldn't have thought sound would carry that well."

"I was in the front garden dead-heading the roses," the old lady replied with an innocent expression. Lenny wasn't taken in. She was probably out there dead-heading imaginary flowers whenever someone called round to next door.

"Who lives there?" he asked.

"Some ramshackle couple," she replied. "I've never spoken to them because they don't seem to want to be neighbourly, but they certainly don't look English." Again, DC Franklin wasn't taken in. She had probably tried to pump them for personal information as soon as they moved in, and they weren't having any of it — especially after what had been discovered on the premises earlier that day.

"Do you know their names?"

"No."

"And how long have they've lived there?"

"I can't remember." How convenient, but then she came up with a bit more useful information. "The house is only rented out. The owners moved abroad."

"Any idea where, or what agency it's with?"

"Nope." This was going nowhere. "But I saw the ambulance take one of them away, and the other one was taken out in a body bag. What happened?"

"We don't have any firm information as yet, Mrs Lucas. What are the neighbours like in this house?" This was more up her street.

"The old git at the back is as deaf as a post. There's no point in trying to talk to him. And the other four flats are either students or foreigners. Probably both, if you ask me, coming over here and getting an education they can't get where they come from."

Bigoted old bag, thought Lenny, before asking, "Did you see anyone arrive at number three today before the ruckus broke out?"

"I wasn't quite quick enough to see," she replied guilelessly. "I had to make a trip to the little girls' room, and by the time I came out it had all kicked off."

"Any idea what nationality your neighbours at number three are?" Franklin used the present tense so as not to give anything away.

"No idea," she replied. "I hardly ever saw them, and I couldn't hear the words when they were rowing. These houses were built to prevent noise getting out; not like the flimsy boxes they put up nowadays. Might as well build them out of Weetabix."

After this comment she clammed up. There was evidently no more to be got from the old lady so, handing her one of his cards and advising her to call him if she remembered anything that might be useful, Lenny indicated, with a slight movement of the head to Leo, that they were about to leave.

"Have they arrested anybody?" was her parting question, her curiosity suddenly coming to the fore again. "There certainly seems to have been a large number of officers going in and out."

"We're told nothing, Mrs Lucas. We're just told to go and ask everybody whether they saw or heard anything."

Lenny pulled the door of the flat closed as they went back into the hall, then muttered, "Evil old witch. I'd bet my bottom dollar that she's got ears like a bat when it comes to snooping on neighbours. We'll have to track down the agency responsible for that letting. I'll bet you there aren't any regular inspections on that place. Nice one staying schtum, as if you didn't understand anything."

"Playing dumb can come in very handy at times."

"I bet it does. Leo, you're turning me into a gambler," Franklin concluded as he rang the bell of flat two, knocking on the wood at the same time. If the occupant was as deaf as Mrs Lucas had said he was, they'd have a job getting him to hear them.

At this double summons a muffled voice sounded through the wood of the door. "Hold your horses. I'm coming. I'm not deaf, you know."

The man who answered the door was equally as elderly as Mrs Lucas, but he had a merry twinkle in his eyes, and he whispered to them as he indicated for them to enter, "Don't let on to her next door that there's nothing wrong with my hearing. I just can't stand her spiteful gossip, so I've gradually become 'deafer' as the years have gone on. Now, I can't seem to hear anything at all that she says."

"Nice one," commented Franklin, stepping over the threshold, his warrant card in his hand.

"Mr Spender," replied the old man, "Not 'Big', any more, I'm afraid."

"I should think you've heard that joke a few times, haven't you?"

"You could say that. Have you come about all that commotion next door? I did go out to look when the ambulance turned up, and it looked quite serious. Those two were always having words, but nothing like the volume here this morning, and the screaming fair chilled my blood."

The occupant of flat two had had no view of the front of the property at all, but had seen two figures streaking through the back garden when the yelling had stopped, and confirmed that they had shinned over the rear fence in their efforts to escape.

"Could you identify them if you saw them again?" asked Franklin, with hope in his voice.

"Probably not. Although I was out in the sunshine, I was reading the newspaper, and I had the wrong glasses on. The only thing I can tell you was that one of them was definitely white, the other darker-skinned, if that isn't too racist for today's policing."

"That's fine. Can we show you some faces to see if you can identify them?"

"I doubt I'll be able to do that, but I'm willing to try, if you think it's worth it." Lenny handed him a card and asked him to call into the station and make himself known.

"Do you know anything about the couple next door?"

"Nothing, except that they aren't sociable. When they first moved in, I called round to welcome them to the Avenue, but they wouldn't answer the door. I knew they were in, so I came home, then went back round with a bottle of wine and a note introducing myself, but they never got back to me."

"And how long ago was that?"

"Must've been about the turn of the year. It was cold, that I do remember, so I didn't stand on their doorstep for too long."

32

"That's very helpful, sir. Do you know anything about the occupants of the first and second floor flats?"

"The first floor flats have got a local couple in one. She's expecting a baby, and the other has got a Welsh couple in it. The top floor flats are foreign students — Moroccan, I think. I don't hear a peep from any of them, but they're mostly out during the day."

"Are they out now?"

"I should think so. You can ring their bells if you want to try them, but I doubt you'll get any answer at this time of day."

"Do you know anything about them — where they work, that sort of thing?" Leo joined in the questioning.

"Ee, that's a grand accent you've got there, son. But the answer to your question is 'no'. I'm not much of a one for socialising. I have a few of my old mates round on a Wednesday evening for some dominoes, and another group round on a Sunday evening for a few games of cards, and that's about it. What with my bits and pieces of shopping, the back garden, the cleaning and getting a bite to eat, I don't really have a lot of time, and I do like my telly of an evening. That's enough for me."

"Here's my card, sir." Leo also offered his at this juncture. "Give us a ring if you remember anything else, and we'll get some officers to come round to speak to the occupants of the other two floors when they're at home."

Number five proved to be a house lived in by an elderly couple who had been there since they were newly married, their grown-up daughter, and her two children who had recently come to live with them after the break-up of said daughter's marriage.

This time they were asked in for a cup of tea, and Mrs Denning admitted to being one of the neighbours out on the pavement when the ambulance arrived. "There had been an almighty row going on in there — shouting and screaming fit to put your teeth on edge," she told them whilst pouring tea from a china pot.

"I know that Mrs Lucas from number one had called the police, because she called across the gardens to me when I went outside."

"Did you see anyone arrive or hear anything of what the argument was about?" asked Leo. At that moment an over-exuberant four-year-old boy went past making an "ee-ow" noise and holding aloft a toy aeroplane, while his three-year-old sister stood in front of the officers and pulled the outer corners of her eyes back to mimic Leo's features.

"Beyonce, Eric, go out into the garden and play," she barked. "You'll have to excuse them. They're full of energy."

"Should they not be at nursery or pre-school?" asked Franklin, a moue of distaste temporarily disfiguring his features.

"Our Sara's not long split up with her boyfriend and moved back here. She hasn't had the time yet to sort them out with anything suitable. She's been too busy looking for work."

Lenny's thoughts weren't very charitable as it crossed his mind that it hadn't been daughter Sara's first boyfriend, as Eric was evidently the offspring of a white mother and a coloured father and, if she did find work, it would be the long-suffering Mrs Denning who would end up bringing up the kids until her daughter had sourced another meal ticket, whether she realised it or not.

It was going to be a long day.

When they finally left the house a deafening half-hour later, they were thirty minutes older, but not a jot wiser about what had happened in number three. As they walked down the garden path, they saw a man in leather jacket and jeans, despite the warmth of the day, approaching the door of number three, and Franklin called to him. "Where the hell do you think you're going, mate?"

The officer on duty outside the front door jumped. He had been miles away, thinking of his summer holiday in Ibiza, and had been oblivious to the presence of any of them.

The man walked slowly across the scrubby lawn to them and said in a quiet voice, "DS Jenner, drugs squad and newly appointed crime scene manager, and I've got a sniffer dog arriving here shortly, just so you know. And you are?"

It was going to be a very long day.

CHAPTER
THREE

Hardy found Police Community Support Officers Winston Harris and Claire Strickland in the canteen, the latter still rather whey-faced, an untouched sandwich on a plate in front of her, already beginning to curl at the corners. Harris was evidently made of sterner stuff. He was shovelling shepherd's pie and chips into his mouth as the senior officer arrived, and nearly choked in his efforts to swallow and greet her at the same time. She had a reputation for being short-tempered and for not tolerating fools gladly, and he didn't want to get on the wrong side of her.

"Whoa there, Harris. I'm not so beautiful that I'm worth dying for."

"No, ma'am," he replied, at which Olivia adopted a furious expression and said,

"How could you agree with me? That's hardly the behaviour of a gentleman."

The young officer looked confused until Olivia let a smile loose on her face, and he realised she was just making a joke to lighten the atmosphere. God knows, it could do with it, considering what that morning had delivered to them. Maybe her reputation was just a bit exaggerated. "I don't want to curtail your lunch break, so when you've finished, could you come upstairs to the CID office for a chat about earlier?"

When she got back to her office, she found a man dressed in black denim and a grey suede jacket sitting in her chair.

"Who the hell are you, and what are you doing at my desk?"

"I, dear lady, am Chief Inspector Buller from the drugs squad and I am here to take over this case." He didn't move from the chair, but stared at her as if she were an exhibit under a microscope, so that she was suddenly aware of her somewhat scruffy appearance.

"Firstly, I am no one's 'dear lady' — and, secondly, under whose authority are you here?" she almost shouted. "I am a CID inspector and I am running this case."

"I'm afraid you're sadly mistaken, Inspector. Superintendent Devenish has requested the presence of both me and my sergeant, Mike Jenner, who is, as we speak, settling in as crime scene manager. This case is a co-operation between you, drugs, and HMRC, and I've been asked to head it up. Things would run more smoothly if we could get on with each other, but it's not compulsory."

Olivia bit her lip. So, she was still under a cloud as far as Devenish was concerned; he still didn't trust her. Presumably, if she didn't accept his decision, her rank would be at risk, if not her job. She'd have to curb her temper and live with it, although uneasily. She knew co-operation between different departments and agencies was necessary, but she thought that the murder should have some prominence.

Taking a deep breath, she asked, as politely as she could, if he would leave her office for a short while as she was expecting a visit from the officers who were first on the scene.

"I don't think I can comply with that request, Inspector. As SIO, I really should be here for that."

You bastard, she thought, although not voicing her opinion. There was a knock on her door, and she called out, "Come in," while indicating with her head that she wanted Buller to vacate her chair. Again, he made no attempt to do so, and she moved rapidly to perch on another desk so that it didn't look so much as if she had been ousted.

Harris and Strickland moved into the room, looking from one occupant to the other, not quite sure what to do, or who to attend to. After a deep inhalation of breath, she said, "This is Chief Inspector Buller from the drugs squad. We will be working in tandem on this case, so you can talk to both of us. Pull up a chair so we can go through exactly what happened this morning." With an effort, she reined in her resentment, but she had a feeling that she and Buller weren't going to get on, and she was already thinking of him as Buller the Bully.

"So, how come you were first on the scene?" Buller asked. "Tell me about it, in as much detail as possible." Hardy's mouth had opened to speak, but she'd been pipped at the post, and now shut it, looking a little like a goldfish. He'd beaten her to the line; in her own office; on a case that she felt she should be running. He was blatantly undermining her authority.

"We got a call that there had been a complaint about shouting and screaming, and we'd only just left the station, so we said we'd take it." This came from Strickland, her voice still shaky from the shock of what they had discovered.

"Did you see anyone fleeing the property?" asked Buller.

"The only people we saw were neighbours who had come outside to see what all the noise was about, but it was quiet when we got there."

"That's good. Now, tell me what you found when you got inside. How did you get in?"

"The door wasn't locked or latched, so we just walked in."

"What did you see first?"

"The place looked abandoned — no furniture, no pictures, nothing, except for this pair of feet." Strickland stuttered to a halt at this point, and Harris looked at her with concern.

"Go on. Who did these feet belong to? What did you see?"

"I can't. I can't. Don't ask me to talk about it." Strickland was close to tears.

Buller had already had enough of pussyfooting around. "Get on with it. Do your duty."

"Leave her alone," Olivia interrupted. "She's very young and she's very new to the job."

"If you can't stand the heat, get out of the kitchen."

With a sharp intake of breath, Olivia regained control of herself, bit her tongue and asked Harris to continue on their behalf.

"I want Strickland to give me her view of the scene." Buller wasn't giving up, and Strickland put her face in her hands and sobbed.

"Strickland, go home. You're obviously suffering from shock. Harris, you carry on."

"How dare you overrule me," Buller barked but, fortunately, Harris cut across him with his description of the scene that had greeted them in the house.

"It was just inside the first room to the right. There was a woman lying there, her limbs at funny angles. I couldn't work out what was strange about her at first, and then it suddenly came to me that her eyes had gone. They simply weren't in her face any more. There wasn't a lot of light. It was difficult to see details.

"My partner here was sick, and I accidentally trod on one of the woman's eyes," offered Harris. Strickland made a retching sound as he said this, and got a tissue out of her pocket.

"Go on."

"I thought she was dead, but she was moaning quietly, and her fingers were twitching, and I wondered how anyone could be alive after what had happened to her. After calling for medical help, we carried on checking the ground floor and we found the remains of that poor man in the kitchen. Claire was in a bit of a state by then, shaking all over, so I put her into another room where there was an old chair, settled her there, and then made my way through the rest of the house."

"And just where do you think you're going?" roared Buller, as Claire Strickland crept, mouse-like, towards the door.

"She's going home, Chief Inspector. She's not medically fit for work in the state she's in," Olivia challenged him.

"Then she needs to grow a backbone and a thicker skin. Stay here!"

"Go on, Strickland, shoo. Get yourself off home."

The young woman looked stricken and only left when Hardy went over, put an arm around her shoulder, and led her out into the corridor. "Don't come back until you're feeling better," she advised, guiding her towards the staircase.

Re-entering the room, she gave Buller a murderous look and asked Harris to continue his narrative.

"It was the second floor that was the most weird," he said, near the end of his story. "There were three doors, all with this really bright light coming from under them, and when I went in there, the whole place had been knocked into one huge space. All the walls, the floor and the ceiling had been lined with plastic and covered in tinfoil, with insulation sticking out at the seams. Even the windows were covered. There were fans blowing, and a huge extractor going into these flexible metal pipes, which were fed into the chimney breast.

"I suppose that was because of the smell — it was skunk — and the plants were obviously thriving on it. They were really bushy and healthy looking. Anyway, when I'd shown the paramedics where the woman was, and pointed out the man, just so they could check he was dead, I checked the electricity meter, and it had been disconnected, and none of the power was being paid for. Naughty, but nowhere on the same scale as the rest of the stuff in that house."

At that moment, there was a perfunctory knock on the door and Groves burst in looking peeved, saying, "Boss, O'Brien and Westbrook are back, but . . . oh, I didn't realise you had company." She had only just noticed Buller at Olivia's desk.

"And who might you be?" he asked impertinently.

"DS Groves, and I need to speak to DI Hardy urgently."

"Perhaps you'd like to have a little chat with me instead."

"I have no idea who the hell you are, and we are working on an important case," she replied, as Olivia winced at this uncharacteristically confrontational attitude.

"I, my dear, am DCI Buller from the drugs squad and, for your information, I am now the SIO on this case. So, what do you want to say to me?"

Groves blushed at her faux pas and began to stutter out her story. "DI Hardy asked me to link up with two of the DCs, get two lists of names from our records officer, and go out interviewing people to see if I could uncover anything about this morning's find."

"None of you will go blundering off into my territory without my say so," he informed her firmly. "Now, where are these other two DCs, so that I can put them straight?"

"They said they were coming back here," the sergeant answered uncertainly, looking fruitlessly round the office.

"What time is it?" Olivia looked at her watch, and added, "I should check the canteen. Knowing those two, they'll probably be shovelling chips down their throats by now. Gotta feed the inner man."

Buller sneered at the DI, looked lecherously at Groves and said, "Come on, darlin', let's go find these two master detectives and see what they've got to say for themselves. We can get a few things straight while we're at it: like, who's in charge. We'll leave Frumpty Dumpty here to finish off with PC Wooden-top."

As their footsteps faded away, Harris called after them, "I'm a Community Officer, not a PC," and Hardy let go of the breath she hadn't been aware that she was holding, in absolute fury.

"Who the hell does he think he is?" she hissed dangerously.

"He said he was a Detective *Chief* Inspector.," Harris offered quietly. "I think that means he holds all the aces."

"Well, he'd better watch his back. If I get the chance to slip a metaphorical knife between his shoulder blades, I shall bloody well do it. Write your report, Harris. I'm not in the mood for discussion now."

Seating herself at her now vacated desk, Hardy switched on her computer and noticed that the preliminary crime scene report from Forensics was in, along with the crime scene photographs, some of which, it would appear, had been taken by the quick-thinking Harris on his phone, before the paramedics could do their job. God, they were grim, those first photographs: the eyeless face a stomach-churning abomination, the state of the man's body in the kitchen resembling a scene from an abattoir.

"Damn!" she cursed out loud. She'd been so thrown by Buller's attitude that she hadn't had time to ask him if they had any intel on that address. She wasn't aware of any markers, but she'd need to check. She read through the preliminary forensic report as well, and was just about to enquire how things were going at the house when Lauren burst into the room.

"The bastard!" she spat, naming no one, but in no doubt that Olivia knew exactly whom she meant.

"I concur. What's your particular beef? Apart from the obvious."

"That shit just bulldozed into the canteen, dragged Daz and Teddy away from their lunch then gave all three of us an ear-bashing about alerting suspects that we were on to them. Your orders went right out of the window," she snarled, even though she hadn't agreed with them, "and said we were not to concern ourselves with any aspects of this case that involved illegal drugs."

"He can't do that!" Olivia was fuming all over again. "That'll completely handcuff us. This whole thing is about illegal drugs. Why else would those two have been attacked? One of them's dead, for God's sake."

The office door was knocked politely and Desai walked in, just back from the hospital, his face a little anxious. "Hello," Olivia greeted him, letting down the steam on her own personal pressure cooker. "How did

44

you get on with the fingerprints? How's the woman? Have you got an identity yet?"

"I had a bit of a problem with the deceased," he said, his face screwing up slightly.

"How come? How can you have a 'bit of a problem' taking the fingerprints of a corpse?"

"The top two joints of his right index finger were missing."

"Bummer. So what did you do?"

"I used the middle finger instead, but took the left index finger as well just to be sure."

"And? I can hardly stand the suspense."

"Nothing on the PNC. Same with the woman."

"This whole situation gets crazier by the hour. Has she spoken yet?"

"No, she's sedated and she was just off to theatre when I left. Shuttleworth is staying there as ordered until he's relieved and, if there's any change when she comes back, he'll radio in. When she does come round, though, I'd be willing to bet that she'll be in a hell of a state, what with the eyes thing."

"It's bloody grim, isn't it, knowing that you're never going to see anything again, and that you're so disfigured?"

"And we've got a new problem here and his name's Chief Inspector Buller from Drugs," announced Lauren, made bold by her ill-temper.

"Devenish has apparently put him in charge of the case," Olivia informed him before he could ask anything. "And he's installed his sergeant at the scene as crime scene manager."

"What shall I do?" asked Desai.

"Get yourself off, with Sergeant Groves here, to the houses behind Gooding Avenue and see what you can pick up from door-to-door. By the way, Sergeant, what happened to O'Brien and Westbrook after Buller finished chewing them out?"

"Don't ask me. I was just dismissed like a cheap tart at a party. Ask the bully boy when you see him."

"I hope you're feeling more civil when you're speaking to members of the public."

"Sorry, boss." Lauren, after some time, had finally landed on this mode of address for the inspector, both of them disliking "ma'am" and "guv".

When he had dismissed Groves, Buller allowed the two DCs to finish their lunch before discussing the lists that Fairbanks had provided the sergeant with, and of which he had relieved her in her final moments in the canteen. "Now, lads, we're going to go through these names, and I'm going to indicate which ones I'll allow you to talk to. Leave the others to Mike Jenner and me.

"We haven't had any word at all about this particular little factory, so I reckon it's either someone branching out, or a newbie just setting up. I'll put the word out on the street that there's a buyer looking for skunk in bulk, and see what I get back. Oh, and while you're out there, call into all the estate agents and see which of them is renting out the property."

Buller didn't have a problem dealing with men, but it was different when he was supposed to co-operate with women. He was going through a very vitriolic divorce at the moment, and he had never come to terms with women in authority. He was very much of the "keep 'em barefoot, pregnant and in the kitchen" brigade, which was probably why he would not rise any higher in rank that he had already.

He used to be able to keep a lot of his feelings schtum, but since the divorce had got under way it was a different matter. He was now a committed misogynist, believing that women should be kept in their place — a place at the bottom of the heap, or in the case of the police service, making teas and coffees for the male officers.

It was to be expected that he would get on well with Daz Westbrook, who was a great believer in male superiority. He would have done better in taking a lesson from Teddy O'Brien, who believed in equality and always gave "the fairer sex" their crack of the whip. After all, his mother had been sharp as a razor, and nobody had ever got one over on her.

"I'll also get the chopper to take a few sweeps over, see if anyone else is of the same enterprising mind," Buller added. At that early point in their relationship, Daz Westbrook blotted his copybook.

"Do you mean the Helicopter Response Unit?" he asked, with a smirk.

"You know bloody well what I mean, sonny! Don't get smart with me, or I'll kick your arse for you. Now, where was I? Right, if we're lucky, the *Helicopter Response Unit* might pick up something not so well insulated and letting off more heat. That thermal imaging camera that they carry could uncover a fresh turd in a five acre field. And, you never know; we might pick up a few others who are of a similar enterprising mind. The stuff I hate, though, is this skunk. If we could just get it separated out from the old hashish, we could decriminalise that and just go after the stinky stuff. That's the thing that drives kids psychotic. In my opinion."

"I'm of a similar mind," O'Brien agreed.

"Bang the lot of them up," snapped Westbrook. He was as intolerant of anyone who used drugs as Buller was of women, and he wanted to try to save face with the man. "Put the lot of them behind bars and throw away the key. That's what I think, anyway."

"Then maybe you should put in for a transfer to my department," suggested the chief inspector, slightly mollified at this macho attitude.

Westbrook's eyes widened in horror as he lowered his head. He'd never get away with anything again if he worked for this man; not that he got away with much with Hardy, but at least she was willing to hear his side of any story.

Hardy and Groves left on time that evening. They needed some time to get their heads around what Buller, already showing off his misogynistic and racist streaks, would do to the spirit and morale of the team. That both of them were in the firing line, there was no mistaking.

CHAPTER
FOUR

When Olivia got home to her cosy cottage, slowly being encroached upon by new housing estates, she found it empty. There was no Hal and there were no familiar smells of cooking. She had not expected Ben and Hibbie to be home as they were both going out this evening, and not in the confines of Littleton-on-Sea, but Hal's absence was a mystery. Her phone was devoid of voicemails or texts from him. This was unheard of, and she worried that something might have happened to him. Surely he hadn't been involved in an accident?

As she dumped her bag and went into the kitchen to put on the kettle, she noticed a piece of paper on the kitchen table, anchored with the cruet set. It was most unusual for her husband to leave a note for her, but that was what he had evidently done. Snatching it up, she learnt that he had been called in to teach just after she had left that morning. One of the regular English teachers had been involved in an accident, and he would be absent during school hours for the rest of the term. Then, of course, he was teaching English at a language school throughout the summer.

This was not good news. After she had ceased to worry about Hal's safety, Hardy had a rummage around in the freezer, eventually turning up an elderly microwave meal that she stuck resentfully into the machine. She had become very used to him being there when she came home, and having a meal already cooking for her. As the turntable revolved, she hoped he'd hate his new temporary post and would decide that he was better off where he was. She really wasn't looking forward to the next couple of months when her life, as she had known it since Hal had retired, would be turned upside down.

He used to play frequently in a steel band augmented with saxophones and congo drums, but bookings had been dropping off, and he'd had fewer gigs and less practices to attend. This was the main reason for him seeking other distractions, but she had not expected this offer of supply work to be taken up so suddenly, and for such a sustained period. She had thought he'd just get the odd day here and there. *Damn!* She'd have to revive her almost dead cooking skills and get back in the kitchen. That'd teach her to take him for granted.

The ping of the microwave brought her out of this reverie, and she wondered anew why he still wasn't home. A ting of her mobile advised her that a text had just arrived, and she opened it to find a message from Hal about a departmental meeting tonight that he would be expected to attend. It told her that he did not know when he'd be home. *Great!* She had expected to bounce all her frustrations off on him about the events of the day and the unexpected arrival of the obnoxious DCI Buller. Now, all she could do was watch the TV news, as she had absolutely no company whatsoever — just when she needed a shoulder most.

Flicking the "On" button, she grabbed her tiny dish of lasagne and a fork and flopped down on to the sofa. She had just started to load the limp pasta into her mouth when she heard something that nearly made her choke. "Police, today, were called to an address in Littleton-on-Sea on the south coast, where a man was found murdered, and a woman was gravely injured." The screen showed what was probably mobile phone footage evidently shot from a first floor window on the opposite side of the road.

"Paramedics and both uniformed and plain-clothes police officers attended the scene. Reports indicate that a substantial haul of drugs was seized at the property."

"Bloody hell!" she spluttered, getting sauce all down her front. "Talk about keeping something quiet. There's no sodding chance with everybody having a mobile that takes video footage. And no doubt they've been paid for their contribution to sharing information with every Tom, Dick and bleeding Harry."

"Three youths have been arrested in connection with the drugs find at the house, believed to be cocaine and heroin." Hardy swore roundly under her breath at this misinformation, although believing it vital that she knew what real details had got out, and what still remained confidential. She watched to the end, unable to comprehend what she was hearing. It seemed that DS Jenner had been recognised by someone, so that explained the conjecture about drugs, but the presence of the contraband still seemed to be under wraps.

Although it was probably pointless, she'd have to have a word with Buller tomorrow about getting the tobacco and alcohol out discreetly. And who the hell had been arrested, or was this just a product of the rumour mill that was in good working order hereabouts.

They'd have a team meeting first thing in the morning to share information, and she'd speak to him then. But were the three youths real or imaginary? She had to find out. Was someone just pulling the legs of the reporters? Maybe she'd phone in a bit later to check on progress — then she remembered how she'd been dismissed by Buller, and decided that if he was SIO, then he should do his job; it wasn't hers any longer.

As she switched off the set and went into the kitchen to chuck her cardboard container in the bin and her fork in the dishwasher, her mobile rang, and she rushed to answer it, sort of hoping it was Hal, saying that the meeting was already over. The lasagne had barely filled a corner, and she'd be quite happy to eat again if he were coming home to cook. It wasn't, and he wasn't.

When Lauren came through the front door, she heard the welcome chug of the dishwasher, and Mrs Moth, home help and childminder *exemplaire*, came out of the kitchen to greet her. The woman had been a godsend after what had happened with Kenneth, Lauren's soon to be ex-husband, and had started working for her about six months ago. Today, Lauren had phoned ahead to alert her that she wouldn't be late home, and the diligent woman had done her best to arrange for there to be nothing for her to do when she got in. The children had been collected from school, and Mrs Moth had supervised their homework at the kitchen table while cooking a meal for them. She had fed them and then sent them upstairs to get showered.

She came in about one thirty on weekdays, did a little cleaning, and then picked the children up from school. She stayed, doing whatever was needed, until Lauren got home, but maintained her own small flat, stating quite clearly that she wouldn't want to give up her independence. Lauren was more than happy with this arrangement as the woman was quite willing to do extra hours at the weekend if needed. Both her own children were now in Australia, so she relished the contact with young children as a substitute for her grandchildren.

"It's good to see you so early tonight, Mrs Groves. The children will be down in a couple of minutes, and the only thing for you to do is to see them up to bed and empty the plate put in the microwave for you."

"You're a doll, Mrs Moth: just what I needed. I thought I'd let you know that we've just had a big case break, and I'm likely to be late over the next few weeks until we've got everything sorted out."

"Don't you worry your head, my dear; you know I'm here whenever you need me. I'll be off then."

As she left, Sholto and Jade came thundering down the stairs, both with wet hair and in their nightclothes. "Can we watch cartoons, please, Mummy?" She shooed them off into the sitting room — it was just the sitting room, not "the drawing room", as Kenneth had always pretentiously referred to it: a man with a beer background and champagne aspirations, if ever she'd met one — and went off to heat up her food. She really appreciated Mrs Moth cooking for both the children and her. The woman also ate her own meal with the children, but it saved Lauren so much time that she didn't in the least mind.

Once sitting at the table, however, she merely picked at her food, mulling over the attitude of the DCI who had been thrust upon them. After a while, she began to get a bit twitchy and realised she was thinking of the bottle of wine chilling in the fridge.

It was something that was happening with alarming regularity now that she was officially a single parent and not just a woman with a husband working abroad. She was changing. She had hardly ever touched alcohol when she was half of a respectable married couple. But there was something about there not actually being someone who would phone later and ask her how her day had been that left her feeling like a shell, and one that could only be filled by a nice chilled white. Kenneth would hardly recognise her if he came across her now. On some of her off-duty days she didn't even put on make-up and just slopped around in a pair of jeans and a T-shirt.

She wasn't really hungry now, her appetite having disappeared at her memories of Buller, but she couldn't get the corkscrew out just yet. She didn't like to drink in front of the children; it set such a bad example.

Instead, she made herself a cup of strong coffee, slipped her plate back into the microwave in case she should get peckish later, and went into the sitting room to join the children, whose eyes were glued to the screen at the antics of a rather unpleasant creature which wasn't exactly human, but couldn't be categorised as an animal either. Her thoughts, however, were still on the bottle waiting for her in the fridge, and it was a little earlier than usual that she escorted her offspring up to bed.

Assuring them that they could read for an hour, she kissed them goodnight and headed purposefully back down the stairs, the bottle calling her like a homing device. Having both been to boarding school, when their parents were still together, both children were trained not to get out of bed after they'd been bidden goodnight, and only ever did so if they were in need of the bathroom. Knowing that she had an uninterrupted evening ahead of her — and an unusually long one — she removed the corkscrew from the cutlery drawer and opened the fridge door.

When she'd had a glass or so she would put on the evening news, which she always recorded so that she could keep up with what was going on in the world in peace: not that she didn't love the children, but she just wasn't used to them being around all the time, and it took some getting used to.

The first two glasses went down almost like water, and she was beginning to feel rather relaxed when she heard the item on their latest case. Swiftly chugging a third glass, she grabbed her phone and punched in Olivia's number.

"What's all this rubbish about cocaine and heroin; and who leaked information about a drugs find?" she almost bellowed into the handset, and Olivia, at the other end, pulled her phone away from her ear a little. "And who the hell have they arrested?"

"Lauren, what are you so worked up about?" Olivia asked, momentarily forgetting her own little fit of swearing when she had heard the same report. "It was probably someone who recognised Sergeant Jenner going into the house. You know the sort of people who rent some of those flats."

"But they had some visual footage as well," Lauren protested, unappeased.

"From someone's mobile phone, no doubt. You know how Joe Public likes to get in first as far as news goes. Why are you so worked up about this?"

"I'm just wondering what that bastard Buller will say about this tomorrow. He'll blame us, no doubt about it. 'S obvious."

Hearing this verbal inaccuracy, Olivia asked her, "Lauren, have you been drinking?"

"Just a li'l one," she admitted.

"It was more than that. And have you eaten?"

"Not really."

"Then get some food down you and go to bed. You'll feel more balanced in the morning."

Realising that she'd been rumbled, Lauren ended the call before Olivia could get huffy with her. "Who's she to say what I should or shouldn't drink?" she asked herself, pouring and downing another glass, then heading back to the kitchen to make sure she had another bottle in reserve.

Having assured herself that she wasn't about to run out of wine, she crept upstairs, took off her make-up and had a short shower, then slipped into her nightie and dressing gown so that she only had to lock up when she'd had a few more slugs of Chateau Oublier. She chuckled at her own joke as she uncorked her second bottle, realising that drinking in the evening was starting to become more than a bit of a habit since the children had left boarding school. It was almost a necessity, now.

Hal arrived home at nine thirty, his eyes dancing. "Had a good day, have we?" asked Olivia sarcastically, still miffed that he hadn't called her and let her know he'd been called into work, but he didn't even notice.

"Do you fancy a bacon butty?" he asked, ignoring her mood. "Do you know I'd forgotten how much I'd missed the chalkface. I had years seven and eight today, and the head of department spent some time going through this half-term's work with me in her free periods."

"All right for some, I suppose," said Olivia in a sulky voice, but Hal didn't seem to notice this either, and carried on eulogising about his teaching and the profession in general, while he got out the frying pan and a loaf of bread. It didn't look like she was going to get a chance to get the events of her day off her chest. Hal had the limelight, and didn't seem to be in the mood to relinquish it.

Interlude

As darkness fell, there was a faint flicker of light in the old Nissen hut in the woods, the occasional shadow moving between it and the grimy window with the tattered curtains hanging.

Inside, there was a loud moan of pain followed by a sudden scream, quickly stifled as more whisky was poured into the wide-open mouth. Both her legs were restrained as she struggled, and a dirty rag was stuffed into her mouth.

Her screams were more muffled now, even though they rose in intensity and frequency until, with one almighty explosion of agony, it stopped. Other cries sounded out, but a pair of hands dived between her legs and, with one twist, there was silence.

CHAPTER
FIVE

Lauren woke up still sprawled on the sofa in her nightie and dressing gown, both children shaking her nervously.

"Mummy, Mummy, are you ill?" asked Jade in a frightened voice.

"Or did you just come down early to watch some TV?" asked Sholto, who was somewhat obsessed with the medium, now he wasn't restrained by a boarding school timetable, and compulsory games at the weekends.

Lauren realised that the set was still on, and that she had never made it to bed. Thank God she'd had the forethought to take off her make-up and shower before settling down with her wine.

"Mummy, why have you got an empty bottle and a glass beside your chair? Have you been drinking pop?" Jade was still quite innocent, but Sholto gave his mother a sly wink, being the older and more worldly-wise of the pair. With one look at his mother's reaction to this, however, he picked up the give-away articles and headed for the kitchen, urging his sister to go upstairs and get dressed.

"Otherwise we'll miss breakfast and be late for school," he concluded, and the little girl willingly obeyed.

Lauren shook herself, becoming aware of how dishevelled she must look, and the fact that her head was banging and her mouth was as dry as a desert. She headed straight for the kitchen where she threw water over her face, dried it with some kitchen roll and ran herself a glass of water, quickly followed by another. This hung-over state was becoming more frequent as time went by in her post-Kenneth life.

She then put cereal packets, bowls and spoons on the table, quickly followed by the sugar bowl and — horror of horrors — a bottle of milk straight from the fridge. She then put bread in the toaster and fled upstairs to get dressed as quickly as possible, and take a couple of paracetamol to try to control the drummer in her head — make-up she could manage in the Ladies at work, but she had to get the children to school on time, and she mustn't miss the morning meeting. Fortunately, the school operated flexible opening times, and children arrived to actually be fed their breakfast from eight o'clock onwards.

After changing her underwear, she put on clothes clean from the wardrobe and dragged a brush through her hair before returning to the kitchen to put the toast on plates and added butter and jam to the items on the kitchen table. She had to help Jade with her buttering, and then got jam on her clean blouse. "Bugger!" she shouted, only to have both children chastise her for swearing. With a quick "sorry", she raced back upstairs to get another clean blouse. This was surely a great start to the day, and she only hoped it wasn't uphill all the way, from here on in.

The day didn't get off to a sparkling start in Olivia's home either. When she finally got downstairs, it was to an empty kitchen, the smell of coffee and toast lingering on the air, but no signs of Hal. Filling the kettle and putting a couple of slices of bread in the toaster to burn, she tried his mobile number, but it was switched off.

With a muffled curse, she put a couple of spoonfuls of instant coffee powder into a cup, and ejected the toast before it set off the smoke alarm; that was one small triumph in a day with an unaccustomedly lonely start. Wincing with distaste as she sipped the coffee, she surveyed the day ahead of her.

Although Hardy wasn't late into the office, DS Jenner had beaten her to it, and had already got the incident board up and running. He greeted her with a smile and a courteous "good morning", and she thought he was probably not of the same ilk as his senior officer. While she took a quick look at her overnight emails, the rest of the members of her team began to drift in, Lauren last of all, to be closely followed by the abominable showman. Buller called the meeting to order and immediately took up the reins.

"Right!" he began, slapping the palms of his hands together to get their attention. "I've already consulted with Devenish and there's been a request to EIS to see

61

if they have any ID on our chummies." Westbrook mumbled something under his breath just as Olivia broke in.

"I don't usually address my officers like some extra from *The Sweeney*," she informed him. "I usually find plain English suffices."

The man's brow clouded, his eyebrows drawn into a furious frown, as he replied to this confrontational response. "Thank you very much for your input, *Inspector*. I shall bear in mind that I have to use a kindergarten vocabulary to deal with your officers." This was clearly a warning shot across her bows.

"Now, to couch it in more simple terms for the *simple* minds involved, there has been a request put in to the Europol Information Service, to see if they can identify our dead man and injured woman. They don't look British to me, so we might have to get Immigration involved."

He was interrupted again by Leo, who asked him if he would identify *him* as British. "Because I'm third generation, tha knows." Broadening his accent, he continued, "Yorkshire born and Yorkshire bred . . ."

"Strong in th'arm and thick in th'ead," his colleagues concluded for him, in unison.

"Settle down now and pay attention." Buller had raised his voice, ignoring the obvious challenge. He had not expected this sort of disruption to his words of wisdom. "HMRC came at four o'clock this morning, and removed the contraband via the back entrance so as not to draw attention to their activities —"

"And someone called in at four oh-five to report a burglary," interrupted Desai, just by way of information. They were clearly showing respect for their erstwhile guv'nor.

"I will not have this level of insubordination!" Buller shouted, thoroughly irritated that he wasn't being taken seriously or treated with sufficient respect.

"What level would you like?" asked some wag in an undertone, as Olivia stepped in to defuse the situation, the flames of which she had originally fanned, with her *Sweeney* reference.

"Settle down, now, settle down and let the man do his job," she called above the sniggers that had broken out, secretly pleased that she had caused such disruption to what he must have considered would be a straight team talk.

"And the cannabis plants are being, as we speak, taken away to be destroyed," he continued, trying to look unruffled, although he had been surprised by this mutinous start to the meeting. His hostile, in-your-face attitude normally cowed junior officers into submission.

"Both victims had tattoos, which have been photographed and sent off in an attempt to put a name to their owners, and I have information from the hospital that the woman is going to be allowed to wake up, in her own time, today, so I want somebody to be ready to go over there and interview her."

"And if she doesn't speak English?" asked Lauren, a little of the anger she still felt about the news report the evening before still remaining.

"Then we work out what language she speaks and bring in an interpreter."

"What about that news bulletin that said cocaine and heroin had been found at the property?" Lenny Franklin wanted to get in his two penn'orth.

"We let the media think what they want to think. They'll have to wait for an official statement if they want accuracy."

"What about the reported arrests?"

"Pure fiction. Now, I have various bodies that I want interviewed today, and I want you to work in pairs . . ." The phone on Olivia's desk trilled at that moment, and she went straight to answer it. Buller stood in silence while she conducted a curt conversation.

"Sorry. I've got to go," she informed him. "It's really rather lucky that we have such a senior officer to head up this case, so that we can be spared. Come along, Groves." She knew she was pushing her luck, but she really *did* have to go, and the timing couldn't have been better, in her opinion.

The young woman in jeans and T-shirt went into the small shop and walked around its shelves for a couple of minutes, before approaching the counter and asking for forty cigarettes, and putting a packet of biscuits beside the till. The cigarettes were the cheapest on sale, and the biscuits were the own brand of the small supermarket chain that had recently bought out the shop. She handed over a twenty-pound note and waited somewhat distractedly for her change, before leaving at a snail's pace.

64

The shop was on the very edge of the town and the manager — who was also the previous owner of the premises — had felt himself lucky to be made an offer by a nationwide chain, as the footfall wasn't great. He had another customer in for a newspaper and some rolling tobacco when he heard yells from outside. It was quite early but it was warm, so he had his door slightly ajar, and he easily heard the calls of distress.

The customer immediately abandoned his newspaper and baccy and rushed off without paying, whilst the manager stood scratching his head about what could be happening. He was no have-a-go hero and, if he lost a sale over the yelling, so be it: it wasn't his loss any more now.

After a couple more minutes a well-built middle-aged woman entered the shop, slightly out of breath. "There's a woman round the corner who's had her baby pinched out of the car," she puffed, planting her elbows on the counter to support her while she recovered from the unaccustomed exercise. "There's a bloke who says he's been in here with her a few moments ago, and he's just phoned the police."

"And you are here because . . .?" he asked, slightly at a loss.

"They might want to bring her in somewhere near the scene of the crime, and the bloke's sent me to warn you, in case they want to use a back room or something."

The man's eyes rolled and he sighed in disbelief. Police in his shop wouldn't do anything good for what trade there still was.

As Lauren clattered down the stairs before the retreating figure of Olivia, she hissed, "I don't know how you had the nerve to do that."

The inspector turned her head slightly and said, "There's a young baby been taken from a car. We need to move quickly. Terry Friend and Liam Shuttleworth are already on their way." This was a reference to two of the uniformed branch based at the station, the former very skilled at getting information out of distressed people and generally calming them down. She was often used to break bad news and deal with the recipient's reaction.

On the short drive, Olivia said bluntly, "You're looking rather wan today. Do you feel OK?"

"I didn't get the chance to put any make-up on this morning. I slept in a bit," Lauren replied, looking pointedly out of the window instead of at the driver.

"No. There's something more than that. Is there something troubling you, or are you coming down with something?"

"Look, I'm fine. Stop fussing," the sergeant insisted in a peeved voice.

"You know you can confide in me, and it won't go any further. I'm very good at keeping a confidence."

"Will you just stop badgering me?" Lauren now turned her head and almost spat the words at the inspector.

Olivia gave her a quick, surprised glance, and said, "Sorry I asked. I was just showing friendly concern," in a conciliatory voice.

66

"When I want someone to confide in, I'll tell you," Lauren replied, whipping her head round to stare out of the passenger window again, as they passed their goal.

Olivia had been directed to Shah's Minimart on Beach Road, a route that joined the shops of the town with the sea, but was in a sort of no-man's-land where tourists and locals usually passed in cars on their way to somewhere else. It was at the other end of the town from the railway station and, although it sold buckets and spades and other plastic beach paraphernalia, picked up none of the foot traffic that streamed off the trains in summer. The day-trip market definitely took the shortest route to the sea and the sand, and didn't usually go exploring off this well-beaten track.

It didn't help that, within the last few years, double yellow lines had been painted along this road, and the locals who used to pop in for a paper or some run-out-of essential, now went to the supermarket as being, not only cheaper, but easier to park, especially as a couple of the bigger supermarkets were offering twenty-four hour opening. The long opening hours of Mr Shah's establishment were now no longer the only choice.

The closest parking was along Jubilee Road, which was always fairly full of residents' cars. A car just pulling out halfway along would do, although there was a bit of a hike back to the shop. The marked car that Friend and Shuttleworth had arrived in was visible much nearer to the corner.

As they left the car, both of them slamming their doors in ill temper, they became aware of a man standing on the pavement a few cars up from them, looking rather lost. Lauren plastered a rather wan smile across her face and approached him, saying, "Can I be of any assistance, sir?"

Without hesitation, he explained his dilemma. "I'm waiting for someone from the police to come and look at this car here." He indicated a badly parked and rather battered model beside him. "There's been a kiddie snatched from it, and they'll need to test for fingerprints and suchlike."

"We're the police," the sergeant explained as Olivia stood sullenly beside her. "You probably noticed our colleagues parking just up the road."

"They were the ones that told me to wait here, until someone else could get to it."

"And you are?"

"Eric White. I was just picking up my paper and baccy from the shop when there was this almighty scream, and I dropped what I was buying and just rushed round here. This woman come along and she took the lass back to the shop to have a sit down."

"If you'll just wait a few more minutes, Mr White, I'll send back one of the uniformed officers to lock and put police tape round the car, and he can summon forensic assistance. Perhaps, then, you could come round to the shop and make a statement?"

"Fine by me. I need my paper and baccy, and I was just keeping guard as requested."

Olivia and Lauren walked round the corner to a shop that had a new sign for that of a nationwide "local" supermarket, another sign languishing against the wall for "Shah's Minimart — Newsagent and Tobacconist".

"God, he was lucky to get out," commented Olivia, indicating the discarded sign. "This has all the looks of a coal mine rather than a gold mine."

"What do you mean by that?" asked Lauren, thawing slightly.

"All the signs of imminent closure," replied Olivia, pushing wide the door.

Inside, Mr Shah was back behind his counter, a sickly smile on his face as he eyed up PC Shuttleworth, who was standing just outside a door that must lead to a back room, not happy at all at this obvious police presence; not that any of his customers were shifty, but because a lot of them just didn't like the police.

"Morning, ma'am, Sergeant," he greeted them. "PC Friend is in what Mr Shah refers to as his 'stockroom', just through here." He indicated the door and then stood almost to attention.

"Can you slip off round the corner and speak to Mr White who is very patiently waiting there to give you a statement, please, Constable? And radio for someone to come and take photographs and fingerprints? Usual procedure," Olivia said while making for the entrance to the rear of the premises. "If you don't mind, sir?" she asked in a perfunctory manner as the shopkeeper nodded for her to go through, and Shuttleworth informed him that that was the DI and a DS going through.

On the other side of the door Olivia and Lauren found a young woman and a large middle-aged woman, both seated on plastic chairs amidst all the boxes and packets of stock. The older woman had her arm around the younger woman's shoulders, and was trying to soothe her while she cried. Terry Friend was crowded against a unit piled high with boxes of biscuits.

"Can I have your names, please?" the inspector asked, trying to look comfortable in the little space left for the two new arrivals.

"I'm Rosemary Kent, and this is Carole Shillington. Her little baby's been nicked from her car," she added, self-importantly. "I'm looking after her."

"And a very fine job you've done, love," commented Friend, with a slightly exasperated expression. "I've got your statement, so I think you can get back home now. I have your contact details."

"Are you sure you wouldn't like me to stay?" the large woman asked wistfully.

"We'll get in touch if we need any more information from you," said Lauren, in a no-nonsense voice. The last thing they needed was this nosebag hanging around filling her gossip tanks through the distress of the mother.

When she'd gone, Lauren had managed to find other plastic chairs from a stack at the back of the storeroom, and brought them forward so that all four of them could sit, although it was a tight squeeze, and all their knees were touching. Terry Friend took a seat gratefully, rolling her eyes dramatically.

"Right, Carole, is it?" began Olivia. "Can you tell us exactly what happened?"

Lauren handed the young woman a tissue so that she could blow her nose and wipe her eyes before starting. "I only came in here to get ciggies and biccies for me boyfriend," she began. "I left Stacey — that's me little baby — in the car seat. I was only gone for a couple of minutes, but when I went back, she'd gone." At this point she burst into fresh tears, and they had to wait for her to pull herself together, Terry Friend patting her shoulder to comfort her.

"She's only six weeks old. Who'd want to take such a little baby? She doesn't know anyone but me, her mum."

"What did she have on?"

"A little pink towelling romper, and I put a shawl over her to keep the sun off of her. Her skin is so delicate. And the shawl's gone as well."

"Anything else?"

"A tiny mob cap with frills round the edges. It made her look so pretty." The memory silenced her, and she sat, just staring at her hands.

"How old are you, love?" asked PC Friend.

"I'm seventeen; eighteen next month."

"Let's get you home. The other constable will take care of any evidence in the car, and we'll get someone to go door-to-door to see if anybody saw someone either at the car or hanging around just before you arrived. It's not beyond the bounds of possibility that someone from a nearby house took her in, in case she got too hot. Did you lock the car?"

"The lock don't work," she informed them in a sniffling voice.

"We'll get you down to the station where you can make a proper signed statement, and we'll probably want you to make an appeal on local television if we haven't found your baby before the end of the afternoon," Lauren told her in a no-nonsense, practical voice.

"But what about me boyfriend?" she asked, suddenly looking more worried than upset.

"He'll not mind when you've told him what's happened. It is his baby, isn't it?"

"'Course it is. What do you think I am?"

"Calm down, and I'll get DS Groves here to bring round the car."

"What about *my* car?"

"We'll get someone to return it to you when we've finished with it. Constable Friend here will go in the back with you."

Lauren took the keys and went back to Beach Road where she asked Liam Shuttleworth to get in touch with Social Services, just in case they were needed.

After a cup of tea, the sober atmosphere of the police station seemed to calm the young mother and, as she drank cup after cup of tea, she told her story and then, when it was prepared as an official statement, signed it placidly.

"We'll get all available officers out on the street looking for her," Olivia assured her, "and I'll have someone go through the relevant CCTV footage to see if anyone can be seen carrying her. There wasn't a pushchair in the car, was there?"

"No, I use a sling when I take her out. We're saving for a second-hand pram at the moment but she hardly weighs anything, and I like the feel of her next to my body," explained the young woman.

"That might just make our job that much easier. Now, shall we get you back home, so that you can have a bit of privacy?"

Carole Shillington looked slightly deflated at this suggestion and it crossed Olivia's mind that she could have been enjoying the attention she had received as an almost pleasant interlude in an otherwise drab and lonely life. "Now, you wait a minute while I get things moving here, then come with my sergeant and me and we'll get you into a car and off home." This would afford a good opportunity to have a look around.

When they had originally arrived back at the station, Olivia had made sure that Devenish knew about the abduction and awaited his accurately predicted reply. He had, of course, ordered that all available personnel should be dispatched to the network of streets from where the child had reportedly been taken, then announced that he would be making a television appeal for the safe return of little Stacey that very evening and would much appreciate it if the parents could be present too for this.

When this request was passed on to Carole Shillington, a frown of doubt crossed her face and she said she didn't reckon that Baz would be up for having his face plastered all over the TV screens of the region,

73

but agreed that she would be there if someone could pick her up and take her to wherever it was being filmed.

"I mean, I don't need a babysitter any more," she said in a half-hearted attempt at jest.

Carole's flat proved to be little more than a bedsit, on the ground floor of the grim, concrete sixties block situated near the council estate where many of the properties had now been sold off. The grey block, however, had few owner-occupiers, and most held a transient population who lived off benefits, drugs and alcohol.

Hardy couldn't help herself, and when they got out of the car, she said, "Is this area really suitable for a young baby?"

"We can't afford anything bigger or better, OK?" Carole was obviously stung by the thoughtless comment, and Hardy was moved to add, "We all have to start somewhere," before buttoning her lip before she did any further damage to their relations with the girl.

"I'll have to go in and let Baz — Barry, that is — know that you're here," she said with a confrontational air.

"Is that Stacey's father?"

"Oh, he ain't here," was their only answer, as she disappeared through the door and poked her head round an adjacent door. "He never told me he was going out." She then turned and invited them in. "We ain't got much, but at least what we've got is clean."

And it was. There was a tiny living room which seemed to be acting as somewhere to eat as well, a minute kitchen and shower room, and a rather undersized bedroom into which a second-hand Moses basket had been squeezed, perched on an old chest of drawers.

"Let me make us all some tea. There's no need to show me, I think I can find everything," chirped Terry Friend, disappearing through a bead curtain into the kitchenette.

"Do you have photographs of Stacey that we could look at? We'll need to take one with us, of course, but you can have it back when we've finished with it." Lauren got straight down to business after a signal from Hardy. Olivia was worried that her comment on arriving at the flat may have soured the poor girl's attitude towards her.

"I've only got one that me mum took of her at the hospital," she said sadly, reaching for a cheap frame on a small coffee table, "But me mum's got a computer, and she took some others on her phone and said she'd transfer them and print them for me."

"And how can we get in touch with your mum?"

"She's on holiday."

"Do you want to tell her what's happened?"

"Not really. We don't get on that well. She doesn't approve of Baz."

"Is there any way we can get a key to her place to access the other photographs. Babies change quite a lot between birth and six weeks."

"I think her next door neighbour's got a key, but she won't let me have one. She doesn't trust Baz not to rob her when she's out."

"I think you ought to phone her and ask her permission for us to enter the house for the photographs. This is your daughter's life we're talking about here," said Lauren with a little more drama than was necessary.

"She doesn't like me disturbing her."

"Would you like us to get in touch with her to try to emphasize how important it is? Then we can ask her to phone her next door neighbour and warn her that someone will be coming round."

"Yes, please. She hates me living here, and she doesn't think Baz is good enough for me." As she eased the sleeves of her long-sleeved T-shirt up her arms a bit in the heat, the edges of bruises began to come in to view. There were a couple of yellowing ones and a fresh, blue one on the other arm. She glanced down to where Olivia was staring and hurriedly pulled her sleeves down again.

"I fell down," she hurried to explain, then blushed, and Olivia wondered how falling down could give you bruises that looked like fingermarks.

"We'll take the photograph because there'll have to be a television appeal, but we promise we'll copy it and return it to you as soon as possible," Lauren assured her, holding out a hand for the precious snapshot.

She handed it over reluctantly, as they promised to speak to her mother as soon as they got round to the office. "All we need now is your mother's mobile number and her address, if you wouldn't mind." The girl gave an address in a rather upmarket part of the town, and all three of the police personnel understood why her mother didn't like her living where she did. They hadn't met Baz yet, but they would all have put money on him not speaking with an RP accent.

At a quelling look from the inspector, they all got up to leave, not having said a word about the place having to be searched as part of standard procedure, and it was only when they were back in the car, her in the driving seat this time, that she explained.

"When we were going round that tiny flat, I saw some discarded pieces of tinfoil, just peeking out from under the bed, and I'm sure I could smell cannabis as well — not really recent, but not dispersed. I reckon a surprise visit to Baz's drum might turn up a few interesting things. And, if that girl's not got a social worker, she obviously needs one. Did you see those bruises on her arm? No wonder she wears a T-shirt with sleeves in this unseasonably hot weather."

"Who are you going to send round to search and to get copies of the photographs from the mother's house?"

"Westbrook and O'Brien, I think, so long as Buller the bully's not got them in detention for not handing over their dinner money." Terry Friend let out a little giggle at this, but Lauren's face remained serious. She didn't like Buller, and she thought he was dangerous.

At five o'clock, a police car came to pick up Carole Shillington to make the appeal, which was going to be filmed in the conference room at the police station. The filming team wanted to get it in the can a little before its scheduled broadcast, so that it could be suitably edited.

Baz was nowhere to be found when the mother was collected, but this was no surprise, as his partner had predicted that he was a little publicity-shy. She showed her youth in that she seemed quite excited at the thought of being on "the telly", and had evidently made an effort with her appearance.

She took her place at the long table at the front of the room and beside Devenish with an air of quiet excitement, her eyes agog at the technicians preparing to record the event, but reality caught up with her as the cameras started rolling and the superintendent began to narrate the tale of the child's disappearance.

As he began his appeal to members of the public for any information they might have that would assist the police in tracing this young, vulnerable child, tears filled her eyes, and her shoulders began to shake. It was as if she suddenly realised that all of this was actually happening. She wasn't just getting herself on "the telly"; she had been deprived of her beloved daughter, and she wanted her back with all her heart.

Devenish was a firm believer that tears from a parent or partner pulled on the heartstrings and made the public more vigilant; more likely to remember something that they might not have thought important, and he silently applauded Carole's sense of the theatrical, although he would not have expressed this opinion so bluntly. Quietly though, he was of the opinion that he couldn't have asked for a better performance than she had given. When there was a final call of "cut", he smiled as he rose to go back to his office, finished with his tiny part in the drama, and oblivious to the fact that all the work was still ahead of his officers. He'd done his bit. What more could be asked of him? This should raise his profile with the top brass, he thought smugly as he trotted back to his eyrie on the second floor.

CHAPTER
SIX

Meanwhile, back at the ranch, Buller had reported that at an evening visit to those in the vicinity of number three Gooding Avenue, any who had not been at home during the day had been spoken to, and the daughter of the Dennings at number five had admitted to seeing someone go into the house during the night.

"She said she had been unable to sleep, and went out into the porch for a cigarette — a habit she was supposed to have given up, and didn't want her parents smelling. Silly bitch!" It was Lenny Franklin who had made the visit, but Buller had wanted the glory of announcing it. Magnanimously, he nodded to Lenny to take up the story. "But don't make a meal of it," he warned him.

Lenny raised a cynical eyebrow and took up the tale. "She was in her nightie, so she stayed at the back of the porch, not wanting any neighbours to see her. You get some right chancers in those flats."

"Get on with it!"

"She was looking down the road, away from this end of it, and she saw this guy sort of slouching along it. Even though it was warm, he had a hoodie on, but as he was approaching a lamp-post, she caught a glimpse of him, and he pulled the hood back as he let himself in. She said he had red curly hair and freckles."

"That's a bit conspicuous, isn't it?" asked Desai.

"That's what I thought. Can any of you think of someone who looks like that on our radar?" There was a negative murmur from the members of the team, and the shaking of heads.

"Right, well, keep your eyes peeled," Buller ordered. "I've spoken to her this morning and asked her to come in and see if we can't get a likeness of this mysterious ginger." This last word he pronounced with hard "g"s. "I've also got a handler with a sniffer dog going round that place a bit later, now that everything's been taken out of it. Yeah, it'll go ape if it's let up to the second floor, but we need to be absolutely sure about the ground and the first floors. Now, I've got your tasks for this morning here . . ."

When they began to disperse, Buller made himself scarce, hinting that he had more important matters to deal with. DS Jenner stayed behind with the two DCs who were last to leave. Lenny Franklin had been paired with Daz Westwood, and they had, unspoken, decided to see what they could get out of the Drugs sergeant.

"Hard man, is he, your guv'nor?" asked Daz, somewhat impertinently.

"Harder than you could imagine."

"Tell us," Lenny urged him.

"I'll not go into detail," responded Jenner coyly, "but he's been shot twice: once in the shoulder and once in the thigh."

"Sounds dodgy." — Daz was so called because he was easily dazzled, and not because his name was Darren.

"It was. A couple of inches higher and he would've been singing with the sopranos. He's had quite a few beatings, a fractured skull and God knows how many drug dealers have threatened to kill him." Jenner fell silent.

"Is that it?" Daz asked in disappointment.

"That's all you're getting from me. Oh, and I'd advise you never to cross him. That would be most unfortunate, and rather unpleasant for you," said the sergeant, heading out of the office.

"What do you mean by that?"

"Just heed my words, or you could be very sorry."

"Bloody party-pooper," muttered Westbrook, and Lenny Franklin raised an eyebrow once more.

They were primed with the best photographs that could be provided of the victims — in the woman's case, an artist's impression — and had been instructed to go round all the supermarkets. As Buller had stated logically, they had to go out sometime just to buy food, even if they went out in the wee small hours to shops that were open twenty-four hours — and they might have gone with a third party if spoken English was a problem.

When Olivia and Lauren got back, the office was eerily empty and Olivia's phone was trilling urgently. Just her luck. It was the superintendent, wanting to be brought up to date on the missing baby case, and she was summoned in no uncertain terms. She might have been frightened of no one, but there was something about Devenish that made her knees shake and the only conclusion she could come to on this one was that she loved her job and didn't want to lose it.

"So, give me an update, Inspector," he snapped, spearing her with his eyes. "Have we had any responses to the appeal yet?"

"All the usual nutters have rung in, and the baby has been spotted in Brighton, Norwich, Birmingham and Inverness to name but a few. I know everything needs checking out, however insane, but I don't think we have got anything concrete yet; nothing that will actually help us locate the baby."

"Not good enough," barked Devenish, "you need to find that baby safe and well, and more to the point, quickly, Hardy! And where the hell was the father during that appeal, or isn't there one?"

"There is, but he's proving hard to pin down."

"Then make like a lepidopterist and get out your box of pins. This is a specimen we *need* to capture."

"Sir!" A heartbeat of a pause and then she continued, "And what about the two people from yesterday?"

"Media silence on that one until we've got more information. Dismissed."

She certainly felt it.

Hardy returned to her office and made the phone call she needed to make to Carole Shillington's holidaying mother. Mrs Shillington was much more concerned for her granddaughter's safety than she was about her daughter's emotional state, and immediately gave permission for the photographs to be copied from her computer, readily submitting her password and agreeing to phone the keyholder next door. "But do excuse any mess," she concluded. "I went off on holiday in a bit of a hurry."

She must have used the last number dialled in, because she was back on Hardy's phone in a few minutes. "I rang my neighbour on her mobile, and she's just gone off on an overnight trip, so you can't have the keys until tomorrow, although she'll be back quite early."

"How early?" She didn't consider it was as vital as she'd made out to the mother, because she didn't reckon that babies changed *that* much in six weeks. She thought a baby was a baby was a baby, if it weren't your own. The things that should help to trace her were the pink romper suit and the flowered mob cap.

"About nine. She's got her daughter dropping her off around half past."

That was all right, then. She'd get someone out there in the morning, and if the kid had changed that much, she could give the photos to the Super so that he could make another appearance on television. That should please him. The only other options open to her were finding a keyholder for the keyholder's property, or actually breaking into it, which would not go down at all well with the brass.

That lunchtime, Lauren left the station before Olivia could ask her if she wanted to go for something to eat with her. That was unusual, and she realised that the sergeant had moved slightly away in their friendship. It was weeks since they had shared a musical evening together, or even mentioned the possibility of one.

She supposed it was just a symptom of getting her social life back together after the break-up of her marriage but she, nevertheless, felt slightly snubbed. She had to take into account that she didn't have a built-in babysitter any more, now that that hussy Gerda had cleared off with Kenneth, but that wouldn't stop her from asking Hardy over to her place. Maybe it was having the children at home now, and not at boarding school. Perhaps she just didn't have the time or the energy with her new responsibilities.

She was still not back in the office by mid-afternoon when DCI Buller came charging in with a face that looked like he'd won the lottery. "How's your luck?" asked the DI, chancing her arm, as he seemed to be in such a good mood.

"Couldn't be better," he almost chirped back. "That sniffer dog really came up trumps. I don't know where the press got their information from yesterday, but it certainly wasn't from us."

"How do you mean?"

"The dog only turned up cocaine and heroin underneath a couple of floorboards: brilliantly fitted back into place, but no match for a trained dog's nose."

"How come the media knew and we didn't?" asked Hardy, very surprised.

"That's what I intend to find out. It wouldn't be from whoever feels they own the drugs so, somewhere out there in that crumbling mass of housing, there's someone who knows full well what's been going on."

"So, what are you going to do about it?"

"I'm going to start with leaning on the local press, then I'm going to dig a bit further afield. It'll no doubt be what they will refer to as an 'anonymous tip-off', but we can only hope." Then he was gone, his eyes sparkling at the thought of a bit of freelance bullying and leaning on people.

But she had some leaning on to do herself, with a few hooky characters who had been brought in that morning: known users who were willing to let out the odd bit of information about their suppliers, provided it paid for a few more wraps or spliffs and it couldn't be traced back to them.

She eventually spotted Lauren at the end of the corridor, in what looked like earnest conversation with Daz Westbrook. Without a second thought, she called, "Put the boy down, Sergeant. I have urgent need of your services," and was surprised when her partner jumped as if she'd been caught out in something irregular.

"Just coming," called Groves, turning on her heel and walking away with a look of innocence on her face.

"What was all that about, then?"

"Nothing important. Just general chit-chat about the case. You just made me jump, that's all."

"And why are you so sensitive all of a sudden?"

"I guess the way that woman was injured has given me the creeps. What an evil thing to do, take out her eyes like that. Whoever did it is an animal."

86

"Agreed. That's why it's so important that we find out who's responsible as quickly as possible. Come on, we've got some guests in our private suites to have a word with and, doubtless, as we're doing it, there'll be a new list being drawn up to include heroin and cocaine users."

"Did the dog get a hit then?"

"From what I hear, he'll be chewing on treats for the rest of the day. Let's get to it."

While they asked up close and personal questions, Lenny Franklin and Terry Friend went back to the Shillingtons' flat. Hardy hadn't managed to secure the officers she'd wanted, so they had been dispatched on a lesser mission. There had been no luck on the baby's whereabouts, and they'd need something either for dogs searching for her, or for Forensics, should the worst happen, and she turn up as a tiny corpse.

As Carole Shillington let them in, they could see through the back window the figure of a man shinning over the fence. "Hey!" yelled Lenny, and then, "Who's that?"

"It's all right, it's only me boyfriend, Baz."

"So, what was so urgent that he couldn't stay around and talk to us?"

"He doesn't like the police," she said, then turned on the tears again. "I miss her so much," she managed to croak out between sobs, and Terry took her by the arm and led her to a seat, while Lenny went through the kitchen and bathroom, looking in cupboards and for anywhere a baby's body could be hidden, then he went into the bedroom and removed the linen from the Moses basket, then lifted it to his face and sniffed.

Going back into the living room, he stated, "This smells fresh."

Carole gave him a blank look.

"Have you recently changed it?" he asked, a ripple of suspicion running through his body. "When did you do that?"

There were a few seconds silence, then she answered, "Before I went out to the shop."

"Why *then?*"

"She'd gone through her nappy in the night, and it was wet."

"What, top as well as bottom?"

"She weed a lot for a little baby."

"She must have."

"Is there anything that might smell of her that we can take with us?" asked the PC, trying not to panic her or set off DC Franklin.

"There's a little teddy that I give her if we're out together," she offered.

"If we could just take that."

The girl retrieved it, still sniffling, while Lenny's face turned stony. "We'd still like a word with your boyfriend. Do you know where he might be?"

"He said he had some business to sort out."

"What kind of business?"

"I don't know what he does," she answered, naively.

"And who does he hang out with?" asked Terry, trying to find a way to get information out of the girl.

"I haven't a clue. All I know is he feeds me and Stacey, and he pays the rent for this place and covers the bills."

At the mention of her daughter's name, she began to sob again. "My poor little Stacey. What has she ever done to anyone?"

"Will you ask your boyfriend to call into the station when he's got time? We'd like to speak to him. And what's his full name?"

"Barry Bailey. I think Barry's short for Bartholomew, though I'm not sure."

"We're going to be able to get the key to your mother's place tomorrow. We've arranged to collect the key and, if necessary, we may get specialist officers round here to have a search." — although there was precious little space to hide anything — *even something so small as a baby's body*, thought Friend, even as she spoke the words. And she knew that Lenny's eagle eye would have picked up anything like blood spots. The PC had to ease the soft toy out of her hands. The girl spoke then, her gaze distant, "His name's Teddy Eddie, and he used to be mine."

"Well, Teddy Eddie," said the woman, "you're coming along to help the police with their enquiries." That produced a wan smile, as they left.

When they were back in the car, the bear was slipped into an evidence bag, and Lenny spoke. "I've got a feeling in my bones that this one's not going to turn out good. And those bits of foil have disappeared from where I was expecting them to be from what you said about earlier."

"Pessimist."

"Realist."

CHAPTER
SEVEN

Lauren was very quiet after the interviews, and said she had to go because she had an appointment, giving no details and scuttling off as if she had something to hide. Olivia returned to her desk to get her paperwork up to date. The interviews had taken some time and, as luck would have it, she was on her own in the office when a call came in from PC Liam Shuttleworth, who was on duty at the hospital at the bedside of the still unidentified woman from Gooding Avenue.

He was in a state, and could barely make himself understood, stuttering and failing to get some words out altogether. "Slow down, Liam. Whatever's happened? Is the woman dead?" Olivia thought this was unlikely, as she had been moved to a single room just off the ward.

"It's w-worse than that," he managed.

"How could it be worse?"

"She was starting to stir, but nothing else was happening, and I just had to go. I couldn't wait any longer."

"You couldn't wait any longer for what?"

"I needed a slash."

"Liam!"

"Sorry, ma'am. I needed to . . . urinate, and I had to stay for a bit longer than I'd intended," — so, he'd had to have a dump — "Anyway, when I was on my way back, there was this terrible wailing that turned into screams."

"And what had happened?"

"She must've woken up, or come to. They reckon it was because she couldn't see, so she put her good hand under the bandages, and then it started. When I got back there were two nurses in the room and they'd called a doctor. I know I've seen some things, but I've never heard anything like this before. It sounded like the poor woman was in hell." She probably was, and would be for the rest of her life.

"So, what happened next?"

"There were these nurses, trying to hold her down and put the bandages back, and then this doctor come flying in. He had a syringe already in his hand, so someone must have told him what was happening. And one of them held her body down while another one held on to her arm while he gave her an injection to calm her down."

"Did she say anything, Liam? This is very important. Did you ask the nurses?"

"I've called you first."

"Well, get back to them, and that doctor, and find out anything that you can that you missed."

"Yes, ma'am."

"And ring me back as soon as you've got their statements. I'll send someone to relieve you. You sound like you could do with a bit of time to pull yourself together, and it must be near the end of your shift anyway."

PC Shuttleworth phoned back within half an hour, but the only thing he had to report was that the woman hadn't yelled anything in English, and that no one within earshot had recognised the language. "OK, Constable. I've asked for another officer to be sent over to relieve you. Did the doctor say anything?"

"Only that they'd have to keep her sedated for a little while longer. It was the most horrible thing I've ever seen, the way she was feeling around for where her eyes used to be, and the despair in her voice . . ."

"I know it's not easy, but try to put it out of your mind, Shuttleworth, although I'll bet she's having nightmares, wherever her mind is at the moment."

Lauren had been moving furtively. She had what she could hardly think of as a date, but definitely an assignation. She'd already phoned ahead to Mrs Moth and said that she might be a bit late home, and the woman hadn't asked any questions, thinking that it would be to do with work.

Starting off on her usual route home, she had soon deviated and taken a smaller road that was not so direct. A couple of miles down this was a little pub called *The Six Bells*. It was not over busy, not being very upmarket, and a lot of its customers came from the caravans that the landlord allowed to stay on the field at the back. Beyond it was just open countryside. It had seemed one of the most inconspicuous places to meet with an almost cast-iron guarantee that they would meet no one they knew, or who would recognise them.

She walked nervously from her car, looking from side to side, out of guilt more than any other emotion. When she tentatively opened the door, she could see him sitting already waiting at the bar on a high stool. Her attempt at "nonchalant" wouldn't have fooled anyone, and as the woman behind the bar stared at her, Daz turned around and smiled. "So, you made it then?" he asked, at a bit of a loss to know what else to say. "What'll you have to drink?"

"Just about," she replied breathily, realising how out of practice she was at meeting men socially, when she wasn't on Kenneth's arm and they weren't his colleagues. It had been different at work. She was the senior officer and hardly ever noticed the DC, but he'd started to make a bit of an effort with her lately, flirting, and complimenting her on her appearance.

She'd dismissed it at first, just seeing it as a bit of banter but, earlier on, when he had actually asked her for a discreet drink, she began to realise how much she had missed the physical side of a relationship. She admitted that she found Kenneth's nightly pawing and lunging at her tedious, and she had learnt to be grateful for the peace when he was away, but recently she had started to feel that she would like the intimacy of a new relationship.

Not that she thought she would find it with this particular candidate, but he might provide a stopgap. Olivia would have been shocked if she had confided in her, but she was just like anyone else of her age, and she had needs and desires. Self-medicating with alcohol didn't take all her pain away and sometimes made her needs feel desperate.

"I'll have a small glass of dry, white wine, if that's all right," she replied. Before he could pass this on to the barmaid on duty, the brassy woman cut in with, "We've got Shar Donnay or Leebfrawmilk. There isn't much call for wine in here."

Blushing at having already stood out, she said that Chardonnay would be fine, and slid up on to the stool next to Daz as the woman turned away to uncork an already open bottle at the back of the bar, unrefrigerated and apparently deserted for some time.

Daz dropped his head and leaned towards her. "You look sexy," he whispered, and she had to look away; perhaps he was after the same thing she was.

"Don't be silly."

"I'm not. Don't you realise how attractive you are?"

She thought back to the black eyes and split lip she had sported at the end of the previous year, and how, in her own opinion, she had not been quite so attentive to her appearance than she used to be, and wondered that he had the nerve to be so blatantly dishonest. Still, if it suited both their purposes . . .

The glass of wine was plonked down in front of her, and she noticed a nasty greasy sheen on the surface. This was a venerable bottle indeed. "Where do you want to go?" she asked, looking at the stale drink that was giving off a rather unpleasant aroma, rather than straight at him.

"Aren't you going to drink your wine?" he asked. "We could have a couple of drinks before we go."

"Actually, I don't really fancy a drink." She could have added "here", because her system was calling out for some alcohol to relax her tense shoulders and ward off the threatening headache, and she looked at him with pleading eyes.

"Why don't we go back to mine?" he suggested. "I've got a nice bottle of white in the fridge and we could, um, get to know each other a bit better." He was certainly willing to take the risk if she was.

"Are we talking the same language?" she ventured.

"What do you mean?"

"The sort of language that never gets spoken at work."

"What do you take me for?" She'd previously taken him for an inexperienced and mouthy boor, but she could hardly voice that opinion. The simple fact was, she had need of his body, and she knew she would be taking an enormous risk; but still, so was he. Both their reputations at the station were at risk. If she didn't get some male attention soon, though, she thought she'd explode. She'd tried DIY, and that had left her feeling both empty, as well as lonely, and slightly soiled.

"You don't live with your parents, do you?" she whispered urgently.

"'Course not. I've got my own little place on the seafront."

"Let's get out of here, then. I'll follow you."

As they left the pub Lauren caught, out of the corner of her eye, the barmaid happily swigging back the glass of wine she had spurned.

His place turned out to be a fairly clean and tidy bedsit with a sofa bed, which he flicked open with one hand. "Drop of the old vino?" he asked. "Just to get us going? To get the engines revving, so to speak."

Lauren thought that if her engine revved any more she'd break a piston. Pushing him onto the fold-out bed, she clamped her lips on to his mouth and began scrabbling at his shirt and he urgently moved a hand to unzip his trousers.

Olivia didn't rush home that night. Hal had been gone when she had risen that morning and, no doubt, he would not be home early tonight. She remembered his teaching days well, and that man gave everything to his job. She didn't think it would be like this with supply work, but having landed a temporary contract until the end of the academic year, she knew only too well how deeply he'd get involved in everything. If she wasn't careful, he'd go back full-time, and then where would she be?

It was probably counter-productive to be rebellious like this, but she was determined not to get home before him and, besides, she had a lot of paperwork to catch up on. The only other officer left in the office was Lenny Franklin, and as he was heading for the door, he sidetracked and sat on the corner of her desk. "What can I do for you, Lenny?" asked Olivia, looking up.

"It's that disappeared baby," he stated, without preamble. "There's something there that stinks, but I can't quite put my finger on it."

"But, you've been through the place, and there's hardly a lot of choice of places to stash a dead baby are there?" she replied seriously.

"No, and I even took a good look out of the back window — all paving stones, and not one of them looks as if it's been moved recently."

"So, what is it that gets your instincts up?"

"Well, that young mother is really broken-hearted, and her boyfriend's attitude stinks, not supporting her or anything and bunking off like that, but there's something about the girl that doesn't ring true. She's lying about something; I just don't know what."

"I agree with you, Lenny, but we'll get it out in the open if we just keep at it. To change the subject, how are things at home?"

"As you'd expect. Lonely. Susan's definitely not coming back, and I thought she was looking forward to me retiring, to do all the things we'd planned but never had time for, but she says she can't wait any longer. Life's passing her by, apparently" — this word was spoken bitterly — "and she needs to get on with things while she still can."

"Still at your daughter's, is she?"

"Still."

"And how is her health?"

"She's in remission at the moment."

"Why don't you try to patch things up and take early retirement?"

"Because I simply don't want to. Any spark there was between us was snuffed out years ago, and I can't face the rest of my life with no work to hide in and having to look after a sick woman."

"Lenny! You know there's help available. And how do you expect your daughter to cope?"

"At the moment, I'm past caring. She always took Susan's side about the hours I have to put in, and now I just think they're welcome to each other. They can carp about what an uncaring bastard I am for the rest of Susan's life. She'll probably outlive me."

"Surely you want her back, after all these years."

"That's the last thing I want, actually. She's made her bed, and now she can lie on it. And Frances is in seventh heaven. She's got carers popping in and out most days, and she's got a grant to provide a disabled extension. All the fuss that goes with the illness is now surrounding her, and she loves the limelight, and making me the bad guy."

"That's simply not true, Lenny. You're a very dedicated officer, and I'm sure they both appreciate that. Is there no way you two can work this out?"

"I don't believe there is. We've simply fallen out of love."

"And does she feel the same way?" Olivia felt sad that there was no way back for Lenny and his wife.

"I've never asked her."

"Why don't you, then?"

"Because I'm afraid she'd say 'yes'. I was just as lonely before she went. We had nothing left in common except the bone of contention between us, my job. It would've been no different without the MS."

"I'm sorry, Lenny."

"Nobody's fault. In fact, I'm thinking of joining an Internet site to try to meet a new partner."

"That's a bit radical for you, isn't it? I thought you might just hook up with some woman you met down the pub."

"I don't need to go to the pub so often now that I haven't got a resident nag."

"Oh, Lenny!"

"Goodnight, boss. Anyway, I've got a hot date with an Indian."

"Who is she?"

"A curry."

When Lauren got home that night Mrs Moth gave her a quizzical look. She was less tidy than usual. A lot of the make-up she had managed to apply later in the day was gone, although she still had some traces of it left, but it was her hair that attracted most of her attention. It was decidedly tousled and this was totally out of character. She had been working for the family for some months now, and she'd never seen her employer in such a state of disarray.

"Are you all right?" she asked, sounding concerned, and Lauren was suddenly aware that she had not checked her appearance before she left Daz's bedsit, there not being a mirror obviously on display. Rushing to the one on the hall wall, she was horrified at the reflection that looked back at her. She looked a little as if she had been pulled through a hedge backwards, although she had smoothed her hair back into an approximation of its usual shape. She'd have to be more careful in future.

But was there a future for what she had just done? And did she want there to be? Yes, she decided, she definitely needed some fun in her life: she had been deprived of it for so long, and she had definitely missed sex — although not quite so much of it would have been an improvement when she had been with Kenneth.

"I'm absolutely first class," she replied. "Just a little rumpled. Work has been very trying this afternoon, and I fear I have not tidied myself up before I headed home." She hastily renewed her lipstick and pulled a small brush out of the hall drawer before seeing her childminder off the property. The less time and opportunity she gave her for speculation, the better.

The children had already been escorted up to bed, so she mounted the stairs so that she could kiss them goodnight. Descending, this done, she headed straight for the kitchen. As well as taking the delightfully chilled bottle out of the fridge door, she also checked the microwave where she discovered a plate of chicken and new potatoes, and a note that informed her that there was salad in the fridge. Suddenly, she was absolutely ravenous, and not in the least ashamed. Instead, she felt empowered; she had seen what she wanted, and she had taken it.

She only drank two glasses of wine that night, and went to bed at a much more respectable time. It was true what the Scots believed. Oats *were* good for you.

* ★ *

When Olivia finally got home, it was to find that both Ben and Hibbie had called in, cooked a frozen pizza each, and gone out again. Of Hal, there was no sign.

"Why didn't you just give me a ring, or text me, Hal?"

"My battery was down."

"Don't you have a colleague whose phone you could borrow?"

"I don't like asking when I'm so new."

"So, they don't mind asking you to stay late or go in early, but you haven't got the nerve to ask if you could borrow a phone?"

"I promise I'll let you know in future."

"Just make sure that you do. At least that way I could pick up a takeaway on the way home instead of getting home to find that I've got to start cooking."

"You could always order something by phone."

"That's not the point."

"Isn't it?"

Interlude

They started swarming over it at first light. As dawn broke, the scavengers were crawling over the heaps like flies. Everything was grist to their mill. They were territorial too, but instinctively unsociable. If a new scavenger invaded their space, they would attack and hope to send them packing. This was their world, and they didn't intend to share it with interlopers.

One of the first there was tearing at a black plastic bag, determined to get at the contents. Most of the bags had already torn or split, but this seemed like a good quality thick one and there could be rich pickings inside. The fabric fought his efforts, but finally gave up its secret. He stared down at it, first shocked, then revolted, and he let out an animal-like cry. What should he do now?

Motioning to the others to join him, he indicated his grim discovery and realisation dawned that there was a decision to be made.

CHAPTER
EIGHT

Buller called his meeting to order. He had asked them all to be ready on time, if not early, and he had information for them. First, he asked for an update from the team members that he hadn't managed to catch the day before.

Lenny Franklin was the first to speak. "It looks like we had some duff gen on that house of contraband. I've checked out all the local estate agents, and no one will admit to having a lease out on it or letting it. I stayed on late last night to spread the net a bit wider and when I've checked my emails, if there's still nothing definite, I'll get the name and address of the owner and try to contact them."

"On the abducted baby case, we've had a few sightings, but nothing's turned up yet," offered Olivia. "Today, I've got someone collecting the key to the grandmother's house, if that makes sense, to gain access and take copies of more recent photos from her computer. The mother herself hasn't got a computer or a mobile, and only had a photo of the baby as a newborn. Her mother happens to be away on holiday and her neighbour who holds the key was away for the night. The father's got a record."

Olivia was immediately slapped down. "That's enough from the women's magazine. Just get on with things and don't bother me until you've got something concrete." Buller didn't like torrents of detail, just results. He was just about to start speaking again when there was a shriek from the mid-distance. "Surely not a drunk at this time of the morning," he quipped, before one the DCs started to say his piece.

"Did you hear that the woman who was blinded in Gooding Avenue had woken up?" Desai had decided to be spokesman, as Shuttleworth was in uniform, and at least he had been sitting at her bedside when she was first admitted.

"And?" Buller was not backward in indicating his impatience.

"Not much. Apparently she got her hand under her bandages and discovered what had happened to her eyes, then she got rather hysterical."

"In what language? English?"

"No. We don't know yet."

"Why the bloody hell not?"

"None of the staff recognised what the language was, and the doctor decided to sedate her again for a while."

"Fucking marvellous. So, we're no further forward on who attacked her. You're a real bunch of limp dicks, aren't you? Well, fortunately for you, I *have* got some results. I knew those two were bloody foreigners ever since I clapped eyes on the scene photographs, and I've got a couple of names back from my enquiries.

"I'm not even going to try to pronounce the names, but they've got a record running all the way from

Tirana to Calais, where they were last picked up. Presumably they've decided to contaminate our fair country with their criminal activities. They were mainly arrested for drugs, but they've done their fair amount of petty crime as well — shoplifting, pickpocketing, that sort of thing. They were generally known as Lena and Michail and I reckon they were just laying low here doing a bit of caretaking work for someone while they got their breath back.

"Now, I want all of you out there speaking to your snouts and anyone else I tell you to, to see if you can get a sniff on who they were connected with and . . ."

At that point, the phone on Olivia's desk rang again. "Get it!" the DCI snapped, "and take it in the corridor. I'm trying to solve a major crime here, in case you hadn't noticed." She exited the office with the handset in her hand, only to receive a request to come downstairs to see to Penny Sutcliffe, who was apparently in a bit of a state. "And, by the way," said the caller, "she's found a dead baby on the doorstep at the back of the station."

On reaching the desk, she was directed to the locker room where she found the uniformed officer in tears. "What the hell's this I hear about a dead baby?" she asked, sitting down on one of the benches and putting an arm around the sergeant's shoulders. Penny Sutcliffe shuddered in an effort to pull herself together, and looked up at the DI with flooded eyes. "Tell me about it? What happened? Where is it?"

Penny, who had three children and spent a lot of time on desk duty, swapping shifts as she could, to allow her to avoid having to use too much childcare, swallowed hard and began to tell her story. "As far as I know, it's being taken over to Dr MacArthur in a patrol car. The bag it was in has gone to Forensics to examine the stuff on it."

"What stuff? Start at the beginning." Olivia was decidedly short on patience after her falling out with Hal late the previous evening.

After a bit of throat-clearing, Penny began again. "I was just on my way in for duty, and I saw this really messy rubbish bag over near the big bin outside the back door. Well, naturally, I went to pick it up and put it in the bin, wondering who could have done such a thoughtless thing as not to lift it in, but when I went to pick it up, it felt wrong.

"So, I put it back down again and looked inside, and there it was, with its neck all funny. It made me feel quite sick. There was something underneath it, but I couldn't even bear to look at what it was, in case it was even worse than what I'd just found. Anyway, I managed not to drop it, and took it inside where I alerted Sergeant Fairbanks. He went a bit white when he took it off me and looked inside, then he just told me to go and have a sit down and he'd deal with it.

"I'd had a quick thought as I went over to pick it up that, if it wasn't someone from the station, then surely people hadn't started fly-tipping in the station car park, but I had to go to be sick when he went off. That's some poor woman's child. She must be absolutely distraught."

"Did Monty say what he was going to do?"

"Just that he'd sort the little body and the bag, and that he'd get back to me."

Monty Fairbanks chose that moment to return to the locker room, and informed Olivia that Superintendent Devenish would like a quick word with her, also informing her that he had set an officer to go through the car park CCTV. With a look of sympathy from the sergeant, a shrug of the shoulders and a muttered, "What have I done wrong now?" Olivia bustled off to meet her nemesis.

When the morning meeting of the team was concluded, Olivia had still not returned and, finding herself in the company of Daz Westbrook, Lauren found herself embarrassed for the first time since the night before. He pointedly avoided eye contact with her, and she, keeping up the charade, looked anywhere but at him, and she thought she'd have to get him on his own sometime to see whether the previous evening was going to be a regular secret or a one-off.

Was she just a one-night stand, or did he want her to be his "fuck buddy"? She wouldn't mind if he did. It suited her down to the ground, having regular sex but with no strings attached — a thought that quite shocked her when she considered how moral and upright she had been until quite recently. She would tell no one; not even Olivia.

When she first received the call to go downstairs to see Penny Sutcliffe, Olivia had had hopes, and fears, that they had found Stacey Shillington, and they would now have to trace the abductor or investigate the parents a little further, but on being told that the baby had been a newborn, she had abandoned the idea.

As she ascended, once more, she wondered what Devenish was going to try to pin on her now. As far as she knew, she had been guilty of no wrong-doing or insubordination since he had given her a bollocking over a case at the end of the previous year.

At his yell of, "Come!" in response to her timid knock, a shiver ran through her. Whatever it was, she hadn't done it. He was the sole person who had this effect on her; she wasn't normally timid.

He had her stand before his desk for at least thirty seconds of agonisingly slow silence before he spoke. "How are you getting on with DCI Buller?" he asked, unexpectedly.

"We're very different characters," she replied tentatively, "but we're co-operating on the case."

"Well, I'm going to take you off it."

"What have I done, sir? What has he said because, whatever it is, it's simply not true?"

"He hasn't said anything derogatory about you. He's a damned good officer, even if his views are a little, what I think we might call, old-fashioned. To change the subject, I've been informed that we have had a dead baby, ah, handed in, if I may put it that way. I don't want DCI Buller and his team to be disturbed too much on this one because he's making progress. I would, however, like you and DS Groves to take on the cases of the infants."

"Because we're women, sir?"

"Not at all: because you're bloody good officers too, and I want to split the talent so that we can achieve the quickest and best results all round." Why was he being so complimentary and diplomatic? Because they were women, of course.

"Thank you for your kind words, sir. And who else from the team would be working with us?"

"I'm afraid you'll have only uniformed officers. Now, you know how big and complicated the other case is and, if you involve social services, you'll have other sympathetic professionals on hand to assist you."

Olivia sighed. "Yes, sir. Thank you sir."

"Dismissed."

I certainly have been, thought the inspector.

When she got back to the CID office, she moved her desk and Lauren's so that they were facing each other at the front of the room, and where they wouldn't be too much disturbed by the others. She'd just had time to explain that she and her sergeant had been allotted the two cases involving babies, when Terry Friend came bustling self-importantly into the office.

"The CCTV's been checked," she announced, and Lauren beckoned her over.

"What have you found?"

"Not a lot. There was a car noticed, but its number plates were covered in mud and dirt, so we don't have a full number for it — barely a partial, in fact — but someone did get out of it carrying a bag, which they then put near the bin."

"Anyone —"

"But," Terry continued, "they were unseasonally dressed in a hoodie and a peaked baseball cap, so there was no sign at all of who it was."

"Male or female?"

"Well, they weren't wearing a skirt or a dress, but it could've been either."

"So, although we've got it captured on CCTV footage, we're precisely no further forward?"

"Looks like it. Sorry, ma'am."

"Who's the most computer literate out of all of you?"

"Penny Sutcliffe," the PC replied, without falter.

"How is she?"

"A bit more calm, although still upset."

"There's nothing much I can do about that, but I do want her to go out to a house that has some photographs on its computer, and I want copies of them sent back directly to me. The owner should be away at the moment, so I'll give you the address where she can collect the key." There had been plenty of time for Mrs Shillington's neighbour to get back from her daughter's, and they couldn't afford to waste any time when a baby's life or well-being was at risk. It was already twenty-four hours since baby Stacey had been snatched.

"You get yourself back downstairs and see if any more has come up on the baby's body." Terry scooted off obediently, and Olivia looked across at Lauren. There was something wrong, and she couldn't work out what it was. It might be something to do with the kids and school, or even the old biddy who looked after them, but she couldn't leave it without asking.

"What's on your mind?" she asked across the two desks, only to have Lauren's eyes scoot furtively across to the main body of the room before settling on her, with an unconvincing smile on her face. "Come on, spit it out," she encouraged her, but to no avail.

"There's absolutely nothing bothering me, boss; nothing wrong whatsoever."

"You can't fool me, you know."

Lauren's face was suddenly awash with thunderclouds as she snapped, "Will you leave me alone? I've already told you that there's nothing wrong. Why won't you leave me be?"

God! She was touchy today. Maybe Kenneth had been in contact and upset her. "Pax!" she replied and her phone rewarded her withdrawal by ringing to distract the two of them from a possible falling-out.

It was Terry Friend again, not wishing to tackle the stairs a second time, and excited by what she had just found out. "Initial thoughts are that the plastic bag came from the tip," she said. Littleton-on-Sea's local authority was notoriously lax in its waste management and recycling and, unbelievably, everything was just dumped at the municipal tip in a series of huge mountains of rubbish, with only the tiny amount of what had been put into recycling bins set aside — a pointless, time-wasting exercise that didn't save the tight-fisted council any money anyway.

"Get the duty officers to send what officers he can to sniff around for the car or anyone acting suspiciously, and get whoever went through the CCTV footage on the car park to go through the tip stuff — anything from midnight onwards."

"Will do, ma'am."

Although she'd had a quiet word with Buller about the change in case allocation, he didn't seem to have passed it on to all of his officers, because Desai approached her with the information that he'd had a call from Ali Shah. He had seen the couple from the television appeal for information on their identities, as they had been into his shop.

"Get out to interview him, but give any information, in future, to DCI Buller. DS Groves and I are now exclusively on the abduction and infant death cases."

"Yes, ma'am."

Damn, this was hard, being side-lined like this, but she could only suppose it was because Buller was a "man's man", and so was Devenish, under all that sexual and racial equality bullshit he hid behind. She knew what the man under the façade was like, and he was thoroughly bigoted, unlike Buller, who wore his prejudices on his sleeve for all to see.

It would get him into trouble one of these days, Hardy thought, but he was doing all right for the moment. God help him if he ever worked for a woman officer who outranked him — she'd rip him to ribbons, whilst casually castrating him on the way. As far as Hardy was concerned she didn't have to work with him long-term, so she could just grit her teeth and get on with things. Maybe it was his personality that was grating on Lauren, though? She'd have to ask her when they were somewhere a little more private.

CHAPTER
NINE

Penny Sutcliffe had driven off to get the key from Mrs
Shillington's neighbour so that she could get the
photographs from her computer, glad to have
something else to do beside think about what she had
discovered that morning. It was hardly an onerous task,
but concentrating on the road kept her mind occupied.

The neighbour had been in about half an hour when
she got there and offered her a cup of tea along with
the keys to the house next door, but she refused it. She
was thinking, again, of the little body she had come
across at the start of her shift, and she would not be
able to make small talk, and didn't want to let the cat
out of the bag — she winced as her mind made the
analogy — before the matter had gone public.

She let herself into Mrs Shillington's house, having
noticed what an upmarket area it was in, and how
nicely the interior was decorated and furnished. There
were tasteful pictures on the walls, and a variety of
antiques on the surfaces of various pieces of furniture.
A quick memory of the owner's daughter's address
made her stop in her tracks. How had the two
generations become so detached from each other's
lifestyles?

The neighbour had told her that Mrs Shillington kept her computer on a desk at the back of the property, and she headed off in search of it. She already had the password, and it should not take long to find and send copies of the photographs to the DI.

Being of a curious disposition, while the computer was booting up, she had a quick look out of the back window, moving aside the lace curtains as she did so. The latter were the only tasteless things in here, and she wondered why the occupier felt she needed to protect her property from view, then she remembered that there was a Neighbourhood Watch sticker in the porch window. That might explain it. If she didn't give burglars the chance to case her interior, they may just leave the house alone.

Noticing that the garden was beautifully kept and planted, she realised that there was only one sour note, and that was where the end of a flower bed had been raked up, small plants and a few remnants of soil showing on the patio flagstones. *What a pity. Probably cats*, she thought, before returning to the task in hand.

What a sweet child, was her first thought, as the file opened. There had obviously been more than one visit to this new granddaughter, and as Penny sent the pictures off into the blue yonder, she hoped the child would soon be found. She was a very motherly figure who adored her children and she pondered that, if she won the lottery, she would leave the force — although she enjoyed her job — and just spend her time with them.

It was very soon time to lock up and return the key to the neighbour, where she had to fend off yet another offer of a hot beverage, this time a cup of coffee.

DC Desai, meanwhile, had gone off to the mini-mart to speak to Mr Shah again. As expected, he had to park round the corner again because of the double-yellow restrictions, but it wasn't far to walk.

Mr Shah went into a tizzy as soon as he saw Desai again. "They were in here," he claimed, using his arms for emphasis. "They've been in here a couple of times, but I never thought anything about it. They were just a couple of immigrants who didn't speak English and needed a bit of help, but there was a red-headed gentleman with them, so I didn't have to come out from behind the counter. Just as well, as it was just before closing time and very late. I'm always very careful with customers when it's very late."

Desai already had out his notebook and began to ask questions about the man who was with them, and what they bought. It probably wouldn't be of any use to the investigation, but he thought he needed to go back to the DCI with something concrete. And that was the second mention of a red-haired man in connection with this couple.

"Would you recognise this man again, the one who was with the two whose photos were shown on television?"

"He had one of those, what do you call them, hoodies, on, but when he looked up to see some prices,

116

it fell backward a little bit. That's how I know the colour of his hair. And he had spots on his face."

"Acne?"

"What is this? No, I think you call them 'freckles'." He smiled proudly at his production of the word.

"Would you be willing to look at some photographs from our records, Mr Shah, to see if you could identify this man?"

"Ah, in*dubitably*."

There wasn't a lot to be learnt here, and Desai was soon on his way back to his car, slightly disappointed, but also rather pleased that he had got an agreement for Mr Shah to come in and look at faces. The daughter from number five Gooding Avenue had already popped in, but had not been able to make an identification due, she thought, to the low light conditions in which she had seen him.

As Desai got back to his car, he heard a knocking noise. Looking around him to see where it had come from, he saw an elderly lady knuckling a front window pane and beckoning at him with her other hand. What could she possibly want with him? How could she even know who he was?

He walked up the path, and noticed her figure disappear, presumably to let him in. There was a shuffling noise from the other side of the wood, and the door opened slowly to reveal a woman well advanced in years, her back bent with arthritis, her slippers misshapen at the big-toe joint, her hand not concealed by the door showing knuckles that were more like nuts than joints, so swollen were they.

"Young man," she said, having to angle her head upwards to look at him although he wasn't tall — osteoporosis was a cruel condition — "are you that policeman who came to speak to that girl in the shop?"

"How did you know that?" he enquired. He would surely have recognised her if she had been out and about in the street.

"Oh, I have a network of neighbours that keep me informed about everything. As you can see, I'm not very mobile, and I get most of my entertainment from looking at the people who park along the street. Speculating about them is much more interesting than the television — mindless trash, I call it."

"Can I have your name, madam, and what can I do for you?" Desai was intrigued as he got out his notebook.

"I'm Ada Belcher, and you can come in, for a start, and make us a cup of tea. I have something to tell you." Respect for elders was something that had been imparted to him by his family, so he went past her down the hall to put the kettle on.

When they were seated in her mothball-scented front room and she had told him that she was ninety-five years old, she finally got down to business. "I wasn't in my viewing seat when that young woman arrived — you know, the one that said her baby had been taken from her car? Well, I'm sitting here telling you that there was no child taken from that car. It was a lie."

"How do you know if you weren't at the window?" The DC began to wonder if the old lady suffered from hallucinations.

She speared him with a fierce and knowing eye and said, "When I got back and settled myself down again the car was parked there, but the back seat was empty. When that young girl got back, she didn't even look inside properly before she started yelling."

"Are you absolutely sure about that?" He had to ask. "How is your eyesight?"

"I need glasses for reading the newspaper, but I can see perfectly at a distance, and I'm telling you that that back seat had no child in it."

"Would you be willing to make a statement to that effect?"

"Young man, I'd be willing to stand up in court under oath and testify that the back seat of that car was empty."

While Lauren took a quick trip to the Ladies, Olivia's phone rang and she found a representative of the hospital at the other end. Of course, she should have transferred them straight away to Buller's extension, but she was eager for information on a case she had now been locked out of.

What she was told made her eyes and mouth open in surprise. The woman, Lena, was dead. They weren't sure, yet, what had killed her, but they'd get back as soon as possible with any new information. The death had been discovered about ten minutes ago, and the body had been sent straight for post-mortem so that cause of death could be established.

Of course, with injuries as severe as hers had been and the physical and mental shock of losing her eyes, it could have been that her constitution just wasn't strong enough to carry on, but there was a feeling that something fishy was in the air.

"Why didn't you call as soon as she died?" asked the inspector.

"Sorry. We were rather hoping to have a cause of death for you as well, but the results won't be back for a while yet, and we didn't want to wait any longer, but we have got back the results of a preliminary blood test. Let me explain what we found . . ."

"Let us know as soon as you've got something," she barked, somehow forgetting to tell the medico on the line that they should contact DCI Buller when they called later. How very remiss of her. She smiled as she ended the call.

Lauren had left her desk after hearing the noise that let her know that she had received a text. She took a quick look and saw that it was from Daz Westbrook, and Olivia didn't seem to have noticed what she was doing. Without reading it, she excused herself, saying that she had left something in the Ladies, and rushed as fast as she could to lock herself in a cubicle. Whether this message was positive or negative, she knew it would show on her face, and she didn't want anybody around to see her when she read it.

Once safely behind a locked door, she pulled her phone from her jacket pocket and read the message. "Same time 2nite?"

Sending back a reply that said "Same place 2", she quickly phoned Mrs Moth, her fingers crossed that neither of them got held up, and told her childminder that she would be late again.

As she put her phone back into her pocket, she could feel her cheeks redden. Was she really going to do this again? It seemed her body had taken precedence to the logical and sensible part of her brain. It was a really bad idea to have a relationship with a work colleague, apart from the fact that he was so much younger than her and probably was only using her as a convenience while he was between girlfriends. She just hoped that he could keep his mouth shut, and didn't want to brag about this senior — in more ways than one — conquest.

After throwing cold water round her face to cool it down, she refreshed her make-up before heading back to the office hoping that she wasn't giving out any detectable signals about what she planned to do after work, and with whom. Before she'd left, however, another text came through: "Str8 2 mine." As she went out of the door, her mind taunted her with the thought that he didn't even want to spend the money for one drink before getting down to business. Wasn't that enough proof that he was just using her body?

With her chin thrust out, she walked down the corridor and towards the CID office. She didn't care. She was using him as much as he was using her, and that was a relationship, of sorts, between equals who sought no more than physical satisfaction. At the last moment, she changed her mind and changed direction to the canteen for a cup of coffee before having to face Daz Westbrook in person. Texting she could do, but for looking straight into his face she might need to compose herself a little.

When she did return to her desk, chickening out and sitting down without looking across the office, Olivia was on her phone, her face wreathed in a mixture of excitement and triumph. As she sat down, Olivia called Buller over. Lauren had caught her last words, mentioning the DCI's name, and she wondered what was going on.

Buller swaggered over to the desk, a challenging expression on his face and asked her abruptly, "What?"

"That was the hospital, sir. They contacted me, not having been given your details."

"Well, why didn't you have the call transferred?"

"The person on the other end had some bad news, and I didn't want to interrupt them once they had started."

"What was the news?"

"Lena, our woman from Gooding Avenue, is dead."

"How? When?"

"They've not had time to do a post-mortem yet, but an initial blood test showed very high levels of insulin, and the only way that could have got into her bloodstream was through her drip tubes via the bag."

"How the hell did anyone get past the nurses' station? I told them not to let anyone not in the force" — he hadn't managed to swallow the fact that they were now a service — "in to see her."

"The person who spoke to me on the phone said that they didn't. But they did mention that a doctor popped

122

into the room briefly while Shuttleworth went to get a sandwich and to relieve himself."

"Did we send anyone to relieve *him* for these activities?"

"No, actually we didn't. We just trusted to his common sense to bring something to eat with him and to get a nurse to sit in if he needed to go to the Gents. Thing is, none of the nurses could put a name to the doctor."

His face was perfect thunder. "Jenner!" he roared, "I want you over to the hospital immediately, and you, Leo. Someone's got on to the ward impersonating a doctor and has killed our victim. Now we'll never get a statement from her."

"But I'm crime scene manager," Jenner protested.

"And we've got another crime scene and they're very closely connected. Get over there right away and see how this gigantic cock-up could have happened."

Leo made straight for Jenner's work station without a word of instruction. He knew better than not to react instantly to the DCI. He didn't need chewing out. Jenner rose from his seat without another word of protest. He'd worked with Buller before, and he was well aware of the consequences of not reacting with alacrity.

"And I hope you put them right on who was SIO on this case, Hardy."

"I did, sir. I said I'd been passed over for someone of higher rank and that they should speak to you in the future."

"What time did she die?"

"I didn't write it down, sir. Sorry."

"Who phoned?"

"Again, not sure. There were two calls from different people."

"And you didn't speak to me after the first?"

"Sorry, sir. I didn't think."

"More likely trying to undermine my authority. I shall be having words about you with your superiors. Leo, you stay here. *I'll* go with Jenner."

Leo headed back towards his desk again while Buller hurried over to Jenner's side. "Come along, Sergeant. We've got a bollocking to deliver. No, hang on a minute, I'm not going to waste us on this sort of thing. Jenner, get on to Immigration and see if they've got any intel on someone of the description we've already got. I'm going to contact Europol again for some mug shots that might fit our member of the Red-Headed League. In fact, I'll send you, Franklin, and you, Westbrook. May to September might just do the trick."

Olivia was fuming, realising that she'd revealed more than she wanted to about the telephone calls, but he'd gone off on the hunt for foreign fugitives, and she thought he'd be considerably calmer when he came back, and might finally content himself with giving Shuttleworth a dressing down when he got back. He'd enjoy that.

She was distracted by the return to the office of Ali Desai. He looked excited and headed straight for her desk. "Any joy with the shopkeeper?"

"He said he'd come in to look at some faces, but my real bit of luck was out of the blue. I was just about to get into my car to head back here and this old lady tapped on her front window and gestured me to come inside."

"You dirty little pervert," hissed Lenny Franklin as he walked past with a wink.

"Carry on, Ali. Don't mind Franklin. He's just being facetious."

"She usually sits at her front window," he continued. "She likes to watch the world go by. Anyway, she didn't see Shillington's car arrive because she was visiting the bathroom, but she did see it when it was parked. She's absolutely convinced that there was no baby in it, and that when the mother came back, she barely glanced into the car and just started yelling."

"How's her eyesight, if she's not young?"

"It's excellent. She only wears glasses for reading, and she's all there; her marbles are definitely still rolling."

"Is she willing to come in to make a statement?"

"I'm picking her up this afternoon after her nap."

"Good work, Desai, but bring her in before she even has a sniff of her lunch. This is a crucial piece of information and changes everything. Leo, don't go away. I want you and O'Brien to get out and find — what was his name? — Baz, Barry, Bartholomew, whatever, Bailey and bring him in for interview. There's a distinct smell of fish in this case now, and I want to see if we've got anything in our net. I know you're not supposed to be working for me, but you can tell Buller that you were out checking with users and dealers if he asks, later.

"I'll deal with questioning him when you bring him in, but right now, what I want most of all is that young mother back in here to answer a few questions about what this witness has claimed. It doesn't quite fit with what we think are the facts and could make a big difference to what we are really dealing with."

Lauren looked steadily down at her computer keyboard as Franklin and Westbrook left the office, but didn't give off any weird vibes when Leo and O'Brien went out a few seconds later. Olivia noticed this difference in reaction and gave her a quizzical look. There was definitely something going on here that she didn't know about.

For now, though she had a possible new suspect to pick up who was either lying about her baby being snatched, or a batty old lady to sort out. Only time would tell which of these options was the truth.

CHAPTER
TEN

In the car en route to the hospital, Lenny Franklin was in quite a talkative mood. He spent a lot of time in his own company when not at work these days, and he liked the chance to chat with colleagues, but Westbrook was reluctant to engage in conversation today. He seemed distracted, his mind miles away, and it was only by raising his voice that the elder DC could get through to him. "Where's your head at, Daz? You're on another planet."

Westbrook slowly swivelled his head until he was looking straight at Lenny and replied, "Sorry. Something I've got to think out." It was lucky he wasn't behind the wheel, because he couldn't really have given the road ahead sufficient attention to drive safely.

"What's bothering you? Whatever it is really seems to be eating away at you."

"Nothing. I can't talk about it."

"Surely your Uncle Lenny can help with any girlfriend trouble. I used to be quite a lad, you know."

"It's not girlfriend trouble."

"Well, what else could there be that's more distracting than that. It's not money, is it? You haven't started gambling? Or taking drugs?" Memories of Colin Redwood flooded back.

"Look, would you leave it, Lenny. When I said I couldn't talk about it, I meant it. It's private and I don't wish to discuss the matter." This was said in a very testy voice.

Lenny shrank away slightly from his partner and apologised for his intrusion. "I haven't the faintest idea what the problem is, Daz, but when you're ready to confide, you know that nothing you tell me will go any further."

"I know, Lenny. I'm sorry, but it's just something that I've got to work out for myself."

"Well, we're at the hospital now. Let's get on with the job we're paid to do. There are nurses involved — women in uniform. You'll like that."

Once inside, they headed straight for the relevant nurses' station and were pleased to discover that those on duty now were the same staff that had been there when Lena was found to be dead. Against regulations, they gathered them together briefly and split them into two groups: those who had to be out on the wards, and those that could be at the station for now.

Advising them that they would need them to swap positions, they tackled them both in the same way. Who had seen the doctor either entering or leaving the deceased's room? This narrowed it down to two members of staff, and they let the rest of them get back to normal duties.

The two who had caught a glimpse of the "doctor" were taken over to a quiet corner where they could be questioned in more detail. Nurses Trafford and Green were like a well-rehearsed double act.

"I only caught a quick look at him."

"Me too. The only thing I noticed was that he had red hair."

"And he wasn't over-tall. Just sort of average height."

"Or maybe even below it, but he did have a bit of a paunch."

"And he wasn't wearing a stethoscope round his neck."

"No, he wasn't. And he had freckles."

"Didn't he just. He was smothered in them. And I don't think he had a name badge on either."

"You're right. I didn't see one."

"Which direction did he come from and which direction did he leave in?" asked Lenny, happy just to shoehorn a word in.

"He came through the double doors from the main corridor, but I can't remember which way he left."

"I can. He went out of the door at the other end."

"And how did he get on to the ward? I've noticed that there's a keypad so he could only have got in if he had the code."

"Easy one. He would just have hung around with a chart or something in his hands and then watched when someone else came on to the ward. Some people don't think to shield the numbers their fingers are pressing. It's probably easier to get on to a ward these days with the keypads than it was when people had to be vigilant and challenge any unknown person who entered the ward."

So much for security and technology being the answer to everyone's prayers. Lenny held up his hands. "All right, where do the double doors come from, and where does the door at the end lead?"

"The double doors lead from the main hospital."

"And the door at the end — oh God, it only leads to the fire escape. I didn't even think about that, earlier."

"You're right. He must have got clean away."

"Ladies, was there anywhere he could've had a syringe hidden? Quite a large syringe, I'd think." Lenny was getting in there while the going was good. Their shock at verbalising exactly what had happened had momentarily silenced both of them.

"He could've had any number of syringes in the pockets of his white coat."

"Or he could've had them in whatever he was wearing underneath."

"Daz," said Lenny, in an authoritative voice to cut through the wittering. "Get yourself out of that end door and see if there's any sign of a discarded medical coat, then we can go and check if anyone's lost one this morning, or reported it stolen."

"You'll probably have no luck with lost or stolen coats. The young doctors are always losing their coats and just grabbing any one that's left around."

As Daz went towards the door to the fire escape, Nurse Green suddenly volunteered, "Actually, come to think of it, he wasn't exactly young."

"You're right," agreed Nurse Trafford with a frown. "He wasn't exactly in the first flush of youth, was he?"

130

Good God, thought Lenny, these were another two they'd have to get in to look at mug shots. Perhaps it would save time if they looked only for the red-headed ones. On the other hand, this bloke could have dyed his hair to disguise himself, knowing that people would see the colour, and not notice much else about him. And then there were the freckles. But someone wouldn't add freckles to their complexion to change their appearance, would they? Of course they would. Unfortunately. The man could actually be as mousey and clear-skinned as the next man.

All these thoughts went through his mind in a matter of a few seconds, and it then went blank until he saw Daz coming back on to the ward with a white coat in his hands.

"Lucky I thought to wedge the door open with something," he said, smiling at his success, "Or I'd have had to come back the long way round."

"What did you use?" Lenny had been distracted by the back-and-forthing of the two nurses.

"One of my shoes. They're slip-ons. It's too warm for trainers at the moment."

"You do realise what you've got there, don't you?"

"What? A discarded white coat?"

"DNA — that's what you've probably got. Our first breakthrough on the identity of this mysterious redhead."

"Well, I'll be buggered."

"Not in front of ladies, Westbrook."

Olivia went out to pick up Carole Shillington again. She did not want to alarm her and would confront her with none of her suspicions. She would just say that they needed to ask her a few more questions regarding the incident the previous morning and would not introduce the subject of there not even being a baby in the car until they were in the station and there was nowhere for her to run.

Although Carole's eyes were panicked when she found a police inspector at her door, the cover story worked well, and she was totally unsuspicious when Olivia said they'd just like to clarify a few things in a formal interview as part of the investigation process.

Once at the station, however, Olivia showed her true colours. "Carole Shillington, I am arresting you for attempting to pervert the course of justice . . ." taking a huge gamble on the situation. As the caution ended, Carole merely asked her what she was talking about. This woman was so far from being the sharpest knife in the box as to be more of a spoon.

"I would like to inform you that we have a witness who says that there was no baby in your car when you parked in Jubilee Road, and that there never was a baby in it. The witness has stated that no abduction took place and that you have been lying to us. I shall now take you to an interview room and question you on tape."

Shillington denied the allegations so vehemently that, for a moment, Olivia's certainty was shaken. What if this *was* just the word of a batty old lady? Then she dismissed the thought from her mind. Desai wouldn't have taken her so seriously if he'd had any serious doubts about her mental health. Perhaps they could get

132

her to do some sort of eye test while she was with them to prove how good her sight was. Shillington was, however, completely unshaken in her story that her daughter had been abducted, and was surprised to be led to a cell after her interview.

"You are currently under arrest, and we can't let you go until we're satisfied that you're telling the truth and we have to test out the reliability of this witness statement," Olivia explained, fingers crossed that her gut reaction was the right one. Once they had Baz Bailey in custody the truth was likely to come out, she was certain, but this woman was completely adamant in her denial at the moment.

Ada Belcher was delivered to the station just before lunch, and treated like royalty because of her age and frailty. When she was shown into the interview room a comfortable chair was brought in for her and tea and biscuits were deferentially administered.

As Olivia and Desai entered the room, she looked round with bird-bright eyes and a lopsided smile and said, "Hello, young man. We must stop meeting like this. And who is this charming lady you have brought with you?"

Olivia smiled back at her and got down to business.

"You won't shake me in my conviction that I saw what I saw, and my eyesight's as good as yours — probably better," she stated firmly, after they had gone through the events of the morning.

"Can I just ask you something?" enquired Olivia, quietly plotting a test for the old woman. She rose from her seat and opened the door of the room, just opposite where Mrs Belcher sat.

"Ask away, gel," she was told.

Pointing to the other side of the corridor, Olivia enquired, "Can you see that poster on the far wall?"

"The one about Neighbourhood Watch or the one about Colorado beetle infestation?" asked the feisty old dear. Olivia squinted in an effort to distinguish the two and had to give in. This old dear had really sharp eyes for her age. "I had me cataracts done last year and it's left me with 20/20 vision," Ada declared with pride.

"It certainly has, hasn't it." Now, all the inspector needed was confirmation that this woman wasn't as mad as a hatter — which she obviously wasn't — and it strengthened her position of believing that Carole Shillington wasn't telling the truth.

Leo and O'Brien, meanwhile, took the town centre and its pubs on foot, armed with a photocopy of Bailey's mugshot with the identifying information at the bottom snipped off. Due to the holiday trade, the pubs in the town were open all day, and they'd have to check them all, as well as the cafes where some of the small-time villains and generally socially dysfunctional hung out, either plotting their little scams or just shooting the breeze. They knew he didn't work so there was little chance of pinning him down anywhere else.

Nobody, of course, had seen him, and few admitted to being able to identify him, but they'd expected this would be the case. Anyone "known to the police" or who was homeless, never admitted to knowing anyone, whoever was asking, unless there was a definite sign it wasn't the filth, and there was money involved.

There was only so much orange juice a man could drink, so they were glad to finally stumble across him in The Bridge Cafe, where they had called in to use the facilities. Bailey might not have met them before, but he recognised immediately what they were and, without a second thought, tried to make a break for it out of the back exit.

They were ready for him, however, and grabbed him, at which point he committed that unforgiveable sin of trying to resist arrest. "We only wanted to bring you in for a chat, so why the attempt to run?" asked Leo, as he clicked on handcuffs, then administered the formula. "I am arresting you for —"

"Yes, bloody why? I haven't done nuffink."

"Resisting arrest and assaulting an officer of the law in the rightful pursuit of his duties. You do not have to say anything, but it may harm your defence if you do not mention, when questioned, something which you later rely on in court. Anything you do say may be given in evidence."

"All right, all right, you've got me. So, why were you so anxious to talk to me?"

"We'd like to talk about the disappearance of your daughter from your girlfriend's car." This was O'Brien, who was nursing a bruised chin from the aforementioned resistance.

Leo finally fastened the handcuffs but, before they could leave, O'Brien turned to Leo and asked, "Could you hang on to him for a second while I nip into the Gents? I'm busting."

"Sure. And perhaps you could do the same for me when you come out. I'm filled to capacity as well."

O'Brien went into the urinals shaking his head at the formality of Leo's phrasing. All he'd needed to say was that he needed a slash too.

Back at the station, they booked Bailey into one of its luxury accommodations for one, en suite facilities included, and then went back to let DI Hardy know that they'd brought in their man.

"Well done, both of you. O'Brien, that looks sore. What did you do? Walk into a suspect's fist?"

"Something like that. What are you going to do now?"

"Me? I'm off for some lunch, and I rather hope that my sergeant will join me in a little repast. Lauren? Lauren!"

"What, boss?"

"I was saying that I'm going to leave Bailey stewing for a bit and that I'm off for a bite of lunch for which you might join me?"

"What? Lunch? Yeah, OK. Fine, whatever. Where are we going?"

"Just to the canteen. Is that all right?"

"I'm easy." For some reason, Lauren turned as red as a sunset with which a shepherd would have been absolutely delighted, and reached down for her handbag.

When they'd been served and were seated, Olivia held her fork above her food and asked, "What the hell is wrong with you today? You've not been right since you arrived." Lauren merely forked food, untasted, into her mouth and kept her eyes on her plate. "Come on, tell me. Maybe I can help."

"You can't," she mumbled, not even swallowing before she answered, and went back to shovelling food.

"Is it Kenneth? Has he been hassling you?"

"No."

"Is it the kids? Is there a problem at school?"

"No." Lauren's plate was nearly empty, whereas Olivia had hardly eaten a bite of her steak and kidney pie and chips.

"Well, is it that woman who looks after them for you after school and in holidays?"

"No."

"Whatever is it then? Not money?"

Lauren put down her knife and fork and shouted, "Why don't you mind your own damned business and I'll mind mine?" This outburst drew eyes from all the other diners, and it was Olivia's turn to blush.

"Look, I didn't mean to pry. I'll back off. But, if you ever feel you want to talk about it, whatever it is, you know you can trust me. I'll be waiting."

"I just bet you will." Lauren was filled with a rage that was partly inspired by guilt.

"Is it your health?" Olivia gave it one last shot.

With a hiss of "Leave it!" Lauren stalked out of the canteen, leaving Olivia to finish her lunch in puzzled silence. She might as well eat, as Hal was unlikely to be back on time to cook this evening.

Later, the atmosphere across the desk was prickly to say the least, and when Leo asked the DI when she planned to speak to Bailey, she nearly chewed off his face.

"I'll question him when I'm good and ready and not before: and certainly not on your say so, Constable. Get on with whatever it is you're supposed to be doing and let me do my job in peace."

After this uncalled-for outburst, the whole office was on tenterhooks.

At last, she couldn't put it off any longer, and looked across at Lauren's set face across the desk. "Come on, Sergeant. We ought to question this suspect. We've no real grounds for holding him overnight, and I don't want Devenish down on my back again about mistreating a detainee."

She phoned down to get Bailey put into interview room three and Lauren rose to her feet in silence. Neither had recovered her good mood, and they walked downstairs in silence.

The subject of the interview had a face that matched theirs for stoniness and, as soon as they had entered and turned on the tape recorder, he wasted no time in declaring, "I haven't done nuffink. You can't charge me with anyfink, because I haven't done nuffink."

After the statutory declaration about date, time and those present, Olivia started the questioning. "What did you do with baby Stacey?" she asked baldly.

"I don't know what you're talking about. The kid was took. That's nuffink to do with me."

"She wasn't taken from the car. We have a witness who's willing to make a statement to that effect. What did you do with her, Mr Bailey?"

"I didn't do nuffink with the kid. I didn't have nuffink to do with it. Ask Carole. She was its mother, and she done all the looking after. I just do me best to get enough to pay the rent, the lecky and feed us."

"What did you do with the baby, Mr Bailey?"

"Look, how many times do I have to tell you, I ain't done nuffink."

"We have a witness who had a good view of your car when it was parked in Jubilee Road, and she is willing to swear that there was no baby in the car. What do you have to say to that?"

"I've told yer. I ain't done nuffink."

"Did you hurt Stacey, Mr Bailey?"

"No comment."

Damn, thought Olivia. He'd finally clicked that this was the normal response to questions from the police. She'd have to check his record to see how many times he'd been arrested and charged, and exactly what with. It had slipped her mind earlier, because she was so concerned with Lauren's uncharacteristically hostile behaviour, and she needed to know exactly what he had on record. It would have a bearing on how they questioned him.

"Interview suspended at . . ." Leaving the room, she asked Lauren to check out his previous, and stalked off to see if Shuttleworth was back. He would be at her disposal now, and she wanted to make sure that when he had returned, Buller hadn't ripped him to shreds.

139

With a cruel smile, she asked if Bailey could be returned to his cell for a while. If nothing else that would shake him up a bit more.

Lauren discovered that Bailey had never been involved in violence before. His record was mainly for petty theft with a smidgen of breaking and entering and a bit of possessing puff. It was nothing big time, and Olivia reluctantly returned him to the interview room to ask him about his previous crimes and just get more of a feel for him.

Everything she asked him was answered with the standard "No comment" and after a while she began to feel that she would never get any further with him unless they found Stacey. Had she been stolen by a bereaved mother? How could she be so ridiculous? Desai had come up with a credible witness — or was the old dear actually gaga? Had the baby been killed by one of her parents? Hardy had absolutely no evidence whatsoever to back up this latter conjecture.

Reluctantly, she had the man released, and regretted it only half an hour later.

CHAPTER
ELEVEN

After Olivia had grabbed a quick coffee to gather her thoughts and get the taste out of her mouth of having interviewed a congenital liar, she returned to her desk to find the phone ringing, and Lauren just ignoring it. Grabbing the handset, she gave her partner a slightly sour look only to find that they had a development in the case involving the alleged abduction of the six-week-old baby.

There had been a 999 call only minutes before from Mrs Shillington in an hysterical state. All that could be got out of her was that she had found her granddaughter in the garden and that she needed help right away. She was too incoherent to give any details, and ended the call as soon as she had managed to splutter out her address.

A patrol car and ambulance had been dispatched, and Olivia was able to give her assurance that she and her sergeant would head immediately for the house. "Come on, Sergeant. I don't care how ticked off you are with me, the job needs you now. Mrs Shillington has phoned in to say that she has located her baby granddaughter. I don't know any more details than that, but I think we should get out there. Uniform and medical help are on their way. Don't let anything personal get in the way of you doing your job."

Lauren rose and grabbed her handbag, muttering, "Truce" to the inspector.

"Atta girl. Let's get off out there."

At the house they found that the patrol car and ambulance had already arrived, and one of the car crew let them in. Mrs Shillington was sitting on the sofa, something very muddy on her lap on to which tears dropped. Her mouth was encircled with muddy stains, and make-up ran down her cheeks, as the paramedics tried to encourage her to let go of the bundle that she cradled.

As she rocked herself to and fro she murmured, "No, no, no, no, no."

"Give her to us, Mrs Shillington, so that we can get her to the hospital," one of the female paramedics asked, hopefully.

"No, no," she replied. "This cannot be happening."

"You know it makes sense." Sometimes the worst clichés come out at the most serious of moments. "Let us take her."

Olivia and Lauren looked on, hardly aware that they were holding their breath. It was Lauren who let hers out first, saying, "Can I hold her, please?"

Mrs Shillington looked up at the sound of her voice, as if she were returning from underwater. "Can I hold her?" repeated Lauren. "I'll be very gentle." There was absolute silence in the room.

The grandmother, who wasn't much older than the sergeant, looked at her, a plea in her eyes. "I didn't

142

know anything until this morning, when I got back. I just noticed something wrong in the garden, and thought next door's cat had been using my flowerbed for a lavatory again. I've tried everything I can think of, but she won't wake up."

"I know you have. Now, hand her to me, so that she can be treated with the proper respect."

Mrs Shillington's face seemed to fold in upon itself with grief as she slowly held the little bundle a bit further from her body. "That's right. Let me take her. She needs to be bathed and have a pretty dress put on." Of course, she knew that Dr MacArthur would test her skin first, for any DNA traces left on it by the person who buried her, and who probably killed her, but she didn't want to upset the shocked and grieving woman any further.

"I have a lovely pink frilly one upstairs on the bed. I'd bought it while I was away." She dissolved into fresh tears at the thought of the gift.

"I'll send someone upstairs to get it," Lauren assured her, and nodded to one of the patrol car's officers. "Now, you hand her to me, and I'll see that she's well looked after."

Very slowly, she moved the bundle away from her body and towards Lauren, who gently took it from her, her own eyes creasing up with grief as she looked down on the little dead face. Carefully, she handed the baby to one of the paramedics while the other one moved tentatively towards the distraught woman, encouraging her to come with them, because she needed to be checked out. She was suffering from shock, and would need some sedation to get her through the first few hours of her grief.

While the crew of the ambulance dealt with the grandmother and transferred the baby's body to the ambulance, Olivia stepped into the hallway to make a phone call to the station. "Can somebody let the baby's mother know, and get as many as you can out looking for Baz Bailey. We'll take a statement before we come back," she concluded. Then she turned to Lauren. "We've only just let that bastard go. I hope he hasn't gone to ground. And, well done for persuading her. I think you prevented her from going into hysterics again."

"Let's get that statement," replied Lauren with the merest hint of a smile.

"I'll let you lead the interview. You seem to have a way with her."

After her visit to the hospital, when Mrs Shillington had returned home, she began to give her statement. With a lot of hiccoughing and hesitations, the woman slowly unravelled her memories.

She never watched or listened to the news when she was away, but an officer had contacted her about getting the key to her property, and had had to explain why. She immediately made plans to come home early and was going to go straight round to her daughter's when she had unpacked.

She had only just taken the little dress out of her suitcase when something attracted her attention outside, and she looked out of the window. She couldn't remember what it was for the moment — it had slipped her mind — but she had instantly noticed that one of her flower beds had been disturbed.

Coming downstairs rather cross, she had gone outside to clear up the mess on the path and was just trowelling holes to replace the plants that had come adrift when she noticed a tiny finger in the soil. That's when she had gone cold and begun frantically digging with her hands — which were still filthy, her nails encrusted with earth and compost.

She had uncovered Stacey's little body and time seemed to stop. In desperation, she had tried to give her the kiss of life, soon realising that she was far too late, and becoming aware of how cold the baby's flesh was. She had no idea how long she had sat on the ground, cradling the body of her granddaughter in her arms, but when realisation dawned on her again, she went straight in and tried to report it, but she found it difficult to get out the words.

"I can't believe it," she sobbed, "and in my garden too. You know who is to blame for this don't you? The bastard! The shit!" Her fists began to beat a tattoo on her knees and she began to shake again, recommencing her rocking, but with her arms empty now.

"Did they give her anything to calm her down?" asked Olivia, who had been more concerned with apprehending Baz Bailey again.

"Yes, and there's a bottle on the mantelpiece with some tablets in it which she can take if she has trouble sleeping," Lauren replied, putting an arm round the distraught woman. "Shall we get you to the cloakroom and get you cleaned up a bit, and is there anyone you'd like to sit with you?" Olivia gave Lauren an encouraging look. She was handling this well.

"I want my daughter," she suddenly shrieked. "I want my Carole."

"I'm afraid that won't be possible at the moment. Your daughter is in custody, because we believe she is lying about the circumstances of Stacey's disappearance."

Mrs Shillington, no more than forty, shuffled from the room like an old woman, at this further bad news. While she was tidying herself up there was a ring on the doorbell, and Olivia went to answer it, hoping to God that it wasn't press already, but it was only the woman from next door who had been the keyholder.

"Is there anything I can do to help?" she asked timidly. "Only, I saw from a bedroom window, when she cried out — when she found it; her."

"Perhaps you could make a pot of tea and sit with her. She's pretty heartbroken, and at least you could see to it that she has hot drinks and some food."

"That's no problem at all, but why isn't Carole here?"

Totally ignoring this direct question, Olivia replied, "Just don't answer the door to any members of the press or other media. I'll draw the curtains now, and you keep away from any windows. Perhaps, with no response whatsoever, they can be persuaded to think that Mrs Shillington has gone away for a while." Although the inspector thought there was about an ice cube's chance in hell of that happening, she thought the woman looked the sensible sort who would handle the situation well. She obediently trotted off to the kitchen, and soon the sound of the kettle heating was audible.

The two detectives left the shocked and grieving grandmother with her neighbour, with a word of warning that she would need to come in for further questioning.

Olivia was in a reflective mood and was convinced that Carole knew exactly what had happened to her baby; after all, she would hardly have gone out to the shop knowing that the baby seat was empty. She'd arrange for her mother to be picked up a little later, when the dust had begun to settle about where Stacey's body had been hidden. That, she probably didn't know, but Carole knew very well who had killed her daughter — it might even have been her. And that's why it had been important to get her into police custody. She'd been wrong to let Baz Bailey go. She didn't want to make the same mistake twice. And incur the wrath of The Devenish.

The drive back to the station was a quiet one, not because of their earlier falling out, but because this was the second young baby that had lost its life on their patch recently at the hands of others with evil intent.

When Lenny and Daz got back to the office they had already booked in the white coat and made sure that it had gone to Forensics to be checked for DNA. Buller was delighted with this bit of progress because it took them one step closer to who was responsible for the deaths, illegal drugs and contraband at the house in Gooding Avenue.

The owners of the house had been traced and were surprised that there had been anybody using it. As far as they were concerned, it was shut up, unoccupied and waiting for them to move into it when the husband's contract ended. It had belonged to his father but, as he had been working abroad, he didn't want to sell it before he and his wife had decided whether they wanted to move into it, sell it, or subdivide it for rental.

The recent events had focussed their minds, and they had decided to fly home and do something about it, which was a good thing as far as the street was concerned, because an empty house was a target for crime. Once it was no longer a crime scene, it could be handed over to its rightful owner, and would be occupied again in some way.

They would have to wait for the forensic results on the white coat, but it might get them a step closer to identifying the man with the red hair and freckles. How could he be an unknown with the sort of things he had been up to? He must be on somebody's records somewhere. They didn't even have a name yet.

When Olivia and Lauren got back there was the scent of hope in the air, but one of their worlds was about to come crashing down about their ears.

The reports of the visits to the tip were coming in, and some of them made some interesting reading, and while Olivia was checking these, Lauren's phone rang. They had nearly finished for the day, and she was looking

148

forward to going off to her assignation. She and Daz had not spoken that day, but he had given her some meaningful looks from his desk whenever he found her gaze wandering. She was disconcerted to find that her body was actually tingling in anticipation of pleasures to come when the phone call knocked her sideways.

She heard the voice of her children's school's headmistress and could hear Mrs Moth's voice in the background protesting something that sounded pretty urgent. As it turned out, it was her innocence.

"Mrs Groves?" the voice enquired. "I'm afraid I have to inform you of a serious incident which occurred today."

Without allowing her another word of explanation, Lauren cut in with, "Is it the children. Are they all right, or have they been hurt?"

"I'm afraid it's more serious than that."

"They're not dead, are they?" Once again Lauren cut across the woman.

"Their father came in this morning and told us that you had been injured in an accident, and that he wanted to take the children to see you in hospital."

"What? And you let him take them? Why didn't you give me a call?"

"Because he said you were injured and being treated, so we couldn't get in touch with you."

"But you knew our marriage had failed."

"This is true, but he said he was back in the country on leave, and that you had asked someone to call him to collect the children to take them to your bedside."

"You should have checked first." Lauren's voice had risen, and all eyes in the office were upon her.

"I realise that, now, but we had no reason to disbelieve him. He was so plausible, and it wasn't until Mrs Moth, your childcare assistant, came to collect them that we realised that anything was amiss."

"But, where would he take them? He hasn't contacted me about taking them away."

"I'm afraid I have no information on that."

"Then you're reporting that they've been abducted?" The sergeant's face had drained of all colour.

"I suppose I am."

"You stupid, irresponsible bitch! How could you do something so, so . . .?" Her voice tailed away as she ran out of adjectives to describe what the headmistress had done without checking with a third party first. "You could've called the station to check up on me. You could've called the hospital to see if I'd been admitted, but instead you just fell for his lies and let them go with him? They could be anywhere."

"He seemed genuinely concerned for your welfare. I must admit, he was very persuasive."

"He is. That's why he's so good at his job. That man could lie for England."

Olivia snatched the handset from her colleague and began to talk to the woman on the other end in a more rational manner. After a couple of minutes while Lauren wrung her hands and hung her head, the inspector handed back the handset with the words, "Mrs Moth. She's in a real state. Try not to be too hard on her. This wasn't her fault."

150

She spoke quite kindly to her employee, stating that she understood that none of this was her fault, and that she couldn't be held responsible for releasing the children into the care of her soon-to-be ex-husband, but when she ended the call, she burst into tears.

"Oh, my babies, my babies, my babies. Whatever am I going to do?"

"It's not too late yet to get something out today. Firstly, we'll have to go back to your house to get some recent photographs. Then we'll get them issued, start a search, get the local press involved and get an appeal on the television as breaking news. He'll be picked up.

"And don't worry yourself about what we were working on. These reports can wait till tomorrow, and Baz Bailey will be picked up. They can hold him overnight if necessary. We've got twenty-four hours to question him, and if we're not done by then, we can get an extension of custody."

"I don't give a shit about Baz Bailey. I just want my children back safe and sound. I can't believe Kenneth has done this. I had no idea he was over here on leave." There would be no illicit rendezvous for her tonight.

On their way to her barn conversion home, Olivia asked her, "Have you got an interim supervision order or whatever it's called? I don't know the exact term, because I've never been divorced."

"There's no custody order in place. We've only just started divorce proceedings, although we've applied for it to be a quick one so that things don't get protracted."

"It'll be all right, Lauren."

"That Mrs Hendry's such an airhead. I don't think she should be in a position of authority."

"You can't be worrying about that now. The first things to be sorted out are photographs so that we can get this abduction publicised. Someone will have seen him either before he took them or afterwards, when he'll be even more conspicuous, once his face is out there."

"He can't take them out of the country."

"That's a relief, anyway. Have they got their own passports?"

"Yes. God, actually I'll have to lodge those with the solicitor. I know I've changed the locks, but I'd put money on him getting in some way."

"Better to be safe than sorry."

"Shit, I wonder if he's got Gerda with him."

"There's no point in speculating. Let's just get on with getting what he's done out with the media and then wait for sightings."

For a moment, Lauren lost it again. "Omigod, omigod, omigod, what if we can't find them? What if he's arranged false passports for them and takes them out to that Godawful place where he's working?"

"Calm down. We will find them."

They called first at the school to speak to Mrs Hendry, who was in quite a state herself now she fully comprehended what she had done, and was fretting about her position at the school. What if she lost her job? She should have found some other way of confirming the father's story. But he had seemed so

152

plausible at the time, and she had just been concerned about the children getting to see their mother in hospital. And he had been so charming and believable, seeming genuinely upset for what he said had happened to his wife and getting the children to her bedside as quickly as possible.

But she was perfectly aware that the children had been transferred from boarding school to the church school simply because the parents' marriage had failed. Why had she believed his story without a qualm? Was it because the children were well-mannered and came from a good address? Was it because they all seemed so respectable? She knew this sort of thing happened, but just not to pupils from her school.

When the two detectives did arrive, it was all Olivia could do to restrain Lauren from attacking the head teacher. Forcing her into a chair, she asked Mrs Hendry if she could describe what Mr Groves had been wearing when he had picked up the children, as they would need that information when putting out an appeal for anyone else who had seen him.

"He had on a grey pinstripe suit, white shirt and a navy tie, and looked like he had just come from his office," she told them.

"But he works in the Middle East. Did you listen to nothing I told you when my children started here?" Olivia actually put her hand over Lauren's mouth while shielding her action by putting herself between the two women.

"Mrs Hendry wasn't to know that he was going to abduct them," she said in a soothing voice in the hope that Lauren would not antagonise the situation by shooting off her mouth and getting the hackles up on the already worried and guilty-looking head teacher.

"She was negligent in her duty of care." Lauren managed to call out, having slapped away Olivia's restraining hand. "A couple of phone calls and she could have deduced that he was up to no good."

"Hindsight is always in 20/20 vision. I'm sure Mrs Hendry was too shocked and concerned for your condition when Kenneth paid his visit here." Could her partner really not see that she was hindering rather than helping things? "Mrs Hendry, I'm sure you would like to get off home, so if you would give me your address, I'll make sure that someone calls on you to take down an official statement."

As the woman grabbed her briefcase and made for the door, Lauren just couldn't let her go without another dig. "Do you have children, Mrs Hendry? How would you feel if this were happening to you? How would you feel about the person who had let them be led away without any kind of corroborative information?"

"Can it, Sergeant!" barked Olivia as the headmistress slipped out. "That was not at all helpful. All you've done is put her back up and made her less likely to co-operate. Come on, let's get you back home so that we can get photographs, and then have a word with the superintendent. And what about poor Mrs Moth, probably back at your place with no information and somehow thinking that she should have prevented this from happening?"

***

Earlier, at the other end of the phone, Mrs Hendry had also been in a daze of anxiety. If the weeping figure of Mrs Moth hadn't been enough, the fact that the children's mother was a police officer had made her blood run cold. How could she have been so stupid? But the man had seemed so plausible. He was so respectable, and he seemed genuinely worried about his wife.

There were little touches like his tie being slightly askew, his hair slightly rumpled, as if he had run his fingers though it in despair, and she remembered thinking it had been bad enough for him for his marriage to break up without him coming home on leave to discover that his wife was seriously injured and in hospital. He seemed charming, but at his wits' end. How was she to know that it was all an act to get his hands on the children?

Of course she should have made a few corroborative phone calls before releasing them into his care, but how was she to realise that this was all a plan to get them away from his estranged wife? And now she'd be vilified and probably lose her job just because she had been taken in. As Mrs Moth had continued to cry quietly on the chair on the other side of her desk, a solitary tear had rolled down *her* cheek, testament to the depths of her self-pity and humiliation.

And now that police officer mother had been in and there was bound to be a considerable fuss over her crass stupidity. She would make her pay, and she only hoped that she didn't lose her position and would be

155

able to find another one after she'd been mangled by a professional.

Fortunately, Mrs Hendry had not mentioned the "accident" to the children when Kenneth had made his visit to the school, believing that any information should come from a parent, and Kenneth took full advantage of this situation when the inevitable questions began.

"Where's Mummy?" asked Sholto as soon as they had got into the car.

"Yes, where's Mummy?" echoed Jade.

"She just can't be with us," replied Kenneth, who had little imagination.

"Has she gone somewhere to have her drinking helped?" asked the ten-year-old boy, who saw and understood more than Lauren realised.

Kenneth's thoughts were scattered by this question? What drinking? Had she taken to the booze since he'd left? If she had, then he could surely use this to his advantage. Little imagination he might have, but he was always a good manipulator of situations.

"That was clever of you to work out, son. Yes, she's gone away somewhere where they can make her better, and she said that, as we'd missed Christmas together, I should look after you and give you a summer Christmas just for us."

At least the very last bit was true. He'd worked very hard getting the things together that would give the atmosphere of a house being in the middle of the festive season, and had rented a place that was isolated. The presents and the usual customs should keep them distracted for a few days, at least.

He intended to apply for custody of the children but, in the interim, he was determined to recreate the important celebrations that he had been forced to miss through Lauren's insensitivity and selfishness. Gerda was, this very minute, cooking the turkey with all the trimmings, and they had an artificial tree, suitably decorated, in the back window, and a large array of presents stacked underneath it. He didn't know how long he could keep them here, but he needed enough time to get a solicitor who was sympathetic to his cause, to fight for his custody.

Gerda was three months pregnant, and he wanted them to be one happy family. Places were already arranged in an English boarding school far from the one they had attended before, and he had applied as a single father working abroad. They could fly back for the holidays, and he wouldn't even notice that Lauren was no longer in his life. Then, all he had to do was get the house off her to help towards his expenses, and he'd have it made. He wasn't made of money, and Lauren would have to be made to understand that this was the best way for things to happen.

Sholto and Jade already knew Gerda and, no doubt, Lauren would not even notice they were missing from her daily round, so absorbed was she in her job. She'd come round — eventually.

At the house, he was careful to put the hire car in the garage and enter through the door to the kitchen. Both children made appreciative noises at the smell, and

157

Sholto reached down and rubbed his stomach in appreciation of what was to come. They acknowledged Gerda's presence by waving "hi" to her, and were then ushered into the living room to see the tree.

"Daddy," said Sholto, with a big smile, "that looks so naff in summer."

"How do you think Christmas is in Australia?" Kenneth asked, knowing that this would make his children think.

"It's always summer there at Christmas, isn't it?" asked Jade.

"You bet it is, my little honey."

"And they go for barbecues on the beach on Christmas day, don't they?" This was Sholto again.

"They do, but we're not near the coast out here, so you'll have to make do with a traditional Christmas lunch with pudding and ice cream and crackers and presents and sweets . . ."

"Oh, Daddy, I love you," said Jade, throwing her arms around his waist.

"So, how would you like to come and live with me and Gerda?" he asked, suddenly realising that he was pushing his luck.

"I'd rather live with you and Mummy," replied Sholto, keeping a little distance between them, "like things used to be, before you went away and Mummy started drinking so much wine."

"We'll have to see." He'd have to box a bit clever here. "Now, who wants to open some presents? Father Christmas has been, and I think you'll find your presents from him upstairs in your stockings."

158

Leaving them to rootle around upstairs, he went back to the kitchen to have a word with Gerda. "Are you sure you're all right about this?" he asked, nervous, all of a sudden.

"Of course I am. I looked after them before, and if you want them in your life, then I want them too," she replied, but a bit too off-pat for his way of thinking. What if she was only humouring him? There was another child to take into account now. Was he really being selfish wanting the new child to be just for them, and then having the pleasure of his old family in the school holidays? No, that was no way to think — he was their father, and they had been used to boarding school, happy there.

He'd been watching the house for a little while now, and surely they couldn't be happy with that dried-up old bat caring for them when Lauren was at work? And all he wanted was what was his. He'd always been territorial. And if the law couldn't deliver his children to him legally, then perhaps Lauren really would have to have an accident that rendered her incapable of looking after them — or even dead.

He knew, deep down that the break-up of the marriage was his fault, but he was that thing that is even worse than a woman scorned: a proud and possessive man deprived of what he believes is rightly his. And he'd get his way. Thank God he had thought to turn off his iPhone so that they couldn't locate him by its signal, and buy a throwaway pay-as-you-go that he could literally dump when all this was over.

CHAPTER
TWELVE

It was Olivia who had to locate the most recent photographs of the two children, and to turn up one of Kenneth, and there hadn't been many of those taken since he had started his current job. Lauren was still too distraught and kept ringing Kenneth's mobile number over and over again, as if that would magically make it turn itself on.

"Get a grip, woman. You've got to speak to Devenish when we get back and launch a hunt for those two. You know he has no patience for a woman in tears, or for hysterics. You need to tell him what happened in a rational and logical way, not snivelling and sobbing through your tale."

It had been a long day and, quite honestly, Olivia would be glad to get back to her own home, even if it was empty and echoing with silence. Anything would be better than this swamp of emotion she had struggled through since she had arrived at the office: in fact, it had been ever since Harris and Strickland had stumbled into that benighted house.

She might have argued that all the horrors stemmed from this; that it was the unusually hot June weather that was turning all the bad guys crazy, but she knew that wasn't the case. These old seaside towns were all the same. They had been born in prosperity, a getaway for those of means to visit and bathe, and breathe in the health-giving sea air.

The town had more than its fair share of those who were unemployed due to the local economy, and those who didn't work from choice, deciding, instead, to keep body and soul together through crime and drugs — either dealing them or taking them.

This was no time for idle speculation, though, and she bundled Lauren back into the car and drove her back to the station. She realised her sergeant was unfit to drive as soon as they had received that phone call about the children and would eventually send her back to her oh-so-empty house with a family liaison officer, who could drive her car and then be picked up when Lauren was in a fit state to be left.

At least the alarm had been raised without delay after school had ended for the day, so they could get something on the six o'clock news and get things rolling promptly.

She rushed Lauren past the CID room so that they wouldn't have to tangle with Buller, but she'd have to go in there herself after the sergeant had been escorted home, to check information that she had left stewing. She needed to see those reports from the officers who had searched at the tip, and she needed to check to see if Baz Bailey was back in custody yet. Life was just about impossibly crowded at the moment.

They had all eaten so well that events were unrolling just as Gerda had planned. Kenneth was asleep after too much to eat and a few glasses of wine too many, and the children were completely absorbed in their play. It had been simplicity itself to suggest that they didn't eat dessert until later; just before bedtime, in fact.

In the kitchen she took the tablets she had managed to wring out of the tired, disillusioned English doctor and began, quietly, to grind them up into a fine powder. When they were ready, she mixed them with a little diluted brandy and sucked them up in the syringe she had hidden in one of the kitchen drawers, right at the back. Kenneth would never have dreamed of looking there for anything. The kitchen was women's work, and he would have none of it.

She sucked it up and began to inject it into the solid, sticky pudding. This would disable all three of them, and she would be able to deal with the spawn of that dreadful woman while he slept. She was sure he'd understand that she didn't want anything to do with this second-hand family, and was interested only in their own child.

A pillow should do that job, and then she could persuade him that the two of them should go back whence they'd come and get on with their lives, unencumbered by the past. She needed absolute peace in which to carry out her mission, for she could expect no help or contrivance from him. She knew he would understand after the event that what he wanted was monstrous; that she could have nothing to do with those awful brats.

It would be time to put this little sweetmeat on to steam in a while, and she could look forward to getting him all to herself so that she could have their baby with peace of mind.

Olivia left Lauren to tell the superintendent what had happened and went back to her desk to collect the reports of what the Uniforms had picked up at the tip. It didn't amount to much, but there had been mention of a lot of foreigners around, working in one of the few nurseries that had survived the march of the developers, although no one had any idea where they were staying.

A little poking around in areas not usually inhabited might help that one. She'd have to take a drive out into the countryside, maybe investigate the woodland that still stood to the north of the town. Dr MacArthur had provided a preliminary post-mortem on the dumped newborn and had given it as his opinion that the child was not of English parentage: it probably had a Middle Eastern parent, which was something that wasn't noticed when Penny Sutcliffe had first opened that little bag of tricks and nearly lost her breakfast. "Oh, and in case nobody noticed it, the placenta was in there too, under the baby's body," he concluded. *Yummy!*

The doctor had also got to work pretty quickly on little Stacey Shillington and sent the inspector an email to say that he thought the little girl had been shaken to death. That would be something she'd have to ask

163

Carole about. She must know something. Either she'd done it or Baz was responsible, and she somehow couldn't see Carole herself extinguishing the spark of life in her own child.

Shit! And it was Friday today. That meant that Operation Zee-Tee kicked off this evening. *So much for going home.* She'd have to be on hand to interview people arrested and detained and there would be no rest for her until Monday morning, if then, as there would probably be a backlog of "guests" to clear before they had to be let go.

This had been quite a nice town to work in when she was younger, but it just got rougher and rougher, and there was little difference between this small town now and the city as it had been when she first joined "the force", as it was known then. Over those years it had more than doubled in size, consuming surrounding small villages and other rural communities in its path as if they were just snacks for its ever-growing bulk. In one Internet review of the place as a resort, it had been referred to as "the arsehole of the world". That might be a bit strong, but she got the gist.

Having checked around, the sole officer available to escort Lauren home was Terry Friend, as the only other woman at her disposal at the moment would have been Penny Sutcliffe — who would be off home to her children. So be it. Olivia didn't want to offer her own hospitality to her sergeant because of that falling-out earlier, and didn't think she'd agree to it either.

No, Terry, although not a family liaison officer — yet — would be ideal, and Olivia could hardly ask Lauren to stay on to help conduct interviews now these abductions had taken place. She'd have to go home to get over the shock and await developments. Basically, Olivia was on her own now, to sort out the cases of two unrelated dead babies and a brace of kidnapped children.

She was vaguely aware of Buller saying that he thought the illegal activity in Gooding Avenue was the work of a newcomer, for he and his department had managed to gather no intel on the situation, but she wasn't really interested. She had her own worries, and little did Olivia know that, while she and her colleagues were involved in their Operation Zee-Tee, there were far more evil deeds afoot in her town.

Interlude

He struggled all the way from his home — where they had lifted him — to their destination, but they had gagged him and bound his hands behind his back before finally blindfolding him. He had rolled around in the back of the van so much that he had little idea of where he had been taken; he just knew it wasn't far away.

Eventually he was hustled through what smelled like a garden and through a door into some kind of building. He hadn't seen who had taken him. They had grabbed him as he went outside to put the rubbish in the bin — such an everyday action that he wasn't expecting them, hadn't been on his guard.

He was pushed down into what felt like a wooden chair and, to his surprise, his blindfold was removed. Those who had taken him, however, had shielded their faces with scarves; they just wanted him to see what was going to happen to him.

His wrists were unbound, but each was seized roughly and held firmly on the table-top. A figure in front of him had appeared, producing a hefty hammer and two six-inch nails. "I will show you what happens to those who trespass on my territory," it hissed from behind its scarf and the captive's eyes widened as he tried to scream.

"You used this house on my patch, so now you die in it," the hissing continued, and the man put the point of one of the nails to the back of his right hand. He made distressed nasal noises behind his gag, but he could not stop the inevitable.

Bang!

The first nail drove its way home, and the figure held the point of the other nail over his left hand, as the prisoner squirmed in agony and continued to moan loudly, but not loudly enough to arouse any suspicion. He knew how thick the walls were: that was why he had put his minders in there. Only a full-blooded shout would reach the neighbours, and that was something he was unable to do. Bang!

The second nail was driven through his hand, but he wasn't lost yet. Through the clouds of his pain he knew he would be able to drag the table to the door or bang it around to attract attention. He wasn't completely done for. Not until the still unidentified figure pulled out a craft knife and moved towards him. "I am not cruel man," he continued, still in the hissing voice. "I not let you die slowly from starvation. I help you die a quicker death."

Before he had had a chance to take in what the man meant, he had whipped the knife under one of his hands and slit the wrist. This really was it. He was going to die, he thought, as the man slipped the knife behind his other hand and did the same to his left wrist. No amount of squirming could have avoided it, and the pain from his nailed hands was still making his head swim. As he bled, the man's companion secured his legs to those of the chair, and then they were satisfied that they had done all they could to stifle the competition.

"Die quietly and quickly, my friend. I will not tolerate trespassers in my town," was the figure's parting message, and all three figures slipped out of the door and the captive heard the key being turned.

The cuts to his wrists must have been deep, for already he could feel his life draining away, his head swimming from loss of blood, and the pain still throbbed in his hands, like the ticking of his life-clock, as it marked the end of his existence.

He made a few feeble attempts to move the table and draw attention to himself, but it was too heavy. It had been there since he had first come to the house and was probably solid oak — good English oak. This was one of his last thoughts as his life drained away and down to the floor, into an already spreading pool around his feet.

CHAPTER
THIRTEEN

Lauren had been assured that there would be a television appeal tonight, and that the photographs of both the children and Kenneth would be broadcast. When Terry Friend had arrived home with her, she wanted nothing more than to get rid of her. She needed a drink like she'd never needed one before.

She had tried offering one to Terry but had received the expected "no", that she wouldn't have one while she was on duty. On the pretext of going to the lavatory, she had gone to the downstairs facilities via the kitchen and on tiptoe, where she had extracted an already-open bottle from the fridge and taken it into the cloakroom with her, to swig what was left of it very quickly — and without a glass.

She then called through that she needed to change out of her work clothes and managed to secrete a bottle upstairs with a corkscrew so that she could have another. It also meant that she had access to a breath freshener spray to cover up her clandestine drinking. She knew she couldn't survive tonight without the oblivion of too much alcohol, and she was beginning to realise that she was developing a habit, if not a downright problem.

169

The addictive side of her personality overrode that almost sobering thought, and she sat, bottle at her mouth as she worked out a strategy to get rid of her uniformed "nanny". What was she turning into, now that she didn't have the controlling influence of Kenneth to rein her in when he was at home? In fact, even his presence at the end of the phone line had kept her on the straight and narrow. She had never rebelled as a teenager, choosing to get married young instead, and maybe that side of her was just beginning to show itself now.

She went into the ensuite and briskly washed her face, put down the bottle of wine with the cork stuck in it lightly, and went downstairs to tell Terry that she would phone her mother to come over, without enlightening the PC that her mother lived in the Cotswolds. If only she could get rid of her she could think things through. The children were probably unlikely to come to any harm in Kenneth's care, and she needed to get herself rat-arsed to face the long night ahead without news.

In the rented house, Gerda served the pudding flaming as it should be done — she had learnt that from her time in England — and with a huge tub of ice cream to accompany it. She knew the children would not want to eat it without something to mask the taste, and she also knew she needed to get them to eat enough of it to knock them out. She'd also have to hope that Kenneth had sufficiently digested his lunch and drunk enough to be feeling greedy, if not actually hungry again.

170

The children had played without supervision the whole afternoon and into the evening, while Kenneth had dozed in an armchair and she'd had time to think that although she had looked after the little brats, and had become fond of them for a while, nothing could ever make her love them. Her affair with Kenneth had begun soon after she had become the family's au pair/nanny, and she wanted to wipe out all evidence of Kenneth's previous life with them and Lauren. He was hers, now, and she and he would make a new life together with their child.

Unaware of any of these machinations, all three of them cleared up their ice cream, Kenneth also polishing off his portion of pudding.

"I don't like Christmas pudding," Sholto stated, putting his spoon in his bowl.

"Neither do I," echoed Jade, mirroring his actions from across the table.

"But you must eat it!" Gerda was already feeling panicked. "If I give you more ice cream, will you just eat a little bit of it? After all, it is so English."

"It tastes like poo," said Sholto defiantly.

What should she do if they wouldn't eat any of it? "Tell them they have to eat some of it, Kenneth, after all the time I took to make it."

"You didn't make it, you just steamed it." Even Kenneth was not being co-operative as he helped himself to another portion and refilled his wine glass. She shouldn't have put the drug in the pudding. What could she do now?

"Just a couple of mouthfuls, please," she almost pleaded. "You can have a big portion of ice cream with it."

"Daddy, stop drinking so much wine. You'll get sick like Mummy," said the boy.

"And how long does she have to be in hospital?" asked Jade. "I want to see her."

"Please, just eat a little bit of your pudding — for Gerda, please." Everything was going wrong.

"Shan't!" Sholto was defiant at mention of their mother.

"Eat some of it, you little shits!" Kenneth had reached that stage of drunkenness that led to belligerence.

Jade began to cry, and spooned the tiniest piece into her mouth. Even her brother's eyes filled with tears. "Why are you being like this, Daddy?" he asked, also taking a small mouthful. "I want to see Mummy, too. Will you take us to the hospital?"

"Daddy will take you tomorrow if you eat up all your scrummy pudding." Gerda felt very cunning at this response. Only she knew that they would be dead tomorrow.

"And don't you dare speak to my children like that," Kenneth retorted.

Gerda started back with shock. Why was he reacting like that? Was it just the booze, or was it something about her? Everything was getting muddled and going wrong. Of course, it didn't help the situation that she had had quite a few nips for Dutch courage before she had served the pudding.

"I think it's time we all went to bed," she declared. The children had eaten half of their portions, and that should be enough. Kenneth had had two, and would sleep like the dead, she hoped, as the booze mixed with the sleeping tablets. Or maybe she didn't know him as well as she thought she did. He worked in a dry country. Previously, as the hired help, she was kept out of the way as much as possible when he was at home. The only time she had been alone with him then was during their trysts, when Lauren was at work, and she had not really had the occasion to see how he reacted to large amounts of alcohol. Today he had certainly consumed enough for him to suffer from what she had been reliably informed was referred to in English as "brewer's droop".

"Come on, everyone, upstairs to bed. Kenneth, you help the children while I clear up." Kenneth was barely in a state to get himself to bed, let alone the children, but they would cope, she was sure of it. "I'll be up when everything is cleared away, Kenneth," she cooed.

She needed to stay down here and think awhile. She knew she could manipulate Kenneth's emotions, but she'd have to settle his unease at what she would have done by morning.

CHAPTER
FOURTEEN

Lauren dragged her sorry ass upstairs to bed at quite an early hour. She had drunk too much, but didn't plan on stopping yet, knowing she had an opened bottle upstairs in the en suite. The alcohol had taken the edge off her desperation for news of her children, and she was now quite confident that the forces of law and order would prevail in returning them.

Sitting down on the bed, her mind now slightly numbed from her rapid intake of alcohol, she began to review the last year of her life. It had really blown up in her face. Twelve months ago she had been an ordinary wife and mother, going about her daily work, and getting on with things as best she could. Then, she had discovered that her au pair was sleeping with her husband, and that it had been a long-term arrangement, taking place under her very nose.

If that hadn't been enough to cope with, her errant husband had left his family and gone off with the au pair and she'd had to disrupt the children's lives by removing the children from their prep schools, as Kenneth would no longer pay the fees. She had to employ someone to look after them after school every weekday, and now Kenneth had come back and abducted the children. On top of that she was having a secret physical relationship with a younger fellow officer. What had happened to the ordinary, respectable woman she used to be such a short time ago?

Shrugging everything off as she managed to struggle out of her clothes and was just settling down with a mug of now un-chilled white when the doorbell rang out, so loud in the silence of the house that it made her jump. Who on earth could that be? If there had been any news of Kenneth and the children, surely someone would have rung her.

She staggered to the window and looked down to the front door, and an inebriated smile split her face. Well, stone the crows, it was Daz Westbrook. But wasn't today Friday? Shouldn't he be embroiled with Operation Zee-Tee and all that entailed? She was surprised to remember this detail with everything else that was going on in her life. Opening the window, she called down to her unlikely Lothario, "I'll be there in a minute. Don't go away."

Using her hands on the landing wall, she carefully made her way to the head of the stairs, then clung on to the bannister to maintain her balance. With her free hand she pushed her hair out of her face and pulled down her nightie. She must try not to appear too drunk; she didn't want to repel him and what he had on offer was important to her. Blinking her eyes hard as she got to the foot of the stairs, she shook her head to try to clear it.

"What are you doing here?" she asked groggily. "And how did you know where I lived?"

"I'm a detective," he replied, "and I'm just playing hooky for a while from all the losers who are being brought in to be questioned and charged. Most of the arrests are just for a warning of being in possession of a Class C drug and a statutory fine, and a lot of the rest are merely pissed and need somewhere to sleep it off before being charged with drunk and disorderly. They won't miss me for an hour or so."

"I thought I'd missed our liaison," she replied, summoning up a little enthusiasm for a game or two. "Come on in." As he crossed the threshold, she grabbed at his shirt and pulled it open. He slipped his hands underneath her nightie, and they never made it upstairs, but stumbled into the living room and collapsed onto the sofa in a jumbled, already copulating heap.

She must have been hazier than she thought because, before she knew it, he was getting dressed and readying himself to leave. "Do you have to go already?" she asked, realising that she had been barely conscious while he had worked away. This wasn't at all what she had hoped for.

"Gotta get back," he said nonchalantly, "I'll text you," and she realised that she didn't care. She wanted another drink more than she wanted anything else, and she let him go without another word as to when she'd see him again. When he had gone, she heaved herself back upstairs and started in on the remaining wine in the bottle. She needed to sleep, and there was no Olivia with a handy sleeping tablet to come to her aid tonight.

Back at the station, Olivia had developed a thumping headache due to the falling-out with her work partner and what had happened at the school, and had decided that, because none of the arrests was for anything serious, she would go home and get some sleep, to see if she could shift the pain. She had already taken a couple of painkillers, and would take some more when she got in. She knew she'd be on duty all weekend because of the nature of the operation, and she was not looking forward to it.

It was only eleven o'clock, but at least she could be fairly sure that Hal would be at home — such a pity that the school week had finished, and she would not be around to spend a little time with him. She'd hardly seen him since he had gone back to supply work, and she missed someone who was not directly involved in her job to talk to about it.

As she swung into the drive she could see his car, so he was definitely there. As she went through the door, she called out in a jocular manner, "Honey, I'm home," but received no answer. There was a flapping noise, and the kitten that she had obtained for Hibbie at Christmas, at great inconvenience at that time of year, slunk through the living room, now considerably bigger than it had been when it had entered the household.

Hibbie was never there to look after it, and her mother had got rather sick of falling over it when she went into the kitchen late at night for a glass of water. She knew she should have turned on the light, but she didn't see why she should change her ways just because

177

of an animal. And it pained her, the draught that blew in from the cat flap when she was cooking in the coldest part of the winter. Damn Hibbie! If she ever left home — again — she could take it with her.

Her mood had soured in an instant, as the headache declared that it was not beaten yet, and she went to the kitchen drawer where she kept some paracetamol. She could understand both their son and daughter being out on a Friday night, but where the hell was Hal? He must be at home if his car was outside.

Mounting the stairs, she found Hal dead to the world, in bed. How dare he, when she needed him most? She shouted his name, and then lost her temper. "How can you treat me like this?" she shouted. "I'm in hell at work, we've got some ghastly cases at the moment, and you're never here any more. How can you be so thoughtless? I need someone to talk to about everything otherwise I shall burst. You were only going to do a bit of supply, and now you're simply never at home."

Hal merely raised his eyebrows and stared at her as she realised what she had said. Damn, she was taking him for granted, and she never asked him about his day, but had always expected him to draw her out to release her tension. He didn't need to say anything: his silence spoke volumes.

With an angry stamp of her foot, she stomped downstairs, furious at him for being right, and not even having to tell her she had slipped into thoughtless habits. However, tonight was not the night to look at her like that, she thought, as she uncorked a bottle of wine. Damn this tightrope that she had to walk between work and home. Would she ever get the balance right and make it to the other side in one piece. At this rate, she might make it to the other side, but she might do that on her own, with Hal long gone. Bugger, she'd have to make it up to him, but she really did have to work this weekend.

Hal didn't even stir when she went upstairs for the second time, and she slipped in to bed beside him and dropped into a deep sleep, emotionally exhausted, only to dream of dead babies and women with no eyes.

Gerda sat for a couple of hours girding her loins for the task before her. Eventually she went upstairs and checked on Kenneth. He was sprawled on top of the duvet, still fully dressed and looked like he would not wake for some time. Then, she tiptoed into the children's room — they had been persuaded to share a room so that they would not be scared if they woke in the night and couldn't remember where they were. At least, that's what Kenneth thought. For Gerda it was more a case of being able to dispatch both of them more easily.

They both seemed to be spark-out, and she got a pillow from the third bedroom so that she could smother them while they slept their drugged sleep. This would be the easy bit. It was dealing with Kenneth tomorrow that would be the real test of her powers of persuasion.

In the master bedroom, Kenneth stirred. Something that Gerda didn't know about him was that he was fairly inured to alcohol, and that too much of it disturbed his sleep rather than aided it. He had drunk heavily before he took the contract in the Middle East, originally in an attempt to break his self-destructive addiction. He was a big man, and the proportion of the ground-up sleeping pills had not been enough to floor him.

He opened his eyes, feeling groggy, but began to get to his feet as a floorboard creaked and one of the children stirred, whimpering in their sleep. On automatic pilot, he got to his feet, slightly surprised that he had not got undressed before collapsing on the bed, and made his way to the next bedroom. Gerda had not been there by his side, so it was his duty to attend to whichever of them was, perhaps, having a nightmare.

As he got out on to the landing, he almost fell, but gritted his teeth and carried on towards the room that the children were in, all the while wondering where his new woman was, his mind grasping on to the fact that he was going to fight for the custody of his offspring come what may.

As he pushed open the door, he could not believe his eyes. Gerda was standing over the double bed with a pillow in her hands and, as he watched, put it over Sholto's innocent little face. What the hell was she doing?

Gathering all his wits, he lunged in her direction, and managed to knock her off balance. "What are you doing?" he yelled, waking both children, who immediately started to cry for their mother.

180

"You don't understand, Kenneth," she said, pulling herself back upright and reaching again for the pillow. "Go back to sleep, good little children," she soothed, but there was a murderous glint in her eyes. "They have to go, so that we can be alone with our baby."

"What the hell are you talking about, woman? All five of us will be a family in the school holidays. There'll be plenty of time for the three of us. Would you like to go back to boarding school, kids, and come out to Gerda and Daddy in the holidays? It's very hot and sunny and you're going to have a new brother or sister."

"I want my Mummy," wailed Jade, while Sholto tried to get out of bed to run away, but his legs felt funny and he couldn't stand.

"Help me, Daddy," he implored, and Kenneth looked towards his children, then at Gerda who was already approaching the bed again, pillow at the ready.

"You have to understand, Kenneth, I cannot bring up another woman's children. I have to wipe out anything that reminds me of my days as someone else's servant, and we need time together by ourselves for our own baby."

Kenneth couldn't think straight. What was happening? Was he dreaming? Gerda loved the children, didn't she? She'd agreed that he should apply for custody, and she'd agreed to his plan to take them and make Lauren more compliant.

"Daddy, my legs feel funny. What's wrong with them?"

"Daddy, I want to go and see Mummy. I'm frightened."

"You do understand, Kenneth, don't you, that we can't have these snivelling brats as part of our life together?"

Kenneth was confused as to whether what he was experiencing was real or a very vivid nightmare. The one thing he did know, definitely, was that he wanted it to stop, and all the drugs in his system welled up and came out as pure, blind rage.

He lunged forward, snatched the pillow from Gerda's hands and grabbed her round the arms, enclosing her in his savage embrace and dragging her to the bedroom next door. The children, already exhausted by their outbursts in their drugged state, sank slowly back into a reclining position and went back to sleep.

In the bedroom next door, Gerda was fighting Kenneth's manic hold of her and trying to justify what she had been about to do but, just like Lauren at the end of the last year, she had underestimated the power of his fury when he felt thwarted, and he was also fuelled by alcohol.

He had thrown her down on the floor and then banged her head against its unyielding surface and, before he had even realised he was going to do it, had his hands around her throat and was choking the life out of her. Unable to distinguish fact from fantasy, he just wanted all this to stop so that he could go back to bed and wake up in the morning with everything as normal, or as normal as things could be with the children abducted.

Gerda stopped struggling, at last, and he got to his feet and made his way unsteadily to the children's room to make sure that they were settled and could go back to sleep. This was only a dream, really, and tomorrow he would contact Lauren and make his conditions known to her regarding their children. She would not defy him on this.

As he crawled back on to the bed, the drugs in his system finally triumphed, and he lost consciousness within seconds.

He didn't wake again until after dawn, and when he did return to the conscious world, he felt like death. His head was thumping, his mouth was like sandpaper, and his stomach contents roiled and fought to be released. He had a heavy feeling in his mind as if he'd had a terrible nightmare — it was only when he got to his feet and saw Gerda's legs protruding from the floor at the foot of the bed that he realised that he had not suffered from bad dreams at all, and that everything that he thought was just his sleeping imagination was, in fact, reality.

He slumped down on the side of the mattress and tried to make sense of what he remembered from the night before. His main memory was of Gerda with a pillow over the face of his son, and the madness in her eyes. He remembered, too, the feeling of his hands round her throat as he choked the life out of her, and it finally dawned on him that, not only had he killed her, but he had murdered their unborn child too.

After a few minutes of self-pity, during which tears of remorse rolled down his cheeks — at the loss of the baby, not Gerda — he realised that he couldn't just sit there and feel sorry for himself. He had to do something with Sholto and Jade, and he had to get back out of the country.

Getting dizzily to his feet again, he checked in the children's room and noted that they were still asleep. That at least was a good thing. He then packed up what he could of his possessions and went outside to get the hire car out of the garage. Only when everything was loaded into the boot did he go back inside and wake the children, who had been sleeping so soundly that he didn't doubt that they would drop off again in the car. But before he did that, he closed the master bedroom door on the mortal remains of Gerda and all his hopes and dreams for their future together with their baby.

He then headed for the coast. He would drop off the children at his old home, make his way to the airport and get a last-minute seat. It didn't cross his mind that he might be unfit to drive as he sped along the road that led to the little hamlet where the barn conversion was situated.

He unloaded the black bags he had stuffed quickly with all the new toys and the clothes bought in preparation for this abduction, and put them on the ground in front of the house, then he went back to the vehicle and gently lifted out his daughter, rousing his son as he did so. Plonking them at the front door, he gave a long peal of the bell, then rushed back to the car and drove off with a screech of tyres. He didn't want to be in the vicinity when Gerda's body was found, and he knew he would never get custody now. He had no idea how long it would take for the agent who had leased him the house to put two and two together and how long after that they would find Gerda, but he certainly didn't want to be there when that happened. The only thing he could run towards was work. His passport was in his jacket pocket and there was a battery shaver in his holdall. He could smarten himself up when he got to the airport.

CHAPTER
FIFTEEN

Olivia was woken by the ringing of both the landline and her mobile. Not knowing which to answer first, she picked up both and shared a "hello" between them. In one ear she could hear Lauren's voice, in the other a voice that sounded official.

Snapping, "Hang on a minute, will you; I'm on another call," into her mobile to Lauren, she put down the phone and spoke into her landline.

"DI Olivia Hardy speaking. How can I help you?"

She discovered that it was a call from the station to inform her of a traffic accident just outside the town where a man had been killed, and he had been identified as Kenneth Groves. Did she think she could break this news to her sergeant and bring her in to identify the body?

"I've got her on the other line," she whispered. "I'll call you back." This was the best she could do for now. Going back to her mobile, she spoke calmly into the handset, telling Lauren to be calm and explain slowly why she'd phoned. Did she already know about her husband, and where on earth were the children, if he had been killed? Were they in the car as well? Were they injured or even worse?

"Olivia, the children are back. I don't know how or why, but I've just been woken by the doorbell, and I found them on the doorstep with bags and bags of toys. What's going on? Has Kenneth been arrested?"

"When did this happen?"

"About forty minutes ago. When I opened the door they became hysterical and asked me why I wasn't in hospital, and then they said all sorts of odd things about Christmas and Gerda and a pillow, and it's taken me all this time to calm them down and get them settled into bed. What should I do now?"

"Leave it with me. I'll call it in and I'll be straight over. I'm going to end the call now. Make yourself a cup of tea and I'll be with you as soon as I can." What on earth was going on here? How could Kenneth be dead and the children back at home? She didn't have the faintest understanding of what was going on, but she dutifully called the station and informed them of the children's return before asking for more details of the accident that had claimed Kenneth's life.

She was told that a witness had seen him in the outside lane of the motorway driving at considerable speed on the route to the airport, and then he had just seemed to slump at the wheel and veer across the other two lanes. The witness had been able to brake and stop, but Kenneth had careered into two other cars, the impact from which had knocked his vehicle off the carriageway.

Several cars had stopped, but when they got to him, they found him dead behind the wheel. They had no medical information, as yet, but it was thought by the

187

paramedics who attended that the impact had thrown him so hard against his seatbelt that his ribs had been broken, and that his lungs had been pierced. The shock of the trauma may then have caused his heart to stop. Whatever, he was dead, and there were three others in various stages of trauma.

Having learnt as much as she could, Olivia threw on some clothes with a sad look over to Hal's side of the bed, and went off on her unpleasant errand. This was a totally unexpected end to the incident that had begun with the abduction of the children from their school, and she had no idea how Lauren would feel at this sudden change to her life.

How would she cope as a widow?

As the town woke up to another day, an estate agent who had, about a week ago, leased a remote house to a respectable man and his good lady for the three months of summer, went into the office earlier than usual for a Saturday to check his records. He thought he had recognised the man he had seen on the late news the night before, and he wanted to see if the name was the same. On the other hand, if someone was going to abduct children, would he give his real name for a short-term lease?

When the name didn't tally he wasn't surprised, but decided to ring the station anyway to voice his fears. God forbid that something should happen to the children and he had done nothing. As managing agent, he still retained a key, and after the phone call, when he was assured that someone would come down to his office and have a chat with him, he felt as if he had done his duty as a citizen. Estate agents weren't universally loved, but he was a good man at heart, and maybe this small act would raise his status slightly.

His call had evidently been taken seriously, for it was only about ten minutes later that PC Shuttleworth tapped on the door to be let in, it being still too early for the office to be open. Having assured the agent that his patrol car did, indeed, have satnav, he dutifully signed for the key and went back to his car on a mission to investigate.

He had been the only officer available, as every other member of the service was tied up with sorting out the large number of arrests that had been made the night before and resultant interviews, or had pleaded associated paperwork. The pressure on staff would be even higher tonight, this being Saturday, and this still being Operation Zee-Tee weekend.

The house certainly was out of the way, but it looked well enough cared for, he thought as he pulled up outside it. There was no answer to his knocks and rings on the doorbell, and he eventually got out the key and let himself in. After calling a few times, he decided that there was no one at home and wondered why, if it was the house where DS Groves' two abducted children had been taken. Surely her soon-to-be ex-husband hadn't taken them on a jolly — that would be much too public, and they were bound to be recognised.

To his puzzlement, there were lights blazing on a Christmas tree in the living room, and decorations hung about the room. When he went into the dining room, there were bowls still on the table, and the remains of a Christmas pudding in the middle of it. What had gone on here?

In the kitchen was a forlorn turkey carcase still in its roasting tin. He would have to search upstairs before he drew any conclusions. Through an open bedroom door he spied piles of brightly decorated wrapping paper on the floor. Something here was out of kilter, time-wise.

A boxroom door was ajar, and he pushed it open to find no signs of occupation. That only left the bathroom and what he assumed was the master bedroom. The smallest bedroom also proved unoccupied, and he approached the final door off the landing with caution. "Police!" he shouted. "I'm coming in." Anything could lie beyond this final barrier.

As the door slammed back on his hinges he became aware of the smell of stale alcohol on the air, and the presence of the figure of a woman sprawled on the floor at the foot of the bed. Dropping down to his knees, he felt for a pulse but found nothing. There were no signs of life, and her body was cooling fast. He'd have to call this in immediately, especially as he could see bruises on her neck on closer inspection. Could this be the woman who had leased the house with Kenneth that the estate agent had mentioned?

When Olivia had reached Lauren's huge home, she found her sergeant outwardly calm. Her children were home, and she could not afford to waste any emotion on her errant husband, but she would no doubt be very shocked at his demise. The inspector decided to take things slowly. "Did you see Kenneth when he brought back the children?" she asked, innocently.

"I didn't see hide or hair of him — not that I wanted to," was her reply.

"Did you not think it odd that he hadn't stopped to apologise and perhaps ask you not to press charges?" This question hinted at events about which Lauren had no knowledge, but she was too flustered to think about what it might imply.

"He wouldn't dare. I'd have killed him." Olivia winced at this phrase. Little did she know. A sudden decision made her just go for it.

"Look, there's no easy way to tell you this . . ."

"What? The children are in bed asleep. It can't be anything to do with them."

"Let me put the kettle on, and then I've got something to say."

"Just spit it out. I don't want any more tea or coffee."

"Well, I do. You called me at stupid o'clock, and I've come straight over without any breakfast or even a hot drink."

"Sorry. I'll do it."

"And after we've had a drink, I've got something to tell you."

Olivia tried not to show too tragic a face before delivering her news, but she saw a worried frown cross Lauren's forehead. The sergeant was, in fact, quite anxious about whether her little fling with Daz Westbrook had been discovered. What on earth did she have to say in her own defence? That she was, literally, gagging for it? Had he been missed the night before when he had called round to see her — to fuck her, actually?

She could hardly contain herself whilst Olivia savoured her Colombian coffee. Finally she urged, "Come on, spit it out. I'm on tenterhooks here." *Please don't let this be about Daz and me, please God*, she silently prayed. *Please, please, please.*

Olivia could not understand her impatience, now that the children were home, but addressed her in her most soothing voice. "There's no easy way to break this to you, but Kenneth's dead."

"Is that all?" Lauren's body sagged with relief. She hadn't been rumbled.

"Don't you want to know what happened?"

"As long as he doesn't have the children any more, I don't give a damn, but I suppose you're going to tell me."

"We think he was heading for the airport when he collapsed behind the wheel . . ."

Olivia's mobile rang, and she reached for it from her pocket. "I'll have to take this," she said, grateful to get a breather before going on with her story of Kenneth's end, although Lauren didn't seem particularly bothered. As she listened, her face creased into a frown and with a final, "Thanks for the information," she turned to her friend again.

"There's just been an update. A house that was leased for three months has been traced back to Kenneth and Gerda through the good memory of an estate agent, and Liam Shuttleworth's been out there. He found the place all decked out for Christmas, and the body of a woman on the main bedroom floor. It appears that she had been strangled, but we have no confirmation of that medically, yet."

"Is it Gerda?"

"Nobody knows, but if we don't find any identification, you're going to have to identify the body — you'll have to anyway, unless you know of a particular friend she had while she was working for you."

"She didn't really seem to have a social life. I suppose she was too wrapped up thinking about Kenneth."

"If you wait until we can get the bodies transferred to the mortuary, then you could see them both at the same time."

Still Lauren was calm and in control. "He's got hefty life insurance, you know, and I'm still, legally, his wife. All three of us will be fine, and I'm still earning."

Suddenly her face crumpled. "How on earth am I going to tell the children? They coped really well with him leaving, but this is permanent. They'll never see him again. I just don't know how they'll take it."

"And what was all that about the place being done out for Christmas, I wonder," murmured Olivia.

"It was probably because he didn't see them at Christmas, and he wanted to make it up to them. It would have provided a distraction while they were in his care. My God, how on earth am I going to break it to them?"

"They'll be fine, Lauren. Children are a lot more resilient than we realise."

Lauren's face was drenched with tears now, but she was not sobbing, rather she was thinking hard, working out the best way to tell the children that their father was never coming back.

"Did they ever go to Sunday school? And they go to a Church of England school now, don't they? Maybe you could tell them that he's gone to heaven."

"Jade might swallow that, but I don't think Sholto would. He's just that little bit older." Lauren was considering the idea, though.

"Perhaps he would go along with it because it gave Jade comfort," Olivia suggested, a little seed of hope in her voice. "And remember, if that woman's body Liam found was Gerda's, then it's saved them having to go through him being tried for murder and going to prison."

"That's what I call really looking on the bright side of life." Lauren smiled weakly at her partner, as there was the sound of feet coming down the stairs.

"Call your marvellous Mrs Moth and get her to come over. You shouldn't be alone, but I have to get back to the station. I'll be in touch when I know more. I've got *live* murderers to catch — baby murderers."

The street patrols had been busy the night before but one episode really made its mark on those who took part in it. They had come out of an alleyway on the council estate and seen the shapes of three men at the end of it. Strolling, quite cautiously towards them, the men were only aware of their approach when a shaft of brightness from a street light illuminated their shapes.

194

Two of them were already known to the police as small-time sellers of cannabis and, knowing they had been seen, held up their hands confident that, as they had little on them at that time of night, the punishment would, as usual, be minimal as there was so little evidence.

The third man, however, threw up his hands in horror and began to run as if all the hounds of hell were after him. With a cry of, "Just stay there!" both uniformed officers took off at a tearing run, but he was infused with fear, and it gave him wings. He shot across the recreation ground, down a dark alleyway and then across a main road before disappearing down an access road to the back of the properties in the street.

The two officers chased after him, but for a while he easily outran them and it was only when he crossed the main road, back into bright lighting once more, that they caught sight of him again. "Over there!" puffed one of the policemen. "He's going down the back alley."

"I'll go down the road and cut him off on the other end."

It was as good a plan as any, but the man did not emerge from behind the houses and the officer who had run in after him could see nothing as he looked down its length. He couldn't have just disappeared into thin air. He had to be somewhere. He was just scratching his head in perplexity when he heard the frantic barking of a dog and a high-pitched scream.

His reaction was automatic, and he hared off down the back lane. As he ran the scream turned into a more masculine cry for help and, as he reached a garden halfway down the long terrace, he located it to over the six-foot fence that separated that house's garden from its back access.

Without waiting, the officer pulled himself up on to the fencing and shone his torch over to the other side of it. There, cowering in a corner of the garden was the man they were after, the dog keeping him a prisoner. "Help me before this thing savages me," he cried in genuine alarm.

At that moment his colleague joined him, and was asked to go round the front and get the owner to call his dog into the house so that they could arrest their man. For a couple of minutes he watched the entertaining sight of the dog making a move every time his captive tried to get away. "Do something, mate, he's going to fucking kill me," he yelled, again showing what was more of a phobia than a fear.

Eventually, the patio doors opened and a thickset man called, "Come in, Stanley, and leave the man alone." At the sound of his master's voice, the spaniel trotted off, its tongue lolling out of its mouth and with almost a good-natured smile on its face. "He wouldn't hurt a fly, Officer," the man said, grabbing the old dog by the collar and dragging him into the house. "He only wanted to be friends and lick his face."

The tenant unlocked the back gate and let in the other constable, and he looked at the cowering man with disdain. "Whatever's wrong with him?"

"I can't stand fucking dogs," replied the prisoner, now theirs.

"Chose the wrong house then, didn't you?" replied the constable who had witnessed his terror from the back fence. "Come along with us. You've got some questions to answer, like why you legged it back there."

He was detained, cuffed and searched and that's where the puzzle began. He had no drugs on him whatsoever, or any large sums of money, so what had spooked him so much? He would say nothing other than "no comment" — no change there from normal, though — but finally one of the uniforms realised that he looked a little familiar.

"Aren't you that guy the DCI is looking for? Do you recognise him?" he asked his colleague.

"No. Go on, give us your name, mate."

"No comment."

As the man turned his head, the constable who thought he knew him suddenly got a glimpse of him in profile and exclaimed, "I know where I know you from, matey. You're that bloke whose kiddie got killed, and you're in deep shit."

"That's not very professional," the man finally uttered, as his legs began to shake.

"Baz Bailey" — fortunately the man's name had come back to him — "I am arresting you . . ." He had finally managed to bring the words of the caution to mind, and the officers radioed for a van to come and pick him up and take him into the station for questioning.

"Hey, well done, mate. Where did you remember him from?"

"When he was being released from custody, I just caught sight of the side of his face. He doesn't look much like his photograph from the front, does he?"

"It's the lighting. Everything looks different under this yellow glare."

As he was shoved into the back of the police van, one of the PCs shouted up to the driver, "When you get back, give him a tour of the police kennels."

There was a wail from the back of the van.

The office was a sea of activity when the inspector got to her desk, but someone had stuck a Post-it to her computer monitor informing her that Baz Bailey had been picked up the night before trying to buy cannabis during Operation Zee-Tee, and was waiting for her in a cell — now that was what she called a piece of good news.

Carole Shillington was also still in custody, an officer of the rank of inspector being able to grant an extra twenty-four hours detention, and it seemed like she was ready to make a fresh statement. After the death of her daughter, she had experienced shock, then grief, and had finally reached a state of extreme fury. "I want to talk to that inspector," she yelled at the custody sergeant, having summoned him. "I want to make a new statement about my Stacey."

"Calm down, madam," soothed Penny Sutcliffe in a quiet voice. "Which inspector do you want to talk to?"

"That fat woman," she stated without any embarrassment.

"Her name?"

"I don't know. How many fat women inspectors have you got working at this station?"

Penny strived to smile, and suggested, "Do you mean Detective Inspector Hardy?"

"That's the one. And I want to talk to her now."

"If you'd care to take a seat, I'll call her down to see you. I'm calling her now," Penny informed them, and lifted the handset of the phone.

Olivia was there in a couple of minutes, amazed at her good fortune at getting such an early opportunity to speak to the witness, and guided the young woman into an interview room. Before she had even had the opportunity to sit down, Carole started again.

"I want to tell you exactly what happened to my baby girl," she said in a very loud voice.

"If you'll just calm down, Carole, I'll get a recording rolling and then you can make your statement." Olivia wasn't exactly sure what the young woman wanted to tell her, but it sounded important.

When all the formalities had been observed, Carole twisting and fidgeting in her seat, making little whimpering noises in her impatience, Olivia informed her, "We know that when you made that trip to Mr Shah's shop that Stacey wasn't in the car."

"That's just what I'm here to tell you about. It was that bastard Baz."

"What about him, Carole?"

"She was crying, like she always does at night. Baz was so cross; said he hadn't had a decent night's sleep since she was born. I tried to quieten her down — tried her with a bottle, changed her nappy, cuddled her and

199

walked round with her, but eventually I had to put her back into her Moses basket, and she just started to yell again. I wouldn't have believed something so small could make so much noise.

"Anyway, he just flipped. He got out of bed and took her under the armpits and just started to shake her, yelling, 'Shut up, you little fuck.' . . ." She broke off her statement as a solitary tear rolled down one cheek. "And he just shook her harder and harder until suddenly she went quiet. I wanted to go to her, but I was too scared. Then, he just put her back into her basket and got back into bed."

"And what did you do then?" Olivia encouraged her, as she looked to be running out of steam.

"I waited until I could hear him snoring again, and then I got out of bed to see how she was, and . . . she wasn't moving or breathing, and I just knew that she was dead. That's when I started yelling, and Baz got up and slapped me round the face and told me to shut up about it or he'd go to prison and I'd have nobody to pay the rent or feed me. Then he said we could always have another baby, and I was to go back to bed and do what he said in the morning.

"I got back under the covers, but I couldn't sleep. It all seemed such a nightmare and I couldn't believe it had really happened."

"And what did Mr Bailey tell you to do in the morning?" Olivia knew that they already had enough to charge him with, but she wanted the full story.

"I must have dozed off and he said I woke him by making whimpering noises. It was quite early, but he said I had to go to the little mini-mart in Beach Road and get some fags and some biscuits. Then I was to get the bits of shopping and go back to the car and . . . and pretend she'd been abducted."

"I just stood there looking at her little body in her basket, so he grabbed me by the hair and told me I had to do it, or he'd make sure that something awful happened to me. Then he said he knew where to get some acid, and did I want a faceful of it? He'd make sure that nobody ever looked at me again if he was going to prison."

"And then what did you do?"

"I just felt numb. How could he do that to our little girl? He'd complained every night since I'd brought her home from hospital, and he had a really short fuse, but I never thought he'd do anything like that."

"And you just went along with his plans?" Olivia was really moved by this horrifying tale of everyday life in Littleton-on-Sea.

"What else could I do?"

"And did he tell you what he was going to do with Stacey's body?"

"I never even thought about it. By the time I'd raised the alarm in Jubilee Road, I think I'd even begun to believe the story, because it was easier than believing what had really happened. I just couldn't believe that he'd done something so heartless and cruel as to bury her in Mum's flowerbed."

"And did you believe him when he threatened you with acid?"

"Absolutely. It was only since the end of my pregnancy that I began to see his dark side, and now he's killed my little girl . . ."

Olivia ended the interview and went off to the canteen to grab a strong coffee and get herself mentally prepared for interviewing Baz Bailey, self-proclaimed hard man, bully and baby-killer. She'd get herself together sitting at her desk among the everyday things.

And if she could sweet-talk the higher-ups, maybe she could get Carole off the hook completely. After all, what she'd done she'd done out of fear and under severe duress, which would be taken into consideration. Baz Bailey was the villain here, and not his long-suffering, ill-treated young partner.

CHAPTER
SIXTEEN

At the nearest airport at about the same time, Alice and Brian Gregg were getting off their flight from France and picking up a hire car. Coming back to England like this had been a great inconvenience, but at least it had focussed their thoughts on the unoccupied, or so they'd thought, house in Gooding Avenue. If they just sold it, the capital would be a useful injection to their bank balance. They'd talked about renovating it or dividing it up, and neither seemed to be a useful solution as they would have been time-consuming.

The easiest solution seemed to be to just go back and look over the old place, stay in an hotel, and instruct an estate agent. That way, they'd get the benefit of it without the chance of squatters or vandals. The house may have been used for criminal purposes, but at least nobody had broken in and set fire to it, as happened with so many empty properties, their fate in the hands of the unwanted attention of arsonists.

Once they'd booked into their hotel on the ring road, they drove straight to Gooding Avenue to inspect the condition of Brian's inheritance.

DS Mike Jenner had been kept very busy with cataloguing the scene of the crimes, keeping the incident room board up to date, and making sure that the actions book was used, but it was he who was free to answer the phone when it rang mid-morning, as DCI Buller was taking a call on his mobile.

The control room had just had an hysterical call about number three Gooding Avenue, but the caller had been too upset to make themselves very clear. The only details had been that there was somebody there nailed to a table. Could that possibly be correct?

Alice and Brian Gregg let themselves in at the front door and Brian headed straight for the kitchen to see if there were the makings for a cup of tea. As he entered the room, he stopped dead at what lay before him. There was somebody, apparently slumped at the kitchen table. He made an involuntary cry, and went towards the figure intent on asking what the hell the man thought he was doing in his house, but the man didn't move a muscle.

His instinct was now one of indignation, and he stomped round to the other side of the piece of furniture, tired after his early flight, and not willing to engage in any sort of argument the man felt moved to instigate. Still, the figure didn't move.

As he got to the other side of it he could see large expanses of blood on the table's surface and the floor and, to his utter horror, two large nails sticking out of the backs of the man's hands. "Alice!" he squawked, to attract the attention of his wife, still in the hall looking through doors into the desolately empty rooms.

Alice trudged into the kitchen, heading straight for her husband, then caught sight of the dead man at the table and started to scream.

DS Jenner made frantic hand-signals at Buller to get his attention and, in doing so, caught the attention of Olivia, who was sitting at her desk sipping scalding hot coffee and reflecting on the evils in society and the cheapness of life.

Buller ended his call and faced his sergeant. "What is it now, Jenner?" he barked, in his usual foul mood.

"There's just been a call about a man nailed to a table in 3 Gooding Avenue, guv. I thought you might like to take a look."

"Any other details?"

"The caller was too distressed to say any more. Do you fancy taking a look?"

From behind him a higher-pitched voice answered in the affirmative. "I'd like to. I was in at the beginning of this thing, and I'd like to see what's turned up now."

"DI Hardy, you have other matters to attend to, if I'm not mistaken." Buller wasn't giving in that easily.

"Sod that for a game of soldiers. It's a baby-killer who's already in custody, and I'm quite happy to leave him to stew in his own juices for a while longer. I want him to have plenty of time to contemplate how he's going to be treated in prison, by the other inmates as well as the guards."

"Why should I let you come?"

"Because if you don't I'll piss on your shoes, and I mean that most sincerely. And I'll crap on the bonnet of your car and generally make your life a complete misery — and, believe me, I can."

Buller was suddenly impressed by the sheer balls of the woman, and gave her permission to accompany them.

It took quite a while for Buller and Jenner to get the information about the couple in the house, and Olivia had slipped through the four of them and gone straight into the kitchen, where she sensed the action was about to go on. She was right. There, with six-inch nails through the back of his hands, was their red-haired, freckled man, the table in front of him and the floor at his feet pooled with congealing blood.

The cuts to the wrists weren't obvious to the casual observer but, having seen how much blood there was, she bent down, eager to have a look, as his hands were so near the edge of the table. Two sets of open scarlet lips leered at her, and they had probably, she conjectured, been made with the ubiquitous and readily-available craft knife. Small to carry and easy to obtain, these had been used as weapons for many years.

"Guv," she called, "we've got our red-haired man with the freckles in here. At least now we can get fingerprints, even if we don't have our day in court."

"You sneaky bitch," he retorted, coming into the kitchen. "How dare you get in here ahead of me."

"I was on the case ahead of you, if you remember, so I was just reclaiming my position."

206

"Well, don't let it go to your head, and just you remember who's SIO," was his reply, with the hint of a grin. Maybe she was winning him over at last.

"At least we can find out who he is now, but who the bloody hell did this to him?" he remarked. "It looks like a hit to me. I reckon he'd trodden on some very big toes to have had this done to him."

"You reckon it's gang-related?"

"I do, indeed, Hardy. This whole house reeks of it. If this guy was setting up on his own, he's obviously got on somebody's tits big time. This killing is a message to other aspiring operators — don't infringe on my patch or you're dead. Get back to the station and, when I've got the prints, see what you can find out about him. If we've got nothing on the national record, I'll check with Europol instead. He can't be new to crime; he's just not very far up the food chain and seems to have wanted to branch out on his own."

"Do you think he's responsible for the original two attacks here?"

"Probably," replied Buller, just this minute thinking it over. "Although he'd have needed help, and we've no idea who else might have been involved, although we do have a statement that saw two hooded figures making good their escape over the back fence. I think he's just been dished out his just desserts for infringing on someone else's territory, although that's another story altogether. All we can do is deal with crimes as they happen, and I think we've got our man for the contraband and cannabis farming in this place — or at least one of them." Buller was nothing if not honest.

207

Lauren had been interviewed at home, where she was able to recount what she had been able to get from the children about Gerda trying to put a pillow over their faces and their father dragging Gerda away. She then left the children with Mrs Moth while she was taken to identify Kenneth's and Gerda's bodies. It was one time she was glad she was in the police and not horrified by death, although she was still very disturbed by what Kenneth had done to his young, pregnant lover, despite the fact that it seemed he was defending the children, and the way he had died. She had been given compassionate leave for a few days so that she could deal with the reaction of the children to recent events, and what they themselves had been through.

The sight of the two bodies in the mortuary moved her more than she had thought possible. If only Kenneth had left this girl alone, or even the other way round, they would both still probably be alive. And their unborn child had had no chance. Life could be an absolute bitch sometimes, and she felt unbidden tears form in her eyes. What Kenneth and Gerda had done was unforgivable, but if only he hadn't tried to snatch the children, they could both have gone on living and Kenneth could have had access in the school holidays.

Now she'd have to break the chain of events to the children. At least they weren't used to Kenneth being around very much in recent years. And she had other things on her mind. What was she going to do with her not-relationship with Daz? Should she just cut him loose and get on with her life now she was a widow?

God, how horrible that sounded, but she had no loyalties to anyone except her children. There were plenty of women around that Daz could use for a quick fuck.

On the other hand, did she want him to? It was all too convenient, although she thought there'd be a ruckus when it all came out, unless they were very careful. How uncomplicated life had been in earlier years.

She realised that she had never appreciated the simplicity of her existence when she was at home with the children. She might have said that life was hard and tiring but, compared with what it was now, it had been a breeze, really.

Olivia had Baz Bailey in an interview room and had made it clear that she would accept no bullshit. Lenny Franklin had been grabbed unceremoniously from the office and was now sitting beside her waiting for her to start the recording.

"Before I press the button, Mr Bailey, I want to make it quite clear to you that I have had a full and frank discussion with your partner, and she has brought me up to speed on exactly what happened with poor, defenceless, six-week-old Stacey. If you try to feed me any bullshit I shall come down on you like the proverbial ton of bricks. Do we understand each other?"

"Yes," croaked Baz, his eyes flicking frantically from side to side as if he were looking for some way to escape. *Consequences* was a game he had never liked to play, and the rules in the adult game were so much more difficult to live with.

"Now, if you tell me the truth, it may help in your defence. You are going down for this, and you're not going to have a good time in prison, so the more straight you are with me now, the less time you'll be locked away with all those psychos who don't like baby-killers. Or all those screws who don't take kindly to disposing of an "inconvenience" in the way that you have done. Do I make myself clear to you?"

"Yes," he repeated, sounding as if his throat was as dry as a desert, and looking as if all the moisture he could ever need was now leaking out of his forehead and top lip.

Lenny slid his eyes sideways towards the inspector. He'd never known her sound so menacing. "Shouldn't we wait for his brief?" he asked.

"I'm more than happy to do that," replied Olivia, not removing her gaze from Baz Bailey's perspiring face. "I just hope that Mr Bailey isn't so stupid as to offer a "no comment" interview. That won't go well for him in court.

There was a knock at the door and a slim and expensively besuited man was led in, and sat the other side of the table beside the prisoner, before shooting a grim smile at those opposite him. "Are we ready to start?" he asked.

"We have been for some time, but then we're not as important and busy as you obviously are."

"I say!" he objected, but Olivia ignored him and pressed the button to start the two tapes whirring,

210

giving the appropriate information for this to be used in evidence. "Now, Mr Bailey," she began, "can you tell me exactly what happened on the night that you killed your daughter?"

"You can't say that!"

"Sorry. I wasn't thinking. OK, Mr Bailey, can you tell me what happened on the night before you buried the dead body of your daughter in your partner's mother's garden?"

"You simply can't talk to my client like that."

"Really? Let's start again, then. What happened, Mr Bailey, on the night before your daughter's abduction was faked?"

"It's all right," Bailey interrupted. "I'm going to tell the truth. You can go if you like." He addressed this last to his solicitor. "I ain't going to get away with this, so there's no point in trying to twist things and lie to get me off, because it ain't going to work, see?"

"Mr Bailey, I am here to look after your best interests," his brief interjected.

"And I'm here to get the shortest time inside that I possibly can, by not pissing around the police, OK?" retorted Baz.

"Would you care to share the details of the time indicated to you in my last question?" Olivia pressed on.

"Look, she was screaming. That's all she ever did when I was around, and for most of the night too. I'd got to the point where I just couldn't take the noise any more, and I sort of acted stupidly."

"You didn't think of moving the Moses basket into another room?"

"I didn't think at all: I just wanted the noise to stop. I couldn't sleep: I couldn't even think straight. Carole said how it was all going to be lovely, just the three of us after she was born, but it was like hell on earth."

"So, what did you do, Mr Bailey?"

"I got out of bed, and I picked her up, and then I shook her to stop the noise."

"You shook her the way a dog shakes a toy?"

"I just shook her so that she'd shut up." There was a tension in the room, almost palpable, that none of the other occupants dared to break.

"And what did you do next, Mr Bailey?"

"She stopped yelling, and I put her back in her basket and went back to bed."

"Without checking that she was all right?"

"I didn't think there'd be anything wrong."

"And what happened the next morning?"

"I woke up when Carole started yelling. I didn't know what was wrong."

"But Carole soon told you, didn't she, Mr Bailey?"

"She said Stacey was dead, and I thought, like, it must have been one of them cot deaths."

"You never thought that the shaking you'd given her frail, six-week-old body could have had anything to do with it?"

"Course I didn't."

"So, why then did you suggest to Carole that she should go out to the shop and then pretend that Stacey

212

had been abducted from the car's baby seat while she was out of the vehicle?"

"Why did you do that, Mr Bailey?" asked Lenny.

"Because I knew your lot wouldn't believe someone like me." Bailey looked down at the floor at this statement.

"Only if you told the truth. And Carole went along with this madcap scheme of yours, did she?"

"She didn't know what to do, either."

"So, you killed Stacey and then got Carole to agree to a conspiracy to hide the death?"

"It wasn't like that."

"How was it then, Mr Bailey?"

"Look, I didn't mean to hurt the kid. I just wanted her to shut up for a while and let me get some kip."

"And then you pointedly avoided us from that point onwards, not wanting to face being questioned, and told your partner that if she didn't do exactly what you told her to do, you'd throw acid in her face?"

"It wasn't like that," he whined.

"So, how exactly was it, Mr Bailey?"

"Look, I done it. It was an accident. I didn't mean to kill her. I just wanted to go to sleep in peace. It was like she was torturing me."

"So you killed her?" Baz Bailey started to sob. "Then threatened your partner — your daughter's mother — with violence if she didn't go along with your charade?"

"It wasn't meant to be like this."

"I think my client could do with a break now." Finally the brief spoke again, having been silent throughout the confession. Even he looked faintly disgusted with what he had heard.

Olivia went for a walk outside before she could return to her desk and, inevitably, Lenny beat her to it, so that, when she finally got back to the office, the news that Baz Bailey had coughed to the murder of little Stacey Shillington and that they should have no trouble in getting the CPS to prosecute had gone ahead of her. There was a small round of applause, over which could be heard Buller's normally hectoring tones calling, "Well done, that woman," something that Olivia thought would never normally pass his misogynist lips.

He then called her over and told her that he did now have an identity for their mystery corpse, and pointing out to her that they currently had three unsolved murders. "Four," she corrected him. "You're not including the newborn in that."

Ignoring her, he continued, "And I reckon that the first two are going to be down to our nailed-hand chappie, and some unknown accomplice. I've got an answer on the prints, and he's a Moroccan who came over here on a tourist visa about three years ago from France. He's overstayed his welcome somewhat, but has a record as long as your arm under the name of Muhammed Kharboub. In general, he was referred to as Ali Kebab or Ali Baba, but this is no fairy tale."

"Muhammed?" squeaked Olivia.

"Yep."

"Kharboub?"

"Yep"

214

"Moroccan?"

"Yep!"

"So how come he looked so bloody Celtic? What gene pool do you reckon his mother was dipping her toes into, then? What a red herring those descriptions were."

"But they fooled us, didn't they?"

"And how. Wait till the others hear about this — a red-haired and freckled Moroccan who looks more Irish or Scottish than North African." Olivia gave a wry smile at this enigma that fate had thrown at them, then continued. "Trying to set up on his own, you think?"

"Definitely. We've got an address for him, and I'll send Desai and Leo off to have a look with a warrant. I've already contacted the landlord and got him to agree to meet them there with a key first thing in the morning. We should find all the proof we need to nail him to that address, no pun intended."

"And who do you think did for him?"

"Definitely a gang; no hint of where they might be based. They may be in this county, or they may be from further afield. We'll have to dig a bit deeper for that information, but his death was a clear message to anyone trying to muscle in on this area."

"How did Operation Zee-Tee go?" she asked, casually, as she had been more noticeable by her absence from a lot of the action.

"Take a look at some of the faces round you. It was a rip-roaring success, and we had to use several stations for those detained and waiting for interview. How's your partner?"

Assuming that he meant Lauren, she brought him up to date and informed him that she was taking a few days' compassionate leave. What she didn't notice was Daz Westbrook's ears pricking up at the news, and then immediately applying himself to his mobile phone.

"Looks like we can all get away at a decent hour tonight, then." The DCI really did seem pleased at the prospect.

"Does that mean you'll be leaving this happy little band?" Olivia asked this, trying not to sound sarcastic.

"Not just yet, so, no need to start weeping. I want to get the rest of the forensic evidence from the three people found dead in 3 Gooding Avenue and put a few feelers out first, before I return to my own gang; but don't worry, I can be back here very soon, if needed."

The inspector tried to produce a sincere smile and found it next to impossible. "We shall miss your cheery countenance around the office."

"Don't try to flannel me, but it hasn't been all bad, as far as I'm concerned. I shall remember my time here, but I'm sure Jenner will be glad to get back to his home turf."

When Olivia finally got the chance to apply herself to the paperwork that had built up while she was otherwise engaged, she found that there had been a couple of reports from the officers that had gone up to the tip to see if anyone there knew about the "baby in the bag".

There was a rumour that a party of travellers, who had squatted illegally for a few weeks on some waste ground north of the ring road, were breaking in, in the early hours and scavenging for anything they could sell on. She had a nagging suspicion that they would be able to locate the finder of the little dead body there. Whoever found it didn't want to be identified handing it in, but was obviously moved enough to want it to be declared, and not just crushed or burnt with the waste.

It would be worth paying the settlement a casual visit to see if she could jog anyone's conscience. She could at least acquire some plain-clothed bodies to do this, as Buller looked like he had got his man.

As she mentally selected Daz and Teddy — *an Irishman is always handy when dealing with travellers,* she thought — to do this very early the next morning, there was a roar from Buller. "I don't believe it. Talk about locking the stable door after the horse has bolted."

"What is it, guv?" She thought she was entitled to call him this now that they had reached some sort of understanding.

"That e-fit of our red-headed murderer has just come through. Just a bit late, wouldn't you say? And looking nothing like our DIY enthusiast."

"Are you absolutely sure you've got the right man?"

"You mean, apart from the fact that he was nailed to a table in the house of death?"

"That's the one."

"Just about. There's more intel coming in on him all the time, since we got a name to work with."

"Like what?"

"There's a van registered in his name which has been clocked going back and forth to France on a regular basis. That might explain all the contraband. And he was more than likely killed as a warning to others trying to move in to this patch. That will do for the weed growing.

"But there were two hooded figures seen fleeing from that house over the back fence. I wonder where the hell his partner is, and *who* the bloody hell he is, so we can look for him. We still don't have any identification or even description of this joker."

"Mind your blood pressure, guv. And the murders that started this thing all off?"

"As I said, that could easily be explained away as a warning that didn't work."

"So, you don't think our Moroccan friend did them?"

"You've got me there. I believe he did, but I just can't work out why. If they were caretaking for him, why would he turn on them? Unless they'd been rather loose-lipped about the operation. OK, I know they weren't English, but where you get one or two illegals, there are usually a couple of dozen others. There's something more going on here than we understand or can recognise at the moment, and I want to get to the bottom of it." He thumped the last phrase out, word for word, on the desk's surface to emphasize his frustration at still being in the dark.

"There's something here we don't understand yet?"

"I think there is — in fact, I know there is. We just have to do a bit more digging."

"I don't think he killed them." For a moment Olivia was certain of this.

"Does not compute, Hardy. Of course he did for them. They may have been talking, like I just said, and he couldn't risk being discovered."

"No, there's more to this than meets the eye, guv."

"If you want to believe that, then there are fairies at the bottom of my garden."

"No doubt called Justin and Tristram."

"Don't be facetious to a senior officer, Inspector."

"I'm right," finished Olivia, but she said it in a hushed tone. She was sure there was more to this situation than they had unearthed, but Buller had sounded most convincing in his conjecture that this case was more serious and more complicated than they yet comprehended.

Interlude

She had managed to get clear of the trees and saw the dark shapes of the glass buildings in the darkness ahead. If she could only get in there, she could hide, and emerge when people turned up the next day. Then she could find out what had happened to her baby. They had taken it away so quickly that she hadn't had a chance to hold the little form, let alone look at the face. She didn't even know whether it was a boy or a girl.

When she was three-quarters of the way across the open stretch, she heard the sound of pursuit and tried to quicken her pace, but she was already rushing flat-out over the grass. As hostile shouts came from her pursuers, she caught her foot in a hole in the turf and went flying, finding despair washing over her. What would happen now?

She'd broken the most important rule and come in pregnant. The loose smocks, or overalls or whatever they called them, that they wore for work had allowed her to conceal it until almost the last moment, but they had made her pay for her deception by stealing her child and had done heaven knew what with it. She must find her baby, or tell someone what had happened, so that they could help her look for it.

Would they send her back to where she had come from, now? She really didn't think she could go on with her current existence, and she couldn't face going back. What was to become of her if she couldn't be a mother?

As she tried to get up, unseen hands grabbed at her clothing and brought her down again. Another body landed on hers, and all the air went out of her lungs. Gasping now, to get fresh breath, she squealed as the punching and kicking started: first her legs, then her arms, and panic consumed her. She knew that if she were to survive, they wouldn't want to leave marks, so this was more than a final warning.

Without conscious thought, she identified the boots as steel-capped and, as if detached from her physical being, was aware of bones cracking and snapping from the kicks. Then they moved on to her back and kidneys. Ribs gave way as one of them jumped on her body.

She had heard of beatings like this before, and the recipients didn't live happily ever after — they just didn't live.

Her hair was torn from her head as they moved further up, and she screamed as loud as she could, but no one would hear her out here. She should never have come here.

A kick that connected with an ear left her head ringing, and then one hit her in the temple and, slowly, the light and sound faded until there was nothing. The dark forms around her, excited by their bloodlust, melted away into the surrounding darkness, heading back whence they had come for a good dose of alcohol. Her body would be found, once it had been tidied away, but she had nothing on her to identify her.

As far as the world was concerned, she didn't exist, and in today's society, in this country, it would be assumed that she had been beaten up by a boyfriend and left for dead. That's the way the English people thought of foreigners — half-savage, and with no control.

And this is what these girls wanted to come to? This kind of life? They were protecting them, really, and saving them from a decadent society that was slowly disintegrating. And she had been only a woman. What worth was a woman, unless she earned you money? Sons, you could get from respectable wives. Daughters had no value, except for breeding from, to carry on the family line.

CHAPTER
SEVENTEEN

Olivia arrived home to find that her children were both in, but were sitting looking stunned. "What's wrong?" she asked.

"It's Dad," said Ben.

"He looked like the end of the world had arrived when we got back, then he just got up and said he was going to the church to pray," added Hibbie. "Whatever's wrong with him?"

"Did he say anything about having bad news from his folks?" asked Olivia, her first thought being that something had happened to Ben's parents far away in the Caribbean.

"No, but he did say he needed to talk to you, as he left," supplied Ben.

Olivia was rattled. Hal hadn't been himself for a while now, and she worried that perhaps going back to teaching, whatever he said about it, had worn him down. Kids at school behaved worse and worse as time went on, and he'd had quite a long break from it. This is what she chose to think, because anything else would be completely insupportable, and maybe, unbearable.

Grabbing a bottle of wine and a corkscrew, she sat at the kitchen table. Drinking wouldn't make this go away, but it would sure take the edge off it. The kids sensibly went to their rooms, and Olivia sat and brooded. The kids would have to get themselves something to eat tonight if they wanted it. She had felt a distance grow between her and Hal since he had gone back to work, and his supply teaching had turned into full-time.

He had always been a set of shoulders to cry on when needs be, and to listen to her blow off steam about her colleagues and the stupidity of the system, when she felt moved to. Now, he just didn't seem to be there, and was often physically missing from their home. What had happened to their relationship?

When the bottle was nearly empty and the clock showed nine thirty, the front door opened timidly, and Hal shuffled in looking utterly bereft. Olivia rose from her chair and ran over to him, flinging her arms around him and burying her head in his shoulder. "Whatever's the matter? What's happened?" Without giving him time to answer she continued, "It doesn't matter what it is, we can get through it together. We're a team; a good, strong one."

"No, we can't get through this," Hal almost whispered, his breath tickling her ear.

"Tell me, Hal. Whatever it is, I can help."

"No, you can't," he sighed.

"There's nothing bad enough for us not to find a way out of it or round it. Tell me, Hal, before I go mad. I've known there was something wrong for some time."

"This is so bad I don't think you will ever be able to look at me again."

"Come on Hal, baby, what's eating you? How can we fight it if you don't even tell me what it is?"

Hal pulled away from her and stood a foot or so away, his face a blank, his body language full of guilt. "Olivia," he finally said quietly, "I have sinned. I have betrayed you."

"How?" Whatever was Hal talking about?

"I have confessed to the pastor and talked it over with him, and he said that the only thing I could do was to confess to you and pray that you could find it in your heart to forgive me."

All of a sudden, Olivia felt a chill run down her spine and felt goose bumps break out all over her body. "Tell me, Hal," she barked, her voice harsh with foreboding. Surely he wasn't going to say what she thought she knew was coming? Her muscles clenched, ready for denial or flight.

"Liv, I've been unfaithful to you." Almost as a reflex reaction, her right hand shot out and gave him a resounding slap across the face. There. It was said. It was all out in the open, and Olivia had neither the breath to scream in denial or the strength to run away. Her whole body began to shake, and she collapsed slowly on to the sofa like a deflating concertina with all the air squeezed out of it, neither crying nor apologising for hitting him; something that had never happened before.

Hal immediately threw himself down next to her and put his arms round her. "I'm so sorry, my darlin' little flower. I've been so stupid. Please say you'll hear me out and at least consider forgiving me."

Olivia's body suddenly stiffened in his embrace and she grated, "Get out! Get out of my home. I don't want to set eyes on you, you filthy cheat."

"Liv, give me a chance to explain."

"I don't want to hear the details of your dirty little secret. Get out now. Go to her if you want, but get out of my sight."

Hal moved slightly away, tears pouring down his cheeks. "But I don't want to go to her. It was a stupid mistake. It's you I love, and I don't know how I could have been so mad."

"You're like all men — easy enough to reel in, if hooked by the dick."

"Liv, give me a chance to explain."

"No way, José. I want you out of here."

"Liv, don't let the price for this one silly mistake be my family. I'll sleep on the sofa; I'll do anything you want, if you'll just give me another chance."

Olivia was sobbing now. "How could you, Hal, after all the years we've been together? And with work in such a difficult phase?" She said the last phrase without thinking, and Hal immediately became like stone.

"And that's just it, isn't it? For the last I don't know how long, you've got back from work and taken it for granted that I will have cooked a meal for the family, and then just rambled on and on about what a hard day you've had; about how difficult and all-consuming the job is, and how put-upon you are. You never ask me how my day has been. You never asked how band practice had gone or how a gig went. You never asked me if I'd done anything that I'd like to discuss with you — it was always you, you, you; take, take, take."

"Hal!" She almost screamed his name in her shock and surprise at his reply.

"It's true. And then you have that sergeant to stay when she's having a bad time with her marriage and you just take it for granted that I'm all right with it, and ninety-nine times out of a hundred, I am all right with anything, but sometimes — just sometimes — I would like you to consider me first, instead of slightly below Hibbie's cat.

"Did you not feel that something was going wrong when Ben had his crisis and Hibbie ran away? Did it not cross your mind that you might've had your eye off the family ball, and if you didn't dribble it back into play soon, it would go over the sideline and be lost? Well, I've been sidelined, and the kids, too. Olivia, you've become a stranger to us all, not the loving wife and mother that you used to be and, as far as I'm concerned, it's that bloody job that you seem to care about most."

After this impassioned speech there was an eerie silence as Olivia began to absorb what Hal had said, and had to acknowledge that there was a grain of truth in it. She *had* taken it for granted that Hal would always cope when she was elsewhere on a case: she *did* take for granted the fact that the kids weren't disobedient or rebellious. And she hadn't learnt her lesson the year before when they'd had their own family troubles: and even that didn't alert her to the fact that she just expected Hal always to be there as a human backstop and all-round rock.

They stood looking at each other in desolate silence, their faces wet with tears, as they contemplated what was at risk here; what they had nearly lost. And what they might still lose. That both were at fault, there was no question. How to put it right was more complex.

Finally, in a hushed tone, Hal said, "We'll talk? And I'll give up this stupid supply work? It's simply not worth it if it's going to drive a wedge between us."

"Yes," replied Olivia, simply, and they fell into each other's arms, the way a child would with a parent; simply for comfort.

Interlude

Three o'clock on a weekday morning, and not a soul around except for the odd drunk sitting on a bench sleeping off his skinful.

The rusty old van drew up and the engine was killed as the two live occupants sat listening to the comparative silence of the wee small hours. There were also two bodies in the back of the van as well, but these were no longer of this world.

"Did you give her a good working over with that hammer?"

"Face, and hands. Even her own mother wouldn't recognise her now."

"I done what I was asked wiv the bloke."

"Shall we get on wiv this fancy art installation, then?" asked the big man, smiling to reveal a row of broken and uneven nicotine-stained teeth.

"Look, I'm Tracey Emin, me," replied the other — the one with only half an ear on the right side of his head. "If we just act like we've got a couple of pissed mates, no one's gonna take any notice of what we're up to — just anuvver coupla drunks helpin" their friends into a van."

A slight, but brilliantly acted, uncertainty of step giving veracity to their inebriated condition to anyone who saw them, they opened the back doors of the van and took out the body of the man, which they then inserted into the cab from the passenger side, but head first, so that his top half was against the driver's door and would flop out when this was next opened.

Almost with reverence, the one with the disfigured ear took some items out of a pocket, neatly wrapped in an old-fashioned handkerchief, and laid them, like a sacrificial offering, on the man's chest.

As he laid them down, he recited, "Nose first. Then ears, two. And lastly, tongue."

"That's real artistic, that is," commented Broken-Teeth, almost in awe.

"Not bad, is it? 'Er, now?"

"'Er, now. My turn to show off," leered Broken-Teeth, moving back to the rear of the van, as his partner in crime shut the passenger door on their grisly, unofficial Turner Prize offering.

The woman's body had been thrown about a bit by the drive here, but nothing would show after what Broken-Teeth had done to her already badly beaten body. "'Elp me pull 'er rahnd so that 'er 'ead's right up to the doors. It'll 'ave more impact — artistically, like. That's it, now 'er 'ands folded decoratively under 'er chin, like she's been laid out proper.

"Jaysus, 'er face's just a mush, and 'er 'ands look like they've been through some sort of industrial mangle. It looks like you 'ad fun."

"Oh, I did, me old mate; I did, that. And you ain't the only bastard who can sign his work artistically." Broken-Teeth put a hand into his old donkey jacket pocket and pulled out a slightly wilted summer flower. "Seems sorta fitting, like, don't yer fink?"

"Yer no bleedin' Damien Hirst, but it's a nice gesture."

"Right, let's get the door shut on this stiff and then scarper."

CHAPTER
EIGHTEEN

The inspector arrived in the office very early the next morning, having found it very difficult to settle in the cottage after the events of the evening before and, simply because she was cognisant of the fact that she was partly to blame for this latest family calamity, had an awful lot of built-up spleen that she needed to vent on somebody.

She had decided that she would visit the travellers' camp, and may God have mercy on their souls if they weren't co-operative and forthcoming with the information she was after. She had only had time to put the kybosh on Westbrook and O'Brian's visit and skim through the reports she had read the day before, when the door opened and she turned, absolutely flabbergasted to see Lauren approaching her desk.

The sergeant gave a wan smile and said, "I couldn't stand it at home with all that silence during the day, so I got the kids off early to school and decided to come in here just to keep my mind off dwelling on everything that's been happening." If she'd been really honest, she would have confessed that she also wanted to see Daz again in the flesh, even if it was dressed.

Olivia smiled at her and said, "Don't get settled. I'm just on my way to put the wind up a bunch of travellers about that newborn's body dumped in the car park, so you can come with me for added support, if you like. All contributions welcome."

"Wilco, boss." Lauren smiled back, any animosity that had existed between them now dissipated by greater events. "Why are we going so early?"

"To catch them unawares, of course." As far as Olivia was concerned, what the situation lacked without an Irishman, was more than made up for by the presence of a very tetchy woman with a companion who would agree with anything she said if given the nod.

"Are you sure you're up for this?" asked Olivia, as they drove out to the encampment.

"I woke up this morning feeling very positive about the future," replied Lauren, her face serious. "As far as my late husband's concerned, I think what has happened has saved me from a very acrimonious divorce and custody battle, and for that, I'm grateful. I also don't have to go through the unpleasantness of fighting for a decent maintenance payment, I'm still, officially, at least, Kenneth's wife, so all the insurance money will secure me, and my children's, future. It all seems rather too good to be true, if you get my drift."

"I believe I do," came a rather wobbly reply, and Lauren turned to see that Olivia's eyes were awash with unshed tears, her bottom lip, trembling.

"Are you sure *you* are? What's up, boss?"

"Nothing I can possibly share at the moment. Leave it for now. I've got a lot of thinking to do, but I'm glad to hear that you're feeling so positive."

The spokesperson elected by the travellers, after a bit of to-ing and fro-ing, turned out to be a Mr O'Reilly, and for a split second, Olivia doubted her decision to take over this task instead of handing it to Teddy O'Brien and Westbrook, but she put on her fiercest expression and set forth on extracting as much information, and maybe even truth, as possible.

"We're here for any info you may have concerning the body of a newborn baby dumped in the car park at the police station. We know it was newborn because there was still the presence of vernix on it. We also know it wasn't a Caucasian baby, but we need to know who left it there for us to find and we need to establish whether we're looking at a stillbirth or a murder. I favour the latter, as its neck was broken.

"A car was caught on CCTV in the station car park and we're following up on that sighting. Now, what have you got to say for your community?"

"Sure and we know nothing about any babby, madam," stated Mr O'Reilly with a disarming and toothless smile.

"Well, we have information that you *do* know something about it. We know it was found on the tip, and that your community has been scavenging there before first light, to see if there's anything to be picked up that will make you a bob or two. Did you know that you needed a council licence to take items from the tip?"

"Now, I don't see as how you can have any proof of anything of the sort," he replied with another gummy leer.

Olivia quickly crossed her fingers behind her back and asked, "Did you know about the new security cameras that have been installed there? They catch evidence of any illegal removal of property that, by law, belongs to the local authority. And would you like me to identify those persons and prosecute for having no licence?"

She knew she was talking bullshit, but if they were only there just before dawn, they would not have had sufficient light to see if anything was filming them from the ramshackle building that served as an administration hut at the tip.

Lauren suddenly took centre stage, removing the pressure from Olivia and asked, "If we're willing to overlook the CCTV footage, would you be willing to make a statement about what you know of this tiny murder victim — assuming it wasn't one of you who committed the dreadful deed. I'd hate to have to take you all in for questioning on either of these matters."

There was a muttering of resentment and the travellers who had been standing in a close-knit group suddenly went into a huddle, excluding the two women from their discussion. Mr O'Reilly then came to the front of the group again and said, "Firstly, that babby wasn't one of ours — I want to get that clear from the very beginning. And we've decided that you couldn't have got anything from the car park, because we made sure to obscure the numberplate, but if you'd be willing to overlook the footage shot at the tip we'd co-operate.

"Sure you must've known that we wanted justice for the little one by the very fact that we brought it to the station in the first place. We just didn't want to get mixed up with the police."

Olivia made a show of consulting with Lauren, muttering nonsense under her breath, and Lauren got the gist of what was going on and nodded her head in pantomime agreement.

"My sergeant and I have come to a decision," announced Olivia, leaving a gap just long enough to put the travellers on edge, before concluding, "and we've decided to ignore any footage that shows you actually at the tip." How lucky that they hadn't had the wit to work out that no cameras except infra-red would have been able to pick up anything before sunup. "Provided you tell us who found the baby's body and what you know about it being there, we'll forget all about your unlicensed scavenging and leave you with a warning to desist from this activity forthwith, or we will be forced to take sterner measures."

As Mr O'Reilly drew himself up to his full height and puffed out his chest, Olivia let out her breath and uncrossed her fingers. This was the best chance they had of discovering anything about the black bag and its horrific contents before it reached the station car park. Lauren got out a notebook and stood there, pencil at the ready as the leader prepared to speak.

236

"The bag was found by one of the passers-through, and he lost his breakfast when he opened it to see what treasure was inside such a good quality bag."

"Is he here to speak for himself?" interrupted Olivia, only to be given a scornful look.

"Did you not listen to a word I said, woman? I said he was a passer-through, and once we'd delivered his unfortunate find to the station car park, he passed through, on to somewhere else."

"So, what happened when he found it?"

"Well, he knows I'm the leader, so he sought me out and showed me what he'd come across. It was me decided that it should go to you coppers. No one should get away with killing a little one, and if it hadn't survived birth, then there should have been a doctor to take care of it, respectful-like."

"So, no one on this encampment knows anything about how it got here?" asked Olivia as Lauren scribbled furiously.

"That's right, missus, but we've got our suspicions, even though we haven't followed them up. We don't poke our noses in where they're not wanted in case we get a clobbering. We keep ourselves to ourselves."

"Can you tell me about your suspicions?" At least they seemed to be getting somewhere.

"It were Big Tam that saw them first; dim lights in them woods over yonder. There were several of them, and sometimes they'd be visible when we went off just before first light. Always in the same place. Don't know of any actual dwellings over there, but there might be people that we don't know about.

"And sometimes, when I've been out in the woods with Scruffy here" — he indicated a ragged lurcher that had collapsed at his feet with a contented sigh — "I've thought I've heard voices, but I can't make head or tail of what they're talking about. Reckon they must be foreigners. We've just kept our noses out because we believe in live and let live."

"Mr O'Reilly, I appreciate your honesty with us, and we'll look into the matter, but I feel honour-bound to warn you that, as we speak, the Council is probably seeking to obtain an eviction order against your vehicles. Just a word to the wise."

"Fair dos. We'd more or less decided to move on in a day or so. We think that tip's cursed, and we don't want anything more to do with it. There are richer pickings elsewhere, anyway, I reckon. That place was a lost cause."

"I don't suppose there's any point in asking you to come in and make a statement backing up what you've just told me, sir?"

"None whatsoever, my duck. I've said my piece, and that's the end of it."

"Thank you for the information about the lights. I'll get somebody to look into it."

"And now, we'll get on with the business of deciding where to go next." Mr O'Reilly tipped his cap at the two detectives and walked away towards a beaten-up old caravan.

"Come on, Sergeant, let's get back to the office and see if we can unearth a large-scale Ordnance Survey map of the area to check if there are any suspect buildings hiding in those woods that could do with investigating. After we've checked with the up-to-date one on the office wall, first, that is. Maybe there's something there that we've all missed so far."

Out and about at a similarly early hour that morning were DCs Oh and Desai, who had made an arrangement to meet the landlord of Kharboub's seafront flat to inspect its contents. Consequently, a small man with a wispy beard and a bald head was standing on the steps up to the ground floor entrance when they arrived.

He greeted them, announced that he had to be somewhere else for an inspection, shoved a keyring into Desai's hand and beetled off about his other business. "Just leave the key in the flat when you've finished," he called over his shoulder.

"Couldn't be better," said Oh, with satisfaction. "Now we can go through things at our own pace without a landlord looking over our shoulders asking us what we're looking for and what we've already come across."

"Let's get on with it then. It's flat G2, which I assume is the basement jobbie — what some people have the brass neck to refer to as a 'garden flat' when usually it's so dark that it's fit only for a holiday burrow for stray Wombles."

"Don't judge before you've seen," Leo admonished him, and they went down a flight of stairs through an open doorway right next to the party wall. There were, indeed, two flats down there, and G2 did prove to be at the back. As Desai looked out of a window that gave a view from eye-level out to the rear of the premises, he commented that there was a pathway through the small garden. By standing on a wooden chair he was able to discern that there was a rear wall to the property, in which was placed a convenient gate.

"I'll just nip out there and see where that gate leads," volunteered Leo, already heading to the rear exit and out on to a small cemented area which had a few steps to bring it up to garden level. He jogged back a couple of minutes later to report that it led directly on to an alleyway which ran between the small rear areas of the Georgian terrace and a row of nineteen thirties houses just behind.

"What a great way of leaving the flat with no one noticing that you've left the building," was Desai's reply. "He could come and go as he pleased and none of the other tenants would have been any the wiser. He could be as secret as a rat in his hole, with no one noticing his comings and goings."

"Clever choice of accommodation. Now, let's see if we can turn up anything that could be used as evidence."

Leo was already engaged in breaking the lock on a desk drawer, and when he finally managed to slide it opened, whistled under his breath. "Look at this," he called, holding up two or three small notebooks. Inside were pages and pages of what looked just like a series of very small but neat squiggles, which they immediately identified as Kharboub's native tongue. "We'll have to get an interpreter in on these."

"Are you any good at French?" asked Desai, from in front of a small filing cabinet. "There are a lot of what look like receipts and correspondence in here, but they're all in French, and I can barely say *merci* and *s'il vous plait*."

"Make that two interpreters," batted back Leo, "or a French Moroccan who can cope with both. We'll have to get this little lot back to the office in individual plastic folders, get it translated, then moved on to Forensics for fingerprints."

Their padded envelopes were just about stuffed full when Leo noticed a small oak single-drawer filing cupboard resting on the floor under a table. "What have we here?" he asked, lifting it up and putting it on the table under which he had espied it. "Have you got something I can force the lock with? I thought I saw you with a knife."

"Here," said Desai, handing over a normal dinner knife. "I got it from a drawer in the kitchenette when you were outside recceing the garden."

There was a splintering sound and the drawer opened to reveal, not a card index system, but bundles and bundles of currency, both sterling and euros. "Whew! Well, will you just look at that? There must be several thousand pounds here at first glance. And what's this?" he asked, as he caught sight of a piece of paper sticking out from under the notes.

He carefully slid it out with one gloved hand and opened the piece of paper, which proved to be A4-sized. "Somebody didn't like to get rid of anything that might prove useful in the future." It was a letter on headed paper for Littleton Salad Nurseries, confirming the receipt of four "parcels" and noting that all monies were paid to date. The typed name under the signature was one Abdul Amir, Manager.

"I don't know what this means exactly, but it looks mighty interesting," commented Leo, slipping it into an evidence bag while Desai bundled the money into yet another padded envelope and sealed it. "Right, one more look around, and then we'll get out of here."

"Hang on a minute," Desai said as he had a last rummage through the paperwork on the desk. "I've just come across the papers for a vehicle. It's listed as a white Luton van. Wasn't there one parked outside? All we need now are the keys."

"Here!" called Leo in triumph, as he pulled them out of the pocket of a jacket hanging on a hook on the back of the door from the communal hall. "I think we're cooking with gas now. Let's put all this stuff in our car and then give the van a going over. You never know what could be in that."

It was Desai who opened the driver's door when they had finished stuffing the boot with paperwork liberated from the flat and as he swung it back, he backed away in disgust. "Bloody hell!" he yelled, then turned away and retched.

"What is it, Ali?" asked Leo, approaching and taking his colleague's place at the open door. "Shit!" he said, putting a hand over his mouth. "We'd better call this one in. But I think we ought to just check the back of the van first, to make sure we've found everything there is to find. I'll do it," he volunteered, as Desai was looking very pasty, and then wished that he had not been so hasty.

As the large rear doors of the rusty van swung open, the light revealed the body of what had probably once been a woman, but now beaten beyond recognition, particularly the face and hands, and she looked like she'd been laid out as if for a funeral. There was even a lone flower on her body. "And we've got one in here, also," he said in a strange, high voice that was nothing like his usual conversational tones. "Can you call this one in, too?" he asked, still sounding unlike himself, as he lowered his body on to one of the steps of the small flight leading up to the communal front door of the building, joining his partner.

"Let me see," said Desai in curiosity, perking up a bit at the thought of another discovery, but still a bit nervy.

"You might regret it." Leo advised him, still feeling dizzy with the sight that had assaulted his eyes when he had looked into the back of that Luton.

When Olivia and Lauren got back to the office, Buller was on his phone, but strangely silent, his mouth hanging open and his eyes as round as saucers. As he ended the call, instead of asking how his two colleagues had got on, he merely bellowed at them. "Get a Forensics team down to Ali Baba's place on the seafront. I've got to go."

"Go where?" asked Olivia.

"There've been two more bodies found. Desai just called it in. Oh, and get me interpreters in both French and Moroccan. I think we've made a huge breakthrough."

"Hang on a minute, boss. If there are two more bodies, they won't be any more dead if you take a minute or two now just to keep us up to date."

"Kharboub's flat, absolutely stuffed with what look like records of his activities in Arabic and French, and in his van — which, if you remember, I said had a marker on it from HMRC — two more stiffs. Some guy stretched out across the two front seats with his nose and ears missing, and his tongue cut out, all of the bits laid out on his chest like obscene decorations on a human cake, and the body of a woman in the back, battered beyond recognition, and got a fucking flower on top of her as if for more decoration. I don't know who we're dealing with, but they're definitely big boys."

"Bugger!" exclaimed Olivia.

"Gosh!" ejaculated Lauren, clearly showing the difference in their backgrounds.

"I've got to get down there to see what's going on." Buller was almost out of the door in his anxiety to get to the scene.

"Aren't you going to ask how we two delicate ladies are getting on with our enquires concerning the dead babies?" asked Olivia sarcastically.

Buller was so caught off guard that he instinctively said, "How?" before he'd had time to think that now he'd need to wait for an answer.

"We've got a confession of murder on the six-week-old, and we've just picked up what my instincts tell me is a good lead in the newborn case," he was informed triumphantly.

244

"Good," was his curt reply, before he flew off as if pursued by hellhounds.

"Charming!" said Olivia, before asking Lenny if he could go off in search of an Ordnance Survey in large scale of the town and its immediate environs. Lenny knew that the only person who could lay his hands on such an article was Monty Fairbanks, and it didn't take him long to come back, like an obedient dog, with what he had been requested to supply, finding both of the officers inspecting the up-to-date map pinned to the wall.

"There you go, ladies," he said, putting it down on Olivia's desk? "That should keep you two happy, although I can't think why you need it with that newbie up there for all to see."

"It's a secret, Lenny," said Olivia, before Lauren could get her mouth open, "but it's one that we'll share with you if we find what we're looking for."

"Very mysterious," was DC Franklin's comment as Olivia began to open out the map, and then fold it to show just the area they wanted to examine.

"Goodness, this is old," exclaimed Lauren. "Look at all that open land at the north of the town. What's the date on this map?"

"1969," Olivia informed her, flipping over a corner to check. "Look at this, there's a chicken farm just beyond the cemetery."

When this map had been printed, Olivia had only been a toddler, but the lack of housing certainly took her mind back to what the town had been like when she was little, and one of the things that it wasn't, was big.

On mature reflection, she realised that there had been very little housing erected during the sixties; her first memories were of a relatively small town. Then the seventies had arrived, and with them, the brand new police station, a partial but substantial rebuilding of the secondary school, as comprehensive education took over, and a much larger number of residential developments.

In the eighties and nineties, the buildings had spread out like a rapidly spreading cancer, but the planners lacked the foresight to provide sufficient facilities to support such large tracts of cheaply built housing, and all previous problems had simply been magnified under these conditions.

There had been a recession, and a lot of the wrong people had relocated to the area due to the price of the housing and the promise of building jobs to go with these new homes being thrown up, in the creation of the next phase or estate, only to find that their jobs were lost due to the next financial crisis. Schools were selling their playing fields and public open spaces were disappearing.

Olivia mused that waste land was no longer waste land, but had become a "valuable development opportunity" but even this had withered and died, making petty crime the order of the day, along with the worship of the benefits payment and the swindling of "the sick". I'm on "the sick" or "the disability" was a constant claim of people with whom the uniformed officers came into contact. It was the ultimate defence of the work-shy and shady, she thought.

She remembered the road of naval officers' detached houses that had ended in a wooden five-barred gate at the edge of a huge field, giving views over to the next village, Rusterton, and, to the north, across what had now become part of the ring road for the town, as it had been. The reason the place had probably stayed so small at that time was because the only way into it from the west and out of it to the east was a venerable but small, metal swing-bridge over the mouth of the river, and driving through from either end had been a nightmare of waiting and frustration in the world of an ever-increasing pace of life.

Ever since a road had been constructed to allow free access at all times, the carbuncles and sores of sprawling "affordable" housing had crept in, the town now the reserve of the cowboy developer with his chipboard and low-quality materials. This was not a town for executive housing: this was now just "Anytown".

"And there's a dense ring of nurseries and other agricultural buildings." Lauren's wonder at how much Littleton had changed in such a few decades finally released Olivia from her reverie, and she fought her attention back to the subject at hand.

"What we need to look at is these remaining woods just beyond the growing businesses. If we can locate where we think the travellers were parked, we should be able to make out the piece of woodland that hasn't yet been cut down."

"Look at this," crowed Lauren, pointing at an indication of a building just within the confines of the map and, all those years ago, buried deep in the woods. "Get me a magnifying glass. I can't quite read what it says it is."

"We should have old Mrs Belcher here for little jobs like this. Let me have a look. I'll put on my reading glasses."

"Reading glasses? I didn't know you needed them."

Olivia blushed, having kept this a secret for a few months now, and tried never to wear them when there was anyone else around — but her secret was out now, and she'd just have to live with it . . . as long as her other and more shaming secret didn't reach the light of day.

Leaning over the map, she managed to make out the tiny lettering beside the marked building. "It's an old Nissen hut!" she exclaimed. "That would certainly explain where those lights could have been coming from. It needs a recce to check out if we're on to something. Lauren, I want you and Daz to go out there and make like you're just a couple having a stroll in the woods together on a nice, sunny day."

She didn't see the eyes of both of the named officers light up, and carried on looking over the old map, continuing to feel amazed that things had changed so much, as she folded it over to look further south towards the sea.

They took Westbrook's car, and when they were on their way, he asked her tentatively, "How are you feeling?" conscious that she'd had a bad time recently, and unsure whether to twinkle his eyes at her or not. She soon answered his question in no uncertain terms.

"How am I feeling? Horny, DC Westbrook, seeing as you were kind enough to ask."

A smile slowly spread across his face and he turned to look at her. "I believe we have some unfinished business, DS Groves."

"Do we?" asked Lauren, with a leer. "From when?"

"From the moment we were paired together for this particular task. I have a blanket in the boot, and I believe there are some very private spots in those woods."

"Then we'd better do our best to find one after we've done what we've been dispatched to do, don't you think?"

"Yes, ma'am, I do."

"You don't have to call me 'ma'am'."

"I know — but I like it."

"So do I," was her reply, with the most lecherous look she could manage.

"I think we'll have to walk from here," Daz said with a change of subject. "It looks like we've just run out of road, and I wouldn't trust my car on that rutty old track."

CHAPTER
NINETEEN

There were various signs about the straggling entrance to the woodland, reading, "Keep Out", "Private Woodland" and "Trespassers will be prosecuted".

"Some welcome," said Lauren.

"I'm sure they can't be aimed at us. We're the police," stated Westbrook simply and with great faith.

"Are you wearing a Kevlar vest?" asked Lauren.

"No. Why?"

"Well, don't come running to me if someone pulls a shotgun on you."

"Don't be silly. This is the south of England, not the Appalachians."

"Suit yourself. And mind where you're putting your feet. This woodland is a minefield of tripping hazards."

"Good old Sergeant Groves, ever Health and Safety conscious."

After about twenty minutes of stumbling over tree roots and avoiding stray bramble branches, they came across a sort of rough pathway through the undergrowth. Checking with the tiny compass that Lauren always carried in her handbag, it seemed to run from north-east to south-west, and it seemed to be that instinct was telling them both to follow it to the north-east. Had they gone in the other direction Lauren reckoned that they would end up, eventually, hitting the last of the nurseries, then the ring-road.

Westbrook agreed with her, and they set off, keeping as quiet as they could now, in case there was someone ahead of them who may not wish them well. After a few minutes, the trees got closer together, and the undergrowth more dense and lush, and they had to walk one behind the other, the lead taken by Westbrook in a misplaced sense of chivalry.

The way was, however, well-trodden, and no remaining obstacles were encountered on the forest floor. After quite a trudge, a more solid shape loomed up out of the almost subterranean gloom. "I think we've found whatever it is we're looking for," whispered Lauren.

"What is it?" asked the more youthful Westbrook, who was a man who neither watched historical documentaries nor read books chronicling the past.

"Well, it looks to me like an old Nissen hut left over from the war," she informed him, not wanting to let on that she'd known exactly what they'd find. "The fact that it's covered in ivy gives it almost perfect camouflage, although there has been some trimming round the windows, which must be how the light got out for the travellers to witness."

"Sure," commented Westbrook, with not a clue as to what she was talking about. His mind was on later. "So, why would they trim round the windows?" he hissed.

"To save on fuel costs during daylight hours? How the hell should I know? Let's just be grateful that we have a way of looking inside." Lauren's more practical attitude won the day, and they crept forward to peer through the surprisingly clear glass panes.

"No curtains," stated Westbrook.

"No peeping Toms out here — but just look at the beds! They're triple bunks. It's more crowded in there than in a cheap boarding school dorm."

"I wouldn't know about that."

"Stop pulling that working class whine on me and let's see if we can get inside," instructed Lauren with unexpected authority. "Would someone lock the door to a place like this? It's on private land and hardly frequented, and it must be a bore if one of the occupants wants to come back for something; always having to have the key to hand."

"Oh, I do love a bossy woman. Come on, then, Sherlock. Let's see if we can get in. What do you think it's used for?"

"I don't know, but all the beds seem to be in use."

The handle of the door turned easily and without squeaking, confirming that it was used fairly frequently and, fortunately, there was no one at home, so they prowled round apprehensively for a couple of minutes, both taking photographs with their mobile phones.

There was an overwhelming smell of humanity — of scantily washed bodies, of greasy hair, and of old clothes and shoes. There were no personal possessions at all on show, and it was impossible to guess at which sex currently occupied this hut. "Come on Watson, let's make ourselves scarce," hissed Lauren, grabbing

252

Westbrook's hand. "I get the feeling we're chancing our arm a bit too much now."

Once more outside and concealed by a screen of ferns and bushes, Lauren whispered in Westbrook's ear, "Do you think we should follow the path the other way, now, and see where it leads?"

Swatting her away, and hissing, "Don't do that, it tickles," he agreed with her, and they set off, once again, down the well-trodden route to wherever.

"I don't really fancy you getting that blanket out now, Daz," said Lauren in an undertone. "This piece of woodland seems to have rather a lot of people using it, from what we've seen."

"I agree. My place after work, then." The evidence of the occupancy of the old hut and the dank and forbidding atmosphere of the woodland had totally dampened their ardour for more physical activities. Nirvana would just have to wait.

The path continued in a more or less straight line, with the exception of skirting particularly large trees and recalcitrant and dense bramble bushes, until it made a sudden dog-leg to the right. A short way down this change of direction, the undergrowth and trees began to thin, and they found themselves looking out over a width of clear ground with glass houses at the other side of it. There seemed to be quite a number of these, leading to the unequivocal conclusion that they were looking at one of the town's last nurseries.

"What do you think?" asked Westbrook in quiet tones.

"I think that must be a salad nursery and that it would employ quite a few pickers in season."

"And where would they get those pickers, Sergeant?"

"Maybe from an old Nissen hut. I think we need to get a call through to Immigration and see if they've got any information about this place. Put the hut together with the nursery, and you have the ideal situation for illegal immigrants being employed."

"Don't you think someone would have thought to investigate that old hut?"

"It's not even marked on the current map on the office wall. That's why Olivia asked me to go and get an old one. It's just disappeared into the mists of time.

"Well, someone's taken some time to preserve it and put it into fair nick without disturbing the covering of ivy too much. To eyes that weren't actively looking for it, it simply isn't there any more."

"Let's go consult with the inspector, and see if she wants to go any higher up."

When they got back to the station, their eyes were alight not with afternoon delight, but with speculation as to what their discovery had meant, and whether there was a link to any of the other current cases.

"Alle-bloody-luiah," sang Olivia when they had passed on the details of what they had discovered. "Buller'll have an orgasm when you tell him. This'll make his day, if not his year.

"Why so?" asked Lauren.

"Because of what Desai and Leo turned up at Ali Baba's flat. He's already got an ID on the male found

254

dead in the cab of the van, and the documents from the flat itself are currently, as we stand here talking, being translated into English — and there was a letter in there about the delivery of 'parcels' to — wait for it — Littleton Salad Nurseries.

"Buller thought the "parcels" could have been drugs but, from what you've subsequently discovered, I think they could be bodies — illegal ones. His van's already got a marker on it to be investigated by HMRC because of its frequent crossings from a variety of Channel ports. Taking that into account and given that there was no record in the UK about the couple that were murdered in Gooding Avenue, I now think we're finally getting somewhere.

"There was a dead woman also found in the back of the van, and her body's being sliced and diced right now. I think Buller needs to get in touch with Immigration to see what they know or suspect about our local lettuce merchants."

Across the office, Buller suddenly ended a phone call, threw a fist into the air and shouted, "Yes!" in a triumphantly loud voice.

"Won the lottery?" asked Olivia in a droll voice.

"Just about," he called back. "You know that woman that Desai and Leo found first thing this morning? Well, it's just been confirmed that she has very recently given birth: and she's the right ethnic origin. I think we have our mother for the little one found on the tip."

"With that in mind, guv, I think that you need to hear about what Westbrook and Groves have been up to this morning," said Olivia, unable to understand why this statement made Lauren blush furiously.

During a retelling of their finds, Buller's eyes positively danced. "So, that means that if we can tie her body up with that of the baby found at the tip, and we can find evidence that this woman's been working at the nursery, then we're just about home and dry," he crowed, "Especially if we can tie up this sliced-up corpse with Kharboub and his under-the-radar activities." He went straight off to phone the immigration service. If they knew about what the police had uncovered, they might already be planning a raid and would probably like police support, and if they didn't, he would have got in first. Whichever way things went, this would result in a lot of bodies being rounded up and pulled off the streets, or the tomato plants, or whatever.

He finished the call with his balloon slightly pricked as they had been aware of what was going on at the nursery, and had been about to ask for the attendance of the police at their already planned raid, but they told him that there was going to be a simultaneous raid at what outwardly appeared to be a perfectly respectable detached house, just outside the town centre.

The property, by sheer good fortune, had a convenient back entrance and the premises had been, for some time, used as a brothel. The prostitutes, who had been local in the past, were now deemed to be illegal immigrants, the two operations inextricably linked, so Buller was slightly mollified that he would have this raid under his belt as well, before he went back to Drugs.

"The whole thing only came to light when one of the tarts left the curtains open, and neighbours saw what was going on inside the bedroom from a side window on the first floor of their own house. Similarly un-pulled curtains downstairs had revealed a row of chairs occupied by men who appeared to be waiting for something to happen. A concerned phone call to the police and a little surveillance had provided all the evidence that was needed to organise a little visit, and now these visits by two different agencies, were planned for the following Friday at 10p.m.

"Take your pick, ladies. Which of them would you like to attend?" he asked lasciviously.

"I think we'll take the Nissen hut, if that's all right with you, Sergeant," announced Olivia rather primly in view of Buller's expression. He did everything but lick his lips. A brothel was a bit too near the knuckle, at the moment, for her, considering Hal's confession. It would probably be full of married men paying for a bit of extra-curricular jollies that the little woman at home simply didn't need to know about.

Lauren nodded in agreement. "As you wish, ladies, and," looking at his watch, he continued, "may I wish you *bon appetit* for your luncheon. I shall eat rather better knowing that there's a brothel to be broken up."

The afternoon passed in a busy collating of the documents translated, processing the information in relation to the various cases, and raising files in which to contain them. Buller was in his element now, with things finally coming together, and he even went off home in a fairly triumphant mood instead of hanging around like a bad smell, criticising whoever or whatever crossed his path. Lauren was also cheerful as she left the office, and it was only Olivia who remained there, a solitary figure, wondering what her arrival at the family home had in store for her.

What sort of mood would Hal be in? Now that the working day was at an end, her mind returned to her personal life and the problems that had just manifested themselves while she had remained in total, if not quite blissful, ignorance. She hadn't even asked him who her husband had been unfaithful with, so stunned was she. Would he be contrite, defiant — would he even be there? Did he actually have the seed of a budding relationship with this bloody woman, whoever she was? Did she have any designs on her husband long-term? The only way to find the answers to the many questions that buzzed round her brain like swarming bees was to actually go there and face the situation, whatever that turned out to be.

With a heavy heart and in a very subdued state of mind, she finally shut down her computer and slunk off outside to the car park.

Lauren had exchanged texts with Daz Westbrook during the working afternoon, and had left the office exactly fifteen minutes after he did, as arranged. They may not have had a roll on the blanket in the woods, but it would be considerably more comfortable in his flat. It also meant that what would have been in the past was now still in the future, to be looked forward to.

This was getting to be a habit, she thought, but rather than analysing it, she dismissed it from her mind and merely imagined the pleasures to come. Life was too short to examine everything one did with too close a scrutiny. Fun had to come into things somewhere along the line.

When Olivia got home it was to a full complement of family members. The other three were sitting around the kitchen table, and Hal was taking from the oven the biggest shepherd's pie she had ever seen. Her greeting was unsurprisingly quite tentative, and she had no idea whether he had passed on the details of his infidelity to the kids, and they had, perhaps, found it justified and just filed it under "normal" behaviour, given the circumstances, and Mum's apparent indifference.

If she had been taking him for granted for so long, and neglecting her children, too, because she was simply too distracted at work, then maybe she had deserved what she had got. The children had both been through a bad time the previous year; totally different problems, neither of which she had seen brewing on the horizon. Hal's betrayal had also been out of the blue. She had simply taken his frequent absences to be due to giving too much to his new supply job. How wrong could a wife be?

In fact, as a wife and mother, she'd really taken her eye not just off the ball, but off the whole fucking game, and had been letting all of them down. She had been, as she would put it herself, "crap", yet how could she devote more time to these three people that she loved the most in the world, when there were such complex crimes to be solved and such villains to be rounded up? Was there an answer — a solution — or was it one of those unsolvable puzzles that no one could get to the bottom of?

"Come on in and sit yourself down, woman. You're probably starving after a full day's work, and I bet you didn't find time to eat any lunch, did you?" This was Hal, back to his "mother hen" best, and she reacted to it with gratitude. They could have a private talk later when the kids were either upstairs in their rooms or out with friends.

With all four of them present, the atmosphere was convivial in a way it hadn't been for a long time and she was really enjoying her food and the chit-chat going on around her, when there was a long ring on the doorbell and a thunderous knocking on the wood. There was a sudden lull in the conversation, and four sets of eyes moving from side to side as if they were all simultaneously asking themselves who the hell that could be.

Olivia rose to answer it with a simple, "I'll get it," adding, "It's amazing how belligerent these doorstep evangelists can be," which at least raised a smile from the others sitting at the table.

She flung open the front door confidently, only to find a woman, a complete stranger, who must have been in her early thirties, standing waiting, her hand up to knock again. "Can I help you?" she asked.

"Does Mr Hardy live here — the English teacher?"

Dammit! Was this one of the mothers of a pupil who had tracked him down to his home address to see why he hadn't been in today to teach her little angel? "What's your business with him?"

"Are you the wife?" asked the woman, with a slight sneer. "I might've known you were a frumpy little thing who had let herself go. Let me in to see Hal. We need to talk. He can't just desert me like this."

Olivia's mouth had fallen open with shock, and her head was whirling. Was this the woman that Hal had slept with? What could she say to her? What could she do to get rid of her: she wanted to punch her in the mouth — *frumpy and let herself go, indeed!* — but knew this would not be a good idea, given her profession. It would look so bad on her work record, a conviction for assault. And fighting with the woman she now saw as her rival was not very seemly. She couldn't suppress the violence she felt building inside her, though. The trollop! And to turn up here on the doorstep . . .

At that moment, the woman gave her a tremendous shove in the chest and marched past her into the interior of the house, calling, "Hal, where are you? I need to talk to you about the future — our future."

Olivia landed on her buttocks on the hall floor, all the air leaving her body with a loud whooshing sound while, at the same time, she became aware of voices coming from the kitchen: Hal's bass boom mixed in with the higher voices of Ben and Hibbie, all raised in anger, but unable to make out anything that was said.

Hibbie came rushing through first, appalled to find her mother on the floor and immediately helping her to her feet, muttering, "Mad bitch! Did she hurt you, Mum?"

Almost before Olivia had had time to dust herself down and inform her daughter that she was uninjured, Ben and Hal came through, one either side of the woman, gripping an arm apiece, and ejected her through the front door, from the other side of which the woman began to pound again, and shout.

Olivia immediately grabbed her work phone and rang in a complaint to the station, with a very sparse and thin explanation, then looked at Hal and lost all control, breaking down into sobs of grief and loss, the emotion that the violent feelings had induced in her suddenly turning her legs to jelly and reducing her to helpless weeping

Hal immediately put his arms around her to support her, steering her away from the door and back on to her seat at the table, whilst muttering that all would be well, while she sobbed, "Don't touch me. Don't you dare lay a finger on me, you unfaithful bastard," then holding on to him for all she was worth and whispering, "Don't leave me; don't leave me; please, don't leave me," her head buried in his midriff.

The kids trailed after them back to the kitchen, all appetites disappeared but, at least with two substantial oak doors closed, the clamour that must be supposed still to be coming from Hal's erstwhile mistress was nowhere near so loud. This problem was going to take a lot more resolving than they had realised now this had happened, and Hal prepared himself for a menu serving only portions of humble pie, for some time to come.

"Who the fuck was that lunatic, Dad?" asked Ben, sounding quite aggressive.

"Ditto from me. Who the *fuck*?" echoed Hibbie, both of them using uncharacteristically coarse language.

Hal gave them both one of his quelling glances that said unequivocally "not now" and Olivia turned her gaze on them beseechingly, her face as white as milk. The cat would be out of the bag soon enough. Until then, he'd like to keep them in innocence for a little bit longer before he became the bad guy.

There'd be an awful lot of coming to terms for all four of them, if they were to remain as a happy family unit, and it was all his fault. No! It wasn't. The blame had to be shared, but this was definitely not the time to air that view. He would have to rebuild Olivia's trust and confidence in him and get the kids on side, while subtly introducing the subject of him being taken for granted; used as a sounding board; a whipping boy; a domestic goddess — hah! That one almost made him smile.

That the situation was able to be resolved he had little doubt, but it was going to take some time — maybe even years — and effort from all of them, before they could get back to anything like the way they used to be with each other. Betrayal and infidelity couldn't be mended with a sticking plaster. There had to be long-term healing involved, and a lot of will as well as skill. For now, the best that could happen would be an uneasy truce.

CHAPTER
TWENTY

Seven thirty the next morning found Olivia sitting back at the kitchen table, alone this time, with a cup of coffee in one hand and a lit cigarette in the other. She had given up smoking years ago, but had felt the need this morning, and had bummed one off Ben, whom she knew smoked on the quiet.

She was still in her dressing gown, her eyes bloodshot and swollen, her hair all over the place — in fact, she felt that she definitely resembled the wreck of the *Hesperus* — when there was a firm rap on the glass panel of the back door. Who on earth could that be this time of the morning? Surely not that bloody woman back again?

With murder in her eyes, she flung open the door to find a rather grim-faced DCI Buller waiting outside, and was stunned into silence. "I heard about what happened last night," he said in an unexpectedly sympathetic voice, knowing only too well the toll that the job could take on a marriage. Still without a word, she stood aside so that he could enter.

In total silence, she sat back down in her chair and took a recklessly long drag on the cigarette. Then ruined everything by coughing. "Choke it up, chicken," he advised with a grim smile, then went on, "Look, I've had a word with everyone who had heard about what went off here last night. I don't know the ins and outs of it, and I don't want to. Suffice to say that I made it quite clear that anyone who breathed a word about you having a mort of trouble out here would be strung up by the bollocks. You should have seen the women's faces."

Olivia granted this the smallest of smiles. "I'm not expecting you in to the factory today, because if you came in looking like that, everybody would think you'd taken up cage-fighting, and that's not a very ladylike hobby." Again she smiled slightly. She had had no idea that Buller had this understanding side; it was a revelation to her.

"Now," he continued, before she could get in a word, "I want you to stay off until you know you can come in without breaking down every half-hour" — again a half-smile to let her know that he wasn't being harsh. "Are you still up for these raids on Friday?"

"I couldn't do the brothel. That's just asking too much of myself given the circumstances — everything's too raw . . ." Here, tears did begin to slide down her cheeks.

"The nursery it is for you, then. That's what we'd previously agreed, and it still stands. Look, I'll keep you up to date with any developments on the case, and you get sorted what you need to get sorted. The whole force won't disintegrate without you, whatever you might privately think. Chin up, Hardy. It isn't the end of the world, even if it feels like it at the moment."

She gave him a watery smile in gratitude at what this must have cost this usually so bombastically macho and in-your-face man. "Thanks, guv," she murmured. As he gave her a cheery wave goodbye and closed the door behind him she wondered if Hal was awake yet.

Since his disclosure two evenings ago, he had not slept in the marital bed, and she couldn't decide whether this was a good thing, or a very bad thing. Was it out of common decency and consideration for her feelings, or was it a sign that their marriage was over? She just didn't know where they were at the moment, or what the future held, although his indignation the evening before when that slut had turned up at his house — his actual home where his actual family lived — had been heartening. *Unless it was all an act.* With a sigh of utter despair, she trailed upstairs to get dressed. She'd bum another fag off Ben, have another cup of coffee, then go out to buy a packet of cigarettes of her own.

Her muddled thinking at the moment was that she'd rather die of a smoking-related disease within a family, than go without this drug and live longer, but without her husband. She felt all at sea; up the creek without a paddle; rudderless. How strange that all these analogies were connected with water; evidently a by-product of all the years she had spent living in a coastal town with its own river mouth.

Ben willingly gave her another of his precious cigarettes, for he was not a heavy or even regular smoker, when she promised to pay him back with a third one as interest, later in the morning, and after throwing on an old pair of jeans and a not too smart T-shirt, she returned to her jumbled, racing thoughts and the homely feeling of the kitchen.

When she had sunk another mug of deplorable instant coffee, the flavour of which was actually helped by the unaccustomed taste of smoke in her mouth, she would nip down to the little shop and get herself a packet of twenty, then, when she came home she'd change into something more smart. If Hal had been sniffing around another piece of skirt, then she ought to make a bit more effort with her appearance, in case he was tempted to do it again. The woman had actually called her a frump who had let herself go. She should take this as a warning.

The next couple of days were peppered with high-volume, triumphant calls from the DCI, as the documents were slowly translated, but his first big coup was the van.

"Absolute dynamite, that rusty old white thing was," he crowed.

"Well, it did have two corpses in it."

"No, no, no, you naïve woman! It had a secret compartment in the back with enough room behind it for all the contraband you could ever want, or room for a few cramped-up illegals. I've got a theory. The illegals were all part of a much bigger network — referred to in several pages of writing as 'parcels' — all going to that nursery.

"The drugs the sniffer dogs found at that house were used to keep the illegals under control, and we theorise that they worked under duress at either the nursery or as prostitutes. It they were doped up to the eyeballs, then they wouldn't be able to go out or need wages. They were slaves, paid in narcotics.

"We reckon that the class As that had been getting through were about to increase because there was a network of small-time distributors being set up to sell them on, on the streets. Those two Moroccans were sent a list of names that they were supposed to contact about this — all of them known to us as small-time dealers — and a list of young kids who have been in trouble with us before and were probably heading for a life of crime. Thank God that didn't get off the ground — they all copped it before they had a chance to start.

"The list was evidently delivered by hand, nothing being trusted to the post, and it was on Kharboub's desk still in its envelope; but it had obviously been opened and perused. That would be so that he wouldn't approach any of those who were already in the pay of the big boys. He wanted his own distribution network for what he managed to 'alf-inch from the larger consignments.

"He would only be paid so much for each 'parcel' delivered, so he was probably going to skim all future traffic when it was brought in; cut the drugs with something to reduce purity, but leave him with a nice little earner of his own.

"I told you that several of the Channel ports have got a marker on the van to be stopped when it next passed through their jurisdiction —"

"Hold on a minute, guv. Isn't a lot of this just speculation?"

"Speculation, my arse! It's all going to be provable when we've got these raids out of the way."

"If you say so." Olivia really wasn't in the mood for all this good cheer and self-congratulation. She was more worried about Hal, who had become very silent, and was spending quite a lot of time reading the Bible, as he had been brought up to do.

Lauren hadn't been in touch either, except for one quick call to confirm that the inspector was on sick leave, and that had been it. She hadn't even asked what was wrong with her, so Olivia's relationship with her work-partner was still frosty, both professionally and personally. Things couldn't get much worse.

"Ah, Inspector, you are in. Good." Olivia entered the office the next morning and once more Buller's relentlessly cheery tones assaulted her ears. "Just thought I'd let you know that we brought a drugs dog into Ali Kebab's flat and found small quantities of both cocaine and heroin, and a note that confirmed that larger 'packets' were going to be dispatched in the near future. How's that for confirmation of conjecture for you? Not 'parcels' this time, but 'packets'.

"And the skunk farm was also him going out on his own. As he'd need dealers for that, why not get them to deal in what he had skimmed and cut, too?"

"Congratulations, guv," Olivia replied in a lacklustre voice.

270

"Have you not sorted out that problem with your old man yet? That's not like you."

"No, guv, and no, guv. It's going to be a tough one, but I'll definitely be there on Friday. Just confirm the time and where the teams are meeting, and I'll make sure I'm ready and waiting."

"Chin up, Inspector. I'll bet you can do anything you put your mind to. I hear you two have been together, er, for ever. You can't blow it just because of a teensy-weensy slip-up on the part of a weak and easily led man." He, personally, had allowed his soon-to-be ex-wife three strikes before she was out: out of his home, out of his marriage, and out of his life.

"Bye, guv. See you Friday."

CHAPTER
TWENTY-ONE

On Friday evening, Olivia dressed in dark regulation issue trousers — looser now, as she had lost some weight over the last few days, and a matching police issue long-sleeved pullover. She didn't go so far as to put any sludge-coloured make-up on her cheeks and forehead to enhance the camouflage, but she was feeling the first stirrings of enthusiasm she had experienced since Hal's shattering confession, at the thought of nailing these bastards, as she left the house.

Not long after she arrived, the whole contingent from the police was assembled; a contingent of uniformed officers and as many female officers who were available, as this case involved a number of women, and would need tactful handling. Devenish had evidently been advised by a fellow senior officer to orchestrate this spread of the sexes, as he wouldn't have had the nous to initiate it himself.

Immigration officers weren't far behind them, joining them on the piece of wasteland screened by a row of Leylandii not too far from the Nissen hut. They included a similar percentage of females, so maybe it was the senior Immigration officer who had spoken to

Devenish, so that he didn't misunderstand what their task was this evening, and just who the targets were.

Instructions as to the spread of the officers involved, and the approaches of the target building from a number of directions, were shared in a subdued hiss, and the time was checked. The two raids were to take place simultaneously so that there could be no whistle-blower from one target to another.

"We go in on the stroke of ten, so we'll have to leave here about twenty minutes before, and moving in as silently as possible. I've synchronised my timing with that of the Immigration officer leading the raid on the brothel, and they should be getting into position shortly after us. Now, think 'success'. I don't want any of you wimping out at the last minute. We need to get the people responsible for this behind bars as quickly and as efficiently as possible."

The other raiding party was just coming together, in unmarked cars and down dark alleyways not far from the supposedly respectable, detached Edwardian house that was their target. This had once been a main road, but had been downgraded after the building of the ring road. This would not have decreased its custom, though, as there was a sufficiently private back alley leading to an entrance through a tall wooden gate at the back of the rear garden.

The punters wouldn't know what had hit them, and neither would the girls, probably being in too relaxed a state from the drugs they had been given. As for those who supervised this part of the business, they were in for a surprise, and the surprise included handcuffs and some fairly unsympathetic treatment.

The back entrance was being kept under discreet surveillance, and three officers had in their possession the heavy device known within the service as "the big, red key", which would ensure that there was no delay in their entry.

Rather more discreetly, a small team from the Drugs squad was targeting the greenhouses of the nursery itself, hoping to find evidence, maybe, of drugs being grown here. This had been a sub-plot organised by Buller off his own bat, for he realised that this would be the ideal spot, not only to grow cannabis, but also for Kharboub to have got his seedlings from, maybe smuggling them out a few at a time, or even getting some of the girls to bring them out somehow and exchange them for a spliff to keep them going between hits.

At precisely ten o'clock, in two geographically diverse sites in Littleton, a shrill whistle sounded — a police signal so antiquated as to be more or less forgotten — quickly followed by the pounding of feet and the splintering of wood, and both teams were in.

At a third, the entrance was more sedate. The only lights on behind the sea of glass were ones that helped the plants to grow, and it was hoped that some of those plants would be mind-altering and, ultimately, deliciously profit-making.

As the teams swung into action, police vans positioned themselves to take in those who were brought in for questioning.

274

* ★ *

The brothel raid took the occupants by total surprise. A number of very relaxed, pretty girls along with the requisite number of very panic-stricken men were rounded out of beds or other little hideaways, and led from the house. None of the girls was English, and there would have to be interpreters brought in to question them, but their native tongues would have to be ascertained first.

The most sinister, and for Lauren, embarrassing room was a cellar, a space where there were whips, riding crops and canes hanging from the walls, and a number of leather articles of clothing that she didn't want to inspect too closely, especially a full-head mask that had a zip for a mouth, and looked absolutely terrifying.

The current occupants of this space were dressed in rubber, and Lauren was absolutely horrified to recognise one of the county's chief superintendents. This would fuck up his police career in no uncertain terms. How were the mighty about to fall!

A second transport van had arrived, and the men were put into one, the working girls into another. They were all young and pretty, but with only a few words of English between them. God knows what they'd been through, and what they would face in the future, but Lauren was sure that they would rue the day they chose to come to England for a better life, till the end of their days.

Eventually, the house was sealed until it was known what charges would be brought and against whom and by which authority, and the team made its way back to the station to sort out exactly what they had to deal with. Using the services of a prostitute was not an offence, although living off immoral earnings was, and then there was the matter that none of these young women would have visas and indefinite leave to stay and "work" in the UK.

Then there were the drugs, which were presumed to be quite a large part of this set-up, not just to keep the girls compliant, but for selling on to the punters. The waiting room stank of weed, as did a lot of the working rooms, and a cursory search revealed stashes of tablets and wraps — a veritable sweetie shop for any user with a bit of cash to spare and, possibly, depraved ideas of what constituted a good night out.

Lauren left with the rest of the team, grim-faced and emotionally drained, and wondering how Olivia had got on at the Nissen hut. She was feeling bad about the way she had shunned her friend and partner, purely out of guilt over what she had on her extra-curricular agenda, and shame was also beginning to creep into her heart. Daz wasn't just a colleague on the same team, he was a junior officer who was also much younger than her, a situation in which there was no future whatsoever. Was he worth throwing her career away for? At her age and with two children to bring up? She knew what she had to do, and she'd better get on with it pretty damned fast.

A sleepless and hag-ridden night before the raid had shown her the error of her ways, and she was determined to clean up her act, not only with regard to the amount of alcohol she consumed, but also to the body she was "consuming" on a regular basis. At this point, she determined to apologise to Olivia and, although not explaining what had been on her mind, at least to open up the channels of friendship again so that, if nothing else, their joint working lives would be less fraught with tension.

Olivia, her personal problems temporarily erased from her mind by the adrenaline of the situation, hurled herself through the door of the hut with the rest of the advanced guard, most of whom were Immigration officers plus Buller, looking like the Grand Panjoram himself or, at least, like the cat who had knocked over the cream jug and was reaping the rewards of the spillage. Rounding up this complicated little scam would do his career no harm whatsoever.

As the big red key did its job, and they pounded into the dormitory, what struck the inspector most was that, with all the noise and intrusion, the girls only stirred in their sleep, and surmised that a daily grind of long hours followed by the reward — "wages", if you were feeling particularly sick about the whole thing — of a hit of drugs, kept them pretty subdued and compliant.

She noticed that between each pair of triple bunks hung three baggy work overalls in an institutional grey, and surmised that these were what the girls wore for their work in the nursery.

Some of the girls were now waking and showing signs of panic, and this was where the female officers came into their own, calming them with small gestures of friendliness and soft words that hardly any of them could understand, but it worked.

It was the smell that also got to the inspector. It was a mixture of old fart, body odour and hopelessness. They had presumably all paid a large sum of money — or at least what was deemed to be so in their various countries of origin — to obtain a new life in England, with a job at the end of it, and had found only callousness and slavery as a reward for all their hopes and dreams.

What the future held for them, no one could yet determine, but it certainly wasn't what they'd paid for, and Olivia felt tears sting her eyes at the crushed ambitions of all these poor individuals who had only wanted to live somewhere in freedom and without fear, and had been catapulted into a life that held both, and was possibly worse than what they had fled from.

Immigration had actually provided a coach to transfer the women to a holding centre, to be sorted into countries of origin and provided with interpreters to make their statements, and when the raid was over, the police van was filled only with the service's own personnel.

Olivia sat in the back, preoccupied with how much she took for granted in her own life and how she would have fared in a similar situation to the ones that these women had found themselves in. In her heart of hearts she knew she was very lucky to live in a democracy that didn't suppress girls and women, and knew now that she would forgive Hal. They had so much, whereas some people had nothing where they came from, and little hope of improvement in the future. The only change these women could make was the choice they had made, it had worked out even worse for them, and now they'd probably have to go back to where they came from, unless they could claim asylum.

Hal had definitely put a foot *very* wrong, but they had adequate income, two lovely children, a comfortable home — an enviable life, really. How could she possibly throw all that up on top of twenty years of marriage because he had made a mistake, one he was already regretting bitterly?

DCI Buller never made it back to the station, having gone to the nursery itself to see if there had been any luck there. His hunch had, indeed, been vindicated. In the most remote greenhouse with whitewashed windows was a sophisticated hydroponics system and, in a heavy-duty safe in an outhouse, was a stash of drugs that would have kept the town high for the foreseeable future.

That there had not been a regular security team was a sign of the arrogance of whoever was organising this, keeping outgoings to a minimum, as they felt under the radar and untouchable. Well, now they'd go and feel Abdul Amir's collar, face him with what had been discovered, and see how untouchable he felt then, and whether he was willing to trade information to make his future not quite so onerous as it could be.

That he would go to prison, there was no doubt, but the length of his sentence would be determined by how helpful he might be to the police in the pursuit of their enquiries. Buller was full to bursting point with glee following this after-dark arrest, hoping that this individual might lead him further up the food chain to wherever this atrocious crime emanated from. It might not get him to the big boys, but even a rung up the ladder was a step in the right direction.

The various police officers had a loose meeting about three thirty a.m., and then were dismissed for a few hours' sleep, until they could have a more formal de-briefing during office hours.

After the meeting, Lauren sought out Olivia and just threw her arms around her and murmured, "I'm so sorry I've been a moody and aloof bitch," in her ear, before disappearing off into the car park and home, from whence she sent a dismissive text to Daz Westbrook, pointing out that neither of them could risk their careers by carrying on with the reckless behaviour they had been indulging in, but thanking him for a few memorable moments. It was the only way she could phrase it without telling him that she must have been off her head to ever consider a physical relationship with him, but that the temporary madness had passed.

Five minutes later, she received a one word reply — "OK".

Phew!

Everyone was bleary-eyed the next morning when they met to pool the outcomes of the previous night's raids — with the exception of DCI Buller, who looked like a model of a man totally stuffed with Mexican jumping beans. His eyes flashed, as did his teeth, in uncharacteristic smiles, and he bounced around on his toes like a teenager.

"You didn't have a little sample last night, did you, guv?" called an obviously disguised voice from the back of the room.

"Or a wee dram or two before you came in?"

"Didn't need anything. I'm high on life: drunk with success. And there's no better way of getting off your face than with results that I, although a modest man" — a few noises from the ranks at this wild claim — "hope might end with a promotion for yours truly."

"So, what've we got now?" asked Olivia, with a particularly infectious yawn.

"Amir's spilled his guts. We've got the names of the local heavies who were used to discipline the girls if they got out of line — we'll track them down, no trouble. He knows he's in it up to his neck, and that's the very thing he wants to save.

"From the translations, we've got a list of all of Mr Kharboub's trips to and from the continent, and the number of 'parcels' and 'packets' he delivered to the nursery. We've got the girls' names — unpronounceable, most of them — from the nursery's under-the-counter records, and the same for the house of ill-repute, along with a couple of ledgers that show records of drug sales and sessions with prostitutes, along with supplements for 'extras'" — there was a chorus of leers at this description — "All right, keep it down, lads, you're not in the playground now! Now, where was I? Ah, yes, and all of this, presumably, to be passed on to whoever keeps the books for this lot.

"We've got a sniffer dog visiting the home of Mr Amir this morning, and then going over the whole of the nursery premises in case we missed anything last night. This is going to be a big case. Devenish is already getting measured for the feather in his cap that he thinks will surely be his after what we've . . . *you've* done. I didn't think you had it in you.

"We've had a statement from Immigration that the woman who was found in the van and whom Dr MacArthur confirmed had recently given birth, had slipped in with a larger than usual consignment, and was probably only a few weeks pregnant, but she wasn't one of the prettier ones, so she wasn't expected to 'serve' male clients. And she was a canny one. The overalls they wore to work at the nursery were baggy, and she managed to keep her spreading middle concealed for all of the pregnancy. After all, whoever used to take any notice of staff in the old days? It's the same now with slaves.

"The other girls knew, but made sure that whenever any of the other nursery staff were around, she was never on her own, so that they could help conceal her steadily expanding overall.

"Of course, there was a complete panic when she went into labour, and her yells attracted some attention from their jailers. One enterprising young thug broke its neck just as it was born, and then the body and the other yucky things that came with it were wrapped up and disposed of on the tip. Again, an act of complete arrogance and disregard for any comeback there may have been. They really thought they were untouchable.

282

"But no more. Amir also spilled all the names he knew up the next rung of the ladder, so we can continue enquiries at a slightly higher level, and hopefully, given time, get to the really big boys. I'll be concentrating on that when I get back to Drugs."

"You're not leaving us, sir, and after we'd got so fond of you?" called out Olivia, moved to smile at the imminent return to normal working life.

"I had considered getting a transfer to you lot" — gasps of horror and calls of "oh, no" — "but home is home, and that's where I'm going; back to the good old Drugs Squad.

"Down *The Locomotive*, everybody, at lunchtime. We can only have one because of the drink-driving laws, but the pints are on me. We certainly have something to celebrate."

There was a round of applause at this summing up of what they'd achieved, and this, Lauren mused, had made no mention whatsoever of Olivia and her wrapping up the Shillington baby-murder case.

CHAPTER
TWENTY-TWO

There was quite an air of celebration in *The Locomotive* that lunchtime, and many of the officers had made private arrangements for their partner or a friend to pick them up after work, so that they could have a little more than one drink. Whatever had they done before mobile phones?

When the merry atmosphere had been milked for as long as possible, the officers began to dribble away back to the station and, finally, there were only Olivia and Lauren left. "Don't be too late back, ladies," called Buller as he waved them a cheery goodbye, and Olivia went to the bar to order them two cappuccinos, a spur of the moment decision that she felt had been relayed almost by telepathy from her sergeant.

As she placed the cups on their table and sat down, Lauren held out a hand. "I'm so sorry I haven't been much of a friend recently," she said with emotion in her voice.

"We all have periods when we're a bit off," Olivia countered.

"I know I've been really distant and aloof, but there were reasons."

"Which you don't want to confide in me."

"It was more a case of 'couldn't talk about' because I was, underneath, so ashamed."

"Do you want to tell me anything now?"

"A little. I was becoming dependent on alcohol. I was using it like a tranquiliser to distance me from all the trouble I expected from Kenneth regarding custody of the children, maintenance, and the eventual sale of the house. After he died, I suddenly realised that I didn't need it any more. Kenneth had been my trigger, and he was no longer around."

"Is that all?" queried Olivia, who had often used wine to switch off her head when a case was particularly disturbing, just for the temporary break it gave her from her teeming thoughts.

"No, but I can't tell you any more at the moment."

Inspiration struck the inspector, and she asked, tentatively, "Did Dr Mac tell you about Gerda's condition?"

"He did have a word in my shell-like to let me know before it came out in the inquest that she was three months up the duff, but then Kenneth never could keep it in his trousers, and she would probably have been terribly careless with the birth control, because she wanted a piece of him that she could really own."

"That's very grown-up of you," replied Olivia, wondering whatever else had been bothering her sergeant, if this wasn't it.

"Anyway, I've made my apologies. I hope we can be friends again as well as colleagues, and what about a musical evening in the near future?"

"Yeah . . ." Olivia's one word reply was limp and lacklustre, "but give me a while. You're not the only one who's had problems; and, no, I can't talk about it either. It's too raw at the moment."

"Buller did have a quiet word with me about Hal." Now Lauren sounded nervous.

"I simply don't believe it. If you want anything broadcasting around the whole station — nay, town — just tell a police officer." Olivia's face was a mask of fury, but it dissipated quickly. "Scratch that. At least you know what *I've* been going through."

"What are you going to do about it?" Lauren was curious to discover if Hal's little slip would end in another fractured marriage.

"I have a fair idea of how I want to play it, but I'm not saying anything till it's dealt with."

"Fair enough."

"Come on, drink up. As responsible officers of the law we shouldn't be sitting here in the middle of the afternoon drinking coffee and chatting about the murkier areas of our lives."

You don't even know the half of it, thought Lauren, as she carried her cup and saucer over to the bar and collected her handbag from the back of her chair. The place was nearly empty now, and they were beginning to stick out like sore thumbs.

"What about these thugs who dispatched the man and the woman in the van, and that man nailed to the table?"

"We know who the killers of the victims in the van are, and they'll be picked up and charged. Whatever, justice will catch up with them, but that's nothing to do with us, now. The other bloke semi-crucified in the kitchen — well, I think that's another matter altogether and leads further up the ladder. Buller will follow that up when he's back on home territory. He'll enjoy that."

"So, what do we do now?"

"Sort out our personal lives and take a breather until something else evil this way comes, I suppose." Olivia was already getting ready for a tense evening at home, and her mind was ahead of her, in the cottage and at odds with Hal.

When the inspector arrived home, a little late that night — subconsciously on purpose — it was to find that Hibbie and Ben had gone out in Ben's old banger, and Hal was waiting for her in the hall with a bunch of flowers.

"Come on in, my lovely," he invited, escorting her with a leading arm to the kitchen. The table was laid with a snow-white cloth, placemats, matching — unusual in their house for everyday eating — cutlery, coasters, and wine glasses. There were even side plates to the left of the forks with ringed napkins on them, and finger bowls to the right.

"What's all this in aid of?" she snapped suspiciously.

"Something very important. I've done all your favourite dishes. We're having asparagus with butter sauce — finger bowls and napkins absolutely essential for that — steak with mushrooms and all the trimmings, followed by lemon meringue pie — not a very elegant dessert, but incredibly delicious."

"But . . . what's all this in aid of?"

Hal suddenly dropped down on one knee and pulled a small leather box out of his trouser pocket. As he opened it, he said, his voice deep and serious, "Olivia, will you marry me?" as Olivia stared down in incredulity at the most beautiful ring.

"Don't be silly, Hal. We're already married."

"I meant . . . will you consider renewing our vows; like a fresh start for us?"

The devil on Olivia's shoulder forced her to reply, "I'll have to think about it first." But the ring looked absolutely scrummy, and considerably more upmarket than the one he had originally bought her when they had gone through round one of matrimony. Her resistance started to crumble.

"Will you at least let me put the ring on your finger? Try it for size?"

"Let's eat first. I'll probably weigh about a stone more after that lot, and we need to know it will fit after a blow-out."

"Does that mean 'yes'?"

"I'll tell you after I've sampled your cooking."

"We can have a glorious reception, and maybe go off on a second honeymoon: go over and see the folks . . ."
"Hold your horses. Food first, Casanova."

288

Other titles published by Ulverscroft:

A MURDER TO DIE FOR

Stevyn Colgan

How do you solve a murder when hundreds of wannabe detectives have the same goal? Every year, fans from all over the world descend upon a tiny picturesque English village to celebrate the life of the enigmatic author Agnes Crabbe and her fictional detective, Miss Millicent Cutter. Crabbe fans are quite obsessive; the majority turn up to the festival dressed as Miss Cutter. Spats between rival fan clubs are not uncommon. But when one of the most prominent superfans is murdered on the first day of the festival, the police find themselves trying to solve a crime in which the victim, witnesses, almost everyone in the village, and even the murderer, are all dressed as Miss Cutter. And most of them are also trying to solve the murder . . .

A NECESSARY EVIL

Abir Mukherjee

India, 1920: The fabulously wealthy kingdom of Sambalpore is home to tigers, elephants, diamond mines, and the beautiful Palace of the Sun. But when the Maharaja's son and heir to the throne is assassinated in the presence of Captain Sam Wyndham and Sergeant "Surrender-not" Banerjee, they discover a kingdom riven with suppressed conflict. Prince Adhir was a moderniser whose attitudes — and romantic relationship — may have upset the more religious elements of his country, while his brother — now in line to the throne — appears to be a feckless playboy. As Wyndham and Banerjee desperately try to unravel the mystery behind the assassination, they become entangled in a dangerous world where those in power live by their own rules, and those who cross their paths pay with their lives . . .

THIN ICE

Quentin Bates

When two small-time crooks rob Reykjavík's premier drug dealer, their plans start to unravel after their getaway driver fails to show. Tensions mount between the pair and the two women they grabbed as hostages, when they find themselves holed up in an isolated hotel that has been mothballed for the season. Back in the capital, police officers Gunnhildur, Eiríkur and Helgi find themselves at a dead end investigating what appears to be the unrelated disappearance of a mother, her daughter and their car, and the death of a thief. But Gunna and her team soon realise that all these unrelated incidents are, in fact, linked — while at the same time, two increasingly desperate lowlifes have no choice but to make some big decisions on how to get rid of their accidental hostages . . .

THE PYRAMID OF MUD

Andrea Camilleri

It's been raining for days in Vigàta, and the persistent downpours have led to violent floods overtaking Inspector Montalbano's beloved hometown. It is on one of these endless grey days that a man, a Mr Giugiu Nicotra, is found dead, his body discovered in a large water main with a bullet in his back. The investigation is slow and slippery to start with, but when the inspector realizes that every clue he uncovers and every person he interviews is leading to the same place — the world of public spending, and with it, the Mafia — the case begins to pick up pace. But there's one question that keeps playing on Montalbano's mind: in his strange and untimely death, was Giugiu Nicotra trying to tell him something?